The Oath of the Knights of Freedom

Looming across the starlit sky, the red-robed figure seemed almost as tall as the cross on the knoll behind him. He bowed to the group of speakers beneath the platform, and again to the ranks of listeners.

Then, as he lifted his right arm in a commanding gesture, the guardian of the cross stepped forward to ignite it.

The Knights raised their right arms in unison. Every eye was fastened on the blazing cross—the sign of man's hope they had perverted to symbolize their own cause.

"Brother Knights of Freedom—I salute you!" their leader cried.

"The South will be avenged!"

SHADOW OF EVIL
was originally published by
Doubleday and Company, Inc.

Frank G. Slaughter

SHADOW
OF EVIL

(Original title: *Deep Is the Shadow*)

PUBLISHED BY POCKET BOOKS NEW YORK

SHADOW OF EVIL

Doubleday edition published 1959

POCKET BOOK edition published May, 1975

*All of the characters in this book are fictitious,
and any resemblance to actual persons, living or
dead, is purely coincidental.*

L

This POCKET BOOK edition is printed from brand-new
plates made from completely reset, clear, easy-to-read type.
POCKET BOOK editions are published by POCKET BOOKS,
a division of Simon & Schuster, Inc., 630 Fifth Avenue,
New York, N.Y. 10020. Trademarks registered in the
United States and other countries.

Standard Book Number: 671-78877-9.
Library of Congress Catalog Card Number: 59-13042.
Front cover art by Robert Berran.

Printed in the U.S.A.

AUTHOR'S NOTE

My mother was a strong believer in aphorisms: among her favorites were, "Never trust a man who parts his hair or his name in the middle," and the biblical injunction that "A prophet hath no honor in his own country." When I started writing my first biblical novel, *The Road to Bithynia,* in 1950, I decided to switch to a pseudonym for my more realistic historical novels, perhaps best called "swashbucklers." *Buccaneer Surgeon, Darien Venture, The Golden Ones,* and *The Deadly Lady of Madagascar* were published originally under the pen name of C.V. Terry. They were only moderately successful in the hard-cover edition, but were best sellers in paperback under my own name, both here and abroad.

When I decided to write an intensely realistic novel about the racial question in 1959, I tried splitting another pseudonym in the middle with G. Arnold Haygood while also essaying to be a prophet, with only moderate success, thus proving my mother's wisdom in advising against ever sailing under any colors but my own. Nevertheless the novel has proved to be prophetic and this new edition, extensively revised, is now scheduled to appear all over the world under the author's true name—with no punches pulled. It is my hope that many of the some sixty million readers, who have bought my books in over twenty countries, will see in SHADOW OF EVIL a practical example of how the whole racial question, along with most human dilemmas, can be solved simply by applying the words of Jesus of Nazareth: *"A new commandment I give unto you, that ye love one another; as I have loved you, that ye also love one another."*

Frank G. Slaughter
May 15, 1974

"TODAY I SPEAK FROM New York," he said. "Yesterday I was in Moscow—and already that visit seems a world away. To sum up what I have shown you, let me read the last paragraphs of my column, *As I See It,* appearing tomorrow in the New York *Record* and its affiliates."

The telecast was nearing its end. Knowing he was off camera, Richard Jordan permitted himself the luxury of a yawn while he adjusted the desk microphone and picked up a galley proof. The studio clock told him he had just fifty-five seconds for his wrap-up. The monitor screen beside the control booth repeated the picture now on the network—a movie clip of the Kremlin, framed in wild flurries of snow, with only his voice to remind viewers of his presence.

> Yesterday [he read] I had my last look at the Russian people—a nation that may someday prove itself the greatest force on earth, even if the end product of that force is our destruction. The Soviet Union was born in blood and welded in tyranny. But there can be no blinking its progress, or the determination of its leaders to draw even with the United States and surpass them.

The number-one camera dollied toward the studio desk for his final close-up. Rick straightened, a split second before George Ormsbee leveled a commanding finger from the control panel. Before the telecast, George had announced that Rick's last travel series (which he had taped abroad) had added two whole points to his rating. Tonight, said George, an audience of forty million would tune in to hear this live report from the New York studio. He could not afford to betray his weariness by so much as a slurred syllable.

> Yesterday in Moscow [he read] I saw how a nation could aim all its resources at a single goal. Today in New York, I found my own country as glorious as ever—and as free. I also found it no less divided, no less stubborn in that division—and no less complacent as it faced the future.

The staring eye of number one camera winked out. On the monitor, the final montage shots of Russian might were overlapping in sequence—ending, as a fitting close, with a repeat view of a snow-lashed Kremlin.

> We have met other challenges in our history [he read]. So far, we have surmounted them. Today, as we pass another milestone in the 1960's, we face the greatest challenge of all, our national survival.
>
> We can defend ourselves only with clean hands— with our own house in order.
>
> The words of Jefferson still hold true. These United States, if they are truly united, remain the last, best hope of man.
>
> We have the resources within us—and the wisdom—to finish what our founders began. It is not yet too late to prove we are a democracy in deed as well as name. But the time is short.

His eye was on the second hand of the studio clock. He did not need George's throat-cutting gesture to know the telecast had ended on the nose. Watching a too-handsome announcer read the closing commercial, bracing himself to face the camera for his sign-off, Rick Jordan felt his weariness lift.

Once more, he had spoken his mind without let or hindrance, to what he hoped was a true cross section of America. Tomorrow, the same words would appear in a column that was read from Spokane to Key West. He was glad this would be his last telecast for ten weeks, that a backlog of European columns would give him ample time for his journey South. The true cause of those slowly rising spirits lay deeper.

It was a delayed reaction he always felt when he left the Old World for the New. Despite the solemn warning he had just broadcast to forty million living rooms, he could not avoid a profound sense of release. The flight from Moscow to New York, in sober truth, had been a journey from death to life. America in 1963, regardless of the tensions that divided it, remained the last, best hope of man.

George Ormsbee came out of the control booth, rubbing tired eyes. As program directors went, George was bitter but efficient, a cynic who sneered automatically. Rick Jordan had endured the bitterness because of the man's vast knowledge of a medium that (to a journalist) still smacked of the occult.

"How did it go?"

"Well enough," said George. "Some of the clips were blurred, but they rang the bell. The audio was excellent. You've seldom been in better voice."

"Did I sound tired?"

"Not one bit." George sat on the edge of the desk. "You're turning into quite an actor, Rick. That's my handiwork, of course."

The joke had begun to fray at the edges. Two years ago, with his reputation as a roving columnist established, Rick Jordan had stepped into television by chance, when he had pinch-hit in a newscast for a friend on vacation. George had directed that show; he had done his part to establish the new program that followed—until Rick Jordan's *Profiles of Tomorrow* had become a household neces-

sity each Friday at ten. It was still impossible to convince
the director that the greatest single factor in the program's
success was Rick's own sincerity—or that the sincerity
was more than skin-deep. To George, all television performers were actors, regardless of the product they were
selling. Actors nowadays were made as often as they were
born.

"Did you think I was acting tonight, George?"

"Be honest. Weren't you hamming when you said
Russkis are human?"

"Didn't you read the script? That's what the program
was about. So was every column I wrote behind the
Curtain—" Rick paused to remind himself that one never
argued ideas with George Ormsbee. "Where do you think
they come from? Mars—or their own sputniks?"

"Give 'em enough rope," said George. "And enough
rockets. Maybe they'll leave the earth to us."

"Suppose they point those rockets at our heads?"

"They won't," said George. "Not while ours are point-
ing at them. Not while we've got the United States mint to
buy us friends. Speaking of the mint, your sponsor called
to say he loves you more than ever. And the public's
ten-deep on the switchboard right this minute. So why
should you mind a thing I say?"

"Answer one question man to man, George. Doesn't
anything frighten you?"

"Not while our sponsor's happy," said the director.
"Not while our ratings hold up. Say what you like, and
say it your way. I won't censor a comma."

"You won't because you can't," said Rick.

"So far, you've earned that clause in your contract. If
your ratings drop, I'll be the first to go after your
scalp."

"You'll never get it, George. The day you can look
over my shoulder, I'll return to the *Record* full time.
That's in my contract too. No one tells me what to say on
Profiles—no one ever will."

"Believe me, fellow, I don't even care. Not if the apple-knockers who tune in believe you."

This time, Rick did not rise to the bait. He knew that George Ormsbee used his post-program needle for strictly practical ends—not from sadism, but to generate power for the next broadcast.

"Tonight, I'm wasting no adrenalin on anger," he said. "Not with a transatlantic flight behind me, and another trip coming up tomorrow."

"Is it true you're going South?"

"Yes—to Central City."

"What's the crusade now? Better cornpone for share-croppers? Or free schools and free love for the black man?"

"I'm breaking no lances this time out," said Rick. "I plan to coast awhile."

"It's hard to picture Rick Jordan coasting."

"I'm going to do just one interview, if the paper can arrange it. With a Dr. Peter Moore, a psychiatrist at Valley Hospital. Ever hear of his work?"

"I meet enough nuts in my working day," said George. "Why should I shop outside?"

"I've heard he's too good a man to bury himself at state level." Rick was thinking aloud now, only half-aware of the director's gadfly presence. "He has a surprising record of cures. I may give him a column—to backstop the hospital series I did last summer."

"Did we use *that* on the air?"

"No, George. Sometimes I forget you can't read."

"Sure that's your only errand, Rick?"

"I can hardly pass through Central City without seeing Bob Partridge. Even you have heard of him."

"The prophet of the New South," said George. "Is he still above ground? I thought they'd lynched him years ago."

"I'll grant you that Bob's a lost voice in the wilderness. He's still vocal."

"Are you planning to sing a duet, by any chance?"

"It's a social call—and nothing else. I'm writing no more about integration, if that's what you mean."

"That's just what I mean," said George. "Hal Stacey thought you were."

"Where'd you run into Stacey? When I last heard, he was in Japan."

"Hal travels fast," said George. "Right now, he's dancing at the Golden Glades with his fiancée—and insisting you join them."

"Since when have you turned social secretary?"

"I got his call at air time," said George. "There was no way to pass it on."

Rick frowned. He had learned to take the director's needles without pain. The news that Hal Stacey was pursuing him could not be ignored so easily.

"Did he say what he wanted?"

"Only that it was important."

"Everything Hal wants is important—to Hal."

"Call him from my office. The number's on the pad."

"Thank you no, George; I'm heading for the barn. If he calls back, tell him to go to hell, with my compliments. And if he really has a fiancée, say I admire her courage."

"Are you two feuding?"

"Of course not. I've known Hal Stacey for years. He was a damned fine reporter—before he learned to focus a Leica. Normally, I wouldn't mind him at all. I'm not in the mood tonight."

They moved toward the thick steel door that divided the studio from the everyday. "Don't you trust Hal?" the director asked.

"I trust him like a brother—if I needn't turn my back when we're on a story together."

"Sometimes I think you don't trust me either, Rick."

"How can I—when you won't trust the human race?"

The door swung wide as George nodded to the watchman, admitting them to an outer hallway and a bank of elevators. "I still think you're covering up," said the director.

"About Bob? If Hal thinks I'm taking sides down there, he's using the wrong pipeline."

"Don't forget I own stock in *Profiles*," said George. "With a stake in your future, I'd much rather you didn't visit the magnolia jungle."

"What have you been doing lately? Running old clips of *The Birth of a Nation?*"

The director stood his ground while Rick rang for an elevator.

"I'm still worried," he said. "Especially if you're calling on a stormy petrel like Bob Partridge—if you'll forgive the mixed metaphor."

Rick found he was laughing as he held out his hand. It was hard to dislike George for long, despite his back-stabbing—and his Neanderthal views.

"Stay in your control booth, George," he said. "Leave the world to me. I'll promise to come back in one piece."

"Am I still your favorite director?"

"Of course you are—so long as you can't change the script."

The apartment Rick Jordan called home (when he paused in his travels to check in at the New York *Record*) was only a few blocks uptown. After he had dropped his airplane luggage and turned on the light above his bed, he found he had no desire to rest. The driving emotional pressure of the broadcast had been just the stimulus he needed; the routine sparring with George had relaxed rather than angered him. He wondered if he should walk into Hal Stacey's trap, if only to investigate the bait Hal was offering. At the moment, even Hal Stacey, and an improbable fiancée, seemed preferable to a restless night alone.

It was his first free time on American soil in over a year—and, though he could have wished for other company, he felt he deserved a nightcap and a little music. His work had brought friendship with most of the world's great names; it was a paradox of that work that he should be often alone. Unfortunately, he had found he could not give his best to the column if he gave too freely of himself—and the column had been his life for more years than he cared to remember.

Hal Stacey, he reflected, had never been troubled by such scruples. From the start, as an unlicked cub on the old *Chronicle*, fighting with teeth and toenails for his first byline, Hal had been a simon-pure example of young America on the make. If they had become friends of a sort in those early days, it was only because Rick had been far less certain of his destiny.

A native Virginian, Richard Jordan had crossed the Blue Ridge on a scholarship to enter the University of North Carolina. Both parents had died midway of his college career. His guardian (a Danville banker) had parceled out a meager estate in teaspoon doles. There had been enough for a graduate year at the Pulitzer School: from that steppingstone, Rick had gone into his first city room. In those days, he had been a starveling, rather pugnacious young Southerner, who had entered journalism only because he possessed a nose for news and had no friends to help him elsewhere. He had needed two more years, and the slow climb up from a district to night rewrite, to discover he had blundered into his true vocation.

He was slow to drop his guard when offered friendship; he had yet to know love—though he had solaced himself with love's gayer counterfeits. There were playmates enough (in the city room of the old *Chronicle*) to make life worth living between assignments. Bob Partridge, who had been ahead of him at Chapel Hill, had been his oldest friend—but Bob had stayed in New York journalism just long enough to learn the ropes, then departed for his father's own paper in Central City.

It had taken courage to stick to rewrite after Bob had

gone South, particularly when the elder Partridge had offered him a real reporter's berth on the *Times-News*. Yet, even then, Rick had felt he was on the edge of better things. If Bob was destined to be a leading editor in the South, Rick Jordan could discover his own beat was the universe.

The war had settled his doubting. Hal Stacey had completed the shaping of his urban carapace.

Hal had come straight from Harvard to the *Chronicle*. He had first told Rick that he was using journalism as an easy entree to Broadway. Later, he had wavered between dreams of an art career, marriage with the publisher's daughter, and a stock-market killing that would permit him to found his own news magazine. Later still, after he had donned a war correspondent's uniform at twenty-three, he had found that a talent for photography, joined to a free-wheeling prose style, could pay dividends of its own.

It was not true that Hal had stolen his first Leica from a captured Luftwaffe pilot; the story that he had bribed his way into a Ranger unit, to cover D day from the enemy side, was also part of Stacey folklore. But he had soon learned to present the war in pictures (without precise labels) in a way the Stateside millions loved. . . . Rick Jordan, brooding on those years, could afford to smile at his own impatience. He had envied Hal Stacey from the first—for his good looks, his hand-tailored charm, his romantic conquests. He had envied him most of all for his meteoric success. It was not Hal's fault that a punctured eardrum had saved him from the draft. It was sheer luck that he had reached Milan in time to photograph the death of Mussolini.

Rick's own career had been almost as lucky, though he had followed a more traditional road. Disabled in Italy after the Salerno invasion, he had received an honorable discharge from the Army in hospital. While a leg wound took its mysterious time in healing, he had put on a correspondent's uniform of his own, to write his first story abroad—the kind of reporting Ernie Pyle had later made famous, plus the comment that soon became a Jordan hallmark. When he had lingered abroad in the first uneasy years of peace, he had added a weekly radio broadcast to his column. It had opened the way to the television show that was now part of his legend.

Looking back tonight, he saw his career had matched Hal Stacey's, step by step. The pacing had been deliberate—the half-angry effort of a small-town Southern boy to match his Yankee counterpart. Without the goad of Hal's notoriety, he might have taken his leg wound back to a rewrite desk in New York. It would have been easy to settle for mediocrity thereafter.

Why did he still curse Hal inwardly for that graceful leap on history's bandwagon? Why, when he owed the camera reporter so much, did he continue to distrust him? The answer was simple: Stacey, like many men before him, had simply sold out to the highest bidder. He had traded on a talent for shading fact into make-believe; year after year, he had used a genuine art form, and a glib prose style, to lull the public with symbols of a world that never was, a streamlined heaven that could be won without blood or tears.

On surface, he was still Rick's friend: he had kept up all his contacts in a profession famous for its give-and-take. His footprints had merged with Rick's at most of the world's crossroads, at Quemoy and Suez, at Moscow and Berlin and Dienbienphu. Time and again, Rick had watched Hal's opportunism function as noiselessly as a Swiss chronometer. He had held his tongue and his temper. Stacey and his kind had come to stay among the news gleaners. . . . Now, once again, Hal intended to use him for some purpose of his own. Tonight's invitation to the Golden Glades could have no other meaning.

It seemed obvious that Hal had heard of his impending trip to Central City and had read a hidden meaning into his visit, since Central City was Bob Partridge's habitat. The *Times-News* had been an outstanding paper when

the elder Partridge had surrendered it to his son: Bob
Junior had made it even greater. From the first day of his
editorship, he had called a spade a spade, in an area
where plain speaking was badly needed: his attitude on
the long impasse in the schools (to name but one cause
out of many) had never wavered.

Elsewhere in the Deep South, editors had grown weary
of the stalemate. Of late, there had been a tendency to
play down the tensions, to bury the stories of bombing
and other acts of terrorism that had followed each effort
of "Northern liberals" to break the deadlock. The *Times-
News* had featured each new outrage with banner heads.
Last fall, when the present Governor (a machine-tooled
perennial named Bowie Stead) had closed the white high
schools in Central City, rather than submit to token "race
mixing," Bob had blasted the move in editorials reprinted
from coast to coast.

Most thinking persons in Central City had discounted
Stead's rumbling in behalf of states' rights, and the divine
mission of the white man to reign supreme. Bob Partridge
had refused to shrug off the implications. The school
closings, he said, were only a symptom of a deep political
illness—a sly dodge to keep the favor of the rural voters,
whose hostility to the Negro was far more violent than
that of their city brethren. He had named names after
the next primary, proving that the move had pushed
dozens of bigots into power—men who had been driven
from the public trough in normal times and now dared to
stand again for election, with race hate as their only
asset. . . .

Rick had picked up mere echoes of the argument—but
he gathered that few holds had been barred. Stead had
been burned in effigy on the campus of the State University; there had been flaming crosses on the lawn of the
Partridge home, and bomb threats in the pressroom of the
Times-News. Later, of course, when the usual revulsion
set in, responsible elements among the voters had supported
Bob's views—particularly the parents of suddenly idle

teen-agers who found that once-peaceful homes were straining at the seams. . . . Such support, however, had remained largely tentative. Meanwhile, the rednecks had marched triumphantly into office at State House level— and the future outlook seemed dark indeed.

So much for background, thought Rick: in its way, the Central City story was a too-familiar classic. Born and bred a Southerner, he was wary of hasty judgments in the tug-of-war (now almost ten years old) between liberal and conservative. In Bob's state, it seemed that only the rascals had profited—but the fact remained that the problem of the Southern Negro must be settled on the spot, on the South's own timetable. . . . Too many outside journalists had stormed in with their typewriters, their formulas, and their moralizing. Why should Hal Stacey (of all people) assume that he was about to add to the dust storm?

He reached for the phone, just as it rang. Hal's voice addressed him, as gaily as though they had parted only yesterday.

"George Ormsbee must be failing," said Hal. "Didn't he explain I'm at the Golden Glades with my fiancée?"

"You've always been too busy to marry, Stacey. Who are you deceiving now?"

"The lady's name is Carol King," said Hal. "Her habitat is Central City—and she's the niece of Walter Case, the construction mogul. He's also her guardian, so he'll make the formal announcement later. We wanted you to be the first to know."

"Why?"

"Aren't you my oldest friend, Rick?"

The purr of Hal Stacey's voice brought an unwelcome image of Hal himself—debonair, handsome as a picture star (and vaguely resembling several), positive that his charm could breach all barriers.

"Come off it, Hal. Let's play it straight."

"I want you to meet Carol."

"What comes afterward?"

"Afterward, you may have a single dance with her. She's going South tomorrow——"

"To Central City—by any chance?"

There was the smallest of pauses on the wire. "The studio gave me your flight number," said Hal. "Carol hates traveling alone: I'm sure you won't mind——"

"I don't mind at all, if that's your only reason for calling me."

"Won't it do for now?"

"It'll do nicely," said Rick. "I'll join you in a half-hour."

Rick's apartment hotel maintained a twenty-four-hour valet service. It had standing orders to keep his wardrobe in order against his return. Remembering his last visit to the Golden Glades, he took out a dinner coat—if only for protective coloration. As he adjusted his tie, he surveyed his lean profile in the dressing-room mirror. Like his sober garb, it seemed adequate, if not spectacular.

He would never match Hal Stacey, in either looks or gall: he could still say, in all honesty, that he had earned the title of world citizen. As an international reporter, he had interviewed picture stars and premiers, war lords and one-world apostles: he had no reason under heaven to quail at the prospect of meeting the niece of Walter Case. Yet he felt a tingle of anticipation as he stepped into the elevator. Knowing Hal as he did, it was a tingle not unmixed with dread.

The Case Construction Company was an industrial behemoth: based in Central City, its work was known all over the globe. Rick had watched its engineers lay pipelines in Arabia and dam rivers in Africa; he had seen its town planners busy themselves on the Siberian steppes and the Alaskan tundra. Hal Stacey had illustrated these continuing miracles in a photographic series that had just run its course in a national magazine. One of Hal's better achievements, it was a departure for Case, whose public relations had always been muted, on the theory that the firm's end product was its best advertisement.

Significantly, there had been no photograph of the company head in that colorful camera essay: few newsmen had seen Walter Case in the flesh. Like his colleagues, Rick had concluded that the builder was another of those natural geniuses, immersed in his achievement, with no regard for personal glory. If Hal had broken that self-imposed isolation, the hand of the construction king's niece was a proper reward. Viewed from this romantic angle, it was easy to forgive the camera reporter's pride. Since Hal was anything but romantic, Rick was positive the reason for his summons was more devious.

When he entered the Golden Glades, he found the nightclub had changed its décor: it was now a Scheherazade dream in black and gold, a sultan's tent with divans of tigerskin and a turbaned orchestra. The floor was jammed with the after-theater crowd. The proprietor, who recognized Rick instantly, waved his own head waiter aside and hurried forward to explain that Miss King and Mr. Stacey were dancing.

"Will you come to their table, Mr. Jordan?"

"I'll watch a moment from here, Mario."

The dance floor was bathed in colored spots, leaving the gold-tented circumference in shadow: it seemed worthwhile to study Hal and his alleged fiancée before announcing his presence. Rick found them easily. Hal's tall frame was a head above most of the dancers, and the woman in his arms would have seemed statuesque had she danced less gracefully.

Rick could not see her face at once; he observed only that her dark-red hair was real (if one could judge by her coloring), that the striking green sequin gown was an original. He had expected a classic beauty to match those bare, almost Junoesque shoulders, the proud head with its flaming coronet braid. When she turned in Hal's arms, he saw that Carol King was merely pretty, with a tiptilted nose and a generous mouth that curved in laughter at some sally of her partner's. She seemed one with the music, responding to Hal's guidance with perfect accord. Yet the conviction persisted that her thoughts were elsewhere. Even when she whirled from view in the press about the bandstand, Rick could half-pretend that she had sensed his presence.

Feeling his pulse quicken, he knew the fantasy for what it was. During most of his forty-odd years, he had lost all thought of self in his devotion to his work. Telling himself firmly that a roving reporter could never marry (much less settle down), he had let random heart throbs take the place of love. His life had given him small chance for introspection. It was only at a moment like this—when he stood, as it were, in limbo between Europe and his native shore—that he could measure the true depths of his loneliness.

The spasm of frustration passed, as quickly as it had come. But he was careful to turn into the bar for a solitary drink until he was certain of his aplomb. It was a long time since he had yielded so easily to the need for affection—and the castle-building that was its inevitable sequel. Tonight, when he faced Hal Stacey and his girl, he would need all his defenses in order. When the music ended and he crossed the dance floor, he was girded for battle.

Hal bounced up to meet him with both hands outstretched. The Big Hello was a Stacey staple.

"Better late than never," he cried. "Carol was sure you'd stood us up." He led Rick to his tigerskin lair, presenting him with a flourish.

Carol King extended her hand. Rick noted with approval that she had smiled only with her lips; the eyes were detached, and just as appraising as his own. "This is an unexpected honor, Mr. Jordan," she said. "It was good of you to join us. I know it's routine these days to cross an ocean between meals—but you must be tired."

"I'm not in the least tired," he said, careful to match her tone. "It was good of you to invite me, Miss King."

"The name is Carol," said Hal. "You can call him Rick, my dear—his public does. Besides, this is Operation Ice-breaking. Don't forget you'll be traveling companions tomorrow." He had already thrust Rick down to the banquette, with a practiced hand. Now, with a broad wink, he darted away to join a table of picture moguls, clustered like wary vultures around a starlet whose figure was famous on two continents.

Rick lifted his eyebrows, and met Carol King's glance. "Hal's always forthright," he said. "Tonight, he's outdoing himself. Not that I mind—if you don't."

"Have we been thrown together with a purpose, Rick?"

"In Hal's place, I'd have done likewise," he said.

"He's avoided marriage successfully for a long time," said Carol. "His friends must wonder how I landed him."

"I'd put that the other way. Hal Stacey is a lot luckier than he deserves."

"Isn't that a rather hasty judgment? I'm sure he's kept me a profound secret."

"It's part of my job to put people on the line, Carol. Shall I tell you who you are—and see how right I am?"

"If this is a game," said Carol, "I'm enjoying it."

"Call it my bread and butter," he said. "I might add that I'm seldom taken in." He paused on that, to let the implication register. "First off, you're a Southerner who's lost most of her accent. There's just enough molasses left to keep the franchise. You're what we call quality in my corner of the South, and you deserve that label. You're a career girl, and you've succeeded damned well at your work——" He paused, wondering if this approach was having its desired effect, but Carol King's expression was unchanged.

"So far," she told him, "you're doing wonderfully."

"I won't guess your age," he said. "That would be really ungallant, let's say you're at least ten years younger than Stacey——"

"I've just turned thirty, Rick." Her chin had lifted now, in a laughing burlesque of outrage. He realized that he had yet to penetrate her defenses. "Don't think Hal's been my only suitor. In the last few years, I've turned down all kinds of proposals—in several languages."

"Of course you have. You've lived and worked abroad —and speak French perfectly. German almost as well—"

"Are you understudying that professor in *My Fair Lady?*"

"It's my turn to take a compliment," said Rick. "I've made a hobby of speech patterns. Wasn't your college Radcliffe—or Wellesley?"

"Sorry to disappoint you there," said Carol. "I took one degree at Barnard. And a master's at Carnegie Tech."

"If you're a lady engineer, I'll call myself a failure."

"Thanks for saying lady. Most men don't think a woman can also be an engineer."

"May I ask what branch?"

"I don't drive a bulldozer for my uncle, if that's what's troubling you. I'm a designer. Industrial layouts, for the most part. This is my fifth year at Case. Before that, I worked in Paris and New York——"

"So you work for Case now. I might have guessed." A pattern of sorts was emerging from this impromptu approach. "Are you returning to Central City to close down shop?"

"Because of Hal? Certainly not. We both mean to go on with our work. They've given him a darkroom in the Case Building——"

"Meaning he's now your uncle's press agent?"

"It's a far bigger job than that," said Carol. "Hal is making a photographic record of our projects. He's also reorganizing our information files. Those magazine pieces were only a by-product."

"Is it to be a full-time position?"

Carol looked toward the bar, where Hal had just cornered another personality for earnest discussion. "Can you imagine Hal Stacey doing any *one* think full time?"

"Go on, please. I'm glad to learn we're discussing the same dynamo."

"You are good friends, Rick. You needn't deny it."

He studied her carefully, before risking a reply. A woman's taste in men, he reflected, was one of the unsolved enigmas of living. Clearly, this was no time for candor.

"I've known Hal for twenty years," he said at last. "I've already told you he's luckier than he deserves. Shall we let it go at that?"

"Would it surprise you to hear he's worried—about you?"

"I'm not sure I could survive the shock, Carol."

"He's convinced you're going to Central City to write about civil rights—and he's afraid you'll be hurt. Please take that much on faith."

"Such an assignment can be dangerous these days. I don't need Hal to warn me. Fortunately, I'm flying South tomorrow for quite another reason: I've no thought of writing a word on the subject. After all, we're moving into 1963. It's hardly news that your state has held our highest tribunal at bay for ten years."

Carol King's chin had lifted with her smile, but her eyes had narrowed. "Would you deny it that privilege?"

"By no means—if your state has the court's ruling in mind. True integration in the Deep South must come in time. It's probably impossible in our day."

"We can agree on that, Rick."

"The problem will be settled eventually: your survival depends on it. But it must be worked out on terms both races can respect. You've had too many meddlers now—whether they call themselves NAACP lawyers, touring statesmen, or plain, snooping journalists. I've said it often in my columns."

"Why didn't you tell Hal that?"

"So far, I haven't had the chance. Besides, he wouldn't believe me."

"May I quote what you just said?"

"Of course. Just remember that it's part of Hal's job to suspect any statement I make. After all, we're rivals."

"Many of my friends back home would agree with you," said Carol. "Most of us are aware the present impasse can't last forever."

"What about yourself?"

"*I'm* in the largest group of all, Rick. I simply can't think the problem through—and I resent being hurried."

"Even after nine years?"

"You said yourself it would take a generation—in Central City."

"I won't deny that for a moment."

"Will you promise me to write nothing on the subject, when you see Bob Partridge?"

"You've no right to ask that. As I told you, I'm on quite another errand. If news is breaking when I arrive, I must cover it. How else can I call myself a reporter?"

"I won't quarrel with your job," said Carol. "That's beyond my province. Can you define your errand—or is that top secret?"

"Not at all. I hope to interview a Dr. Peter Moore at Valley Hospital—if the paper can arrange it." He broke off, when Carol King turned pale under her make-up. "Have I said something to offend you?"

He saw that she had found her control, in a single breath—but the fact that she had reached across the table to take his hand betrayed her. It was a pleading gesture that did not belong to Carol King. Brief as the contact was, he felt the impact. It was dangerous empathy, and he held back from it, even as he returned the pressure of her fingers.

"Must you go to Valley, Rick?"

"Why not—if there's a story in Dr. Moore?"

"Must *everything* be copy?"

"You know him, then?"

"We're old friends."

"Will he refuse to see me?"

"I'm sure of it. His methods are his own. He doesn't believe in sharing them."

"Can you explain why?"

"It's his secret. I respect it. Why can't you?"

"I'm a reporter. It's the nature of the brute to expose secrets."

"Even if it meant harm to someone?"

"I can't answer that remark, until you translate it."

"I think we've said enough tonight, Rick."

"More than enough—if you won't meet me half-way."

"I can assure you that I'm not being mysterious on purpose," said Carol. "My reasons for sparing Dr. Moore from the press are genuine. May I save them for tomorrow—and the plane? And will you forget to mention him to Hal?"

"The answer's yes, on both counts," he said. "Though I must say it's odd of us—keeping secrets from your fiancé."

"Valley Hospital is an exception," said Carol, with the ghost of a smile. "Hal is a Yankee from Boston."

"Is Dr. Moore a Southern problem?"

"We're saving him for the plane—remember?"

"I'll remember," he said. "That's my last question but one. Will you dance?"

"I've been waiting for you to ask me."

On the floor, he felt the same teasing excitement when she moved into his arms. It was only when they whirled past the bar that his heart sank in earnest. Hal Stacey was anchored there, deep in talk with the Nobel-prize-winning novelist who had just swept in with his retinue. Busy though he was, the camera reporter found time to offer him a solemn wink, across the great man's shoulder. For the first time, Rick realized that he had done just what Hal expected—even though he had walked into the trap with open eyes.

THE FLIGHT to Central City had made a single stop, at the Raleigh-Durham airport. Stretched full length in the luxury jet, with a wary eye on the passenger runway that led to the rotunda, Rick Jordan could rejoice in his situation. So far, he could not accept Carol King as his friend. It was impossible to believe she was his enemy.

After his brief dance, he had surrendered her to Hal Stacey, and left the Golden Glades. Alone in his apartment, he had passed a restless night, as he reviewed each nuance of their passage of arms. In a snow-smudged dawn, he had pinned down two certainties. Hal Stacey was about to use him as a pawn—and he had fallen in love with Carol (as disastrously as only a bachelor in his forties can fall in love). At the moment, it did not matter too much if Carol was an unwitting accomplice in Hal's design.

Desire was firmly on leash at the moment. In a different situation, he would have acted promptly: nothing could have been more rewarding than stealing Hal Stacey's girl. Unfortunately, until he had the facts at his command, it behooved him to walk with care. . . .

Until that moment of enlightenment (he repeated the conviction, while the first passengers returned from the Raleigh airport, after the ten-minute halt) his role was simple. He would continue to play the cynical reporter—a man who gave his friendship warily, a confidant who was reluctant, so far, to offer himself with his advice.

Another thing was certain (this was the journalist speaking, not the romantic). When Carol had settled on

Hal Stacey as a prospective husband, she had chosen blindly. He could never call her the devil's advocate, whatever her motive in sharing this flight to Central City.

They had talked quite frankly while the great, four-engined ship roared south from New York. Had they been friends of long standing, Carol King could not have spelled out her life story with greater candor.

She had been born in Central City just thirty years ago—the only child of Alice Case (a descendant of one of the oldest families in the South) and Jefferson King, a *beau sabreur* with no ancestors whatever. Jeff King had been an ace in the Canadian Air Force, a barnstorming flier with a flair for airplane design. After the marriage, he had been taken into the empire of Walter Case as an engineering consultant and sent on a ground-breaking expedition in Brazil. Two months before Carol's birth, he had died in an air crash. Her mother (already pining in enforced separation) had survived her birth by just three years. Walter Case, the only living relative who could afford such gestures, had taken over the girl's raising thereafter.

It was Case who had selected her college and her boarding school, who had persuaded her to take a second degree at Carnegie Tech. When she was halfway through Barnard, he had done his best to play down her engagement to Kerry Loring—a millionaire at twenty-one, whose only hobby, before Carol, had been sports-car racing. Case (who could see a bit farther than his niece) had predicted Loring would die behind the wheel before the betrothal could be translated into marriage. Actually, he had perished in the cockpit of his Piper Cub, en route to a race in Maine.

Carol had lost a college year thereafter, in what Central City called a nervous breakdown. For a time (and here, too, she was quite frank) her condition had been far more serious: she had received an extended course of psychotherapy in the private wing of Valley Hospital, with Dr. Peter Moore as her physician. Once she had risen from her depression, recovery had been swift. She had known her cure was complete when she found she could enter a passenger plane without quailing. The act had been part of Dr. Moore's therapy. Even today, she did not quite trust herself to fly alone. ...

"Did you love Loring that much?"

"Remember, I was only twenty. While it lasted, he was everything to me."

"Did losing him make it last that much longer?"

"I can see now that he was just a playboy. If he'd lived, he would have had four wives before he turned thirty. Uncle Walter was right to oppose the engagement—but I hated him all the more for his wisdom."

"You don't hate him now."

"He saved me that year. A push in the wrong direction could have wrecked my whole life. Instead, I found the work I was born to do—and I learned to fight back. It's a good lesson to learn young."

Above the Raleigh airport, her hand had crept into his, just as it had done at Idlewild: it was the only leftover of the fears that had pursued her since childhood. Even this would go in time, after a few more journeys by air. Dr. Moore had said her cure was complete, since she herself had willed it.

When the plane set down, Carol had gone into the airport to telephone. Rick had been grateful for this short interlude, since it permitted him to consult his notes one last time. So far, he had been careful to avoid the subject of Valley Hospital and its presiding genius.

Last year, he had visited a dozen hospitals to prepare his series on mental health, and Dr. Peter Moore had been one name among many. The subject had proved more formidable than he had dreamed: blind alleys had been endless, and he had been reluctant to venture into another. In one sense, Valley Hospital was a rarity—a fine physical plant, administered by a first-class man at

snake-pit level. Yet it had seemed unlikely that even the
most dedicated of psychiatrists could surmount the barriers of apathy and graft erected by the usual corrupt
administration at the State House in Central City. The
pattern had repeated itself too often in state institutions
Rick had visited. Criminals, psychopaths, the unwanted
old (the flotsam that drifted through all cities) usually
ended here. Understaffed and ill-equipped, the asylum
could offer little more than shelter, and an enviroment
not too different from prison.

Or so Rick had thought—until he had read a recent
article in the *American Journal of Psychiatry* describing
Dr. Moore's work at Valley in his own words, and listing
his amazing percentage of cures. The figures in themselves
would have sent him winging South in his first free moment. But it was the brief notation at the end of the
article that had made the visit imperative:

> All patients reported here [Dr. Moore had written]
> were treated with the dynamic method of psycho-
> therapy developed by Dr. Franz Alexander at the
> Chicago Institute for Psychoanalysis. Due credit,
> however, must be given to another factor—a state of
> trust, closely resembling the classic transference
> characteristic of regular analysis, but going far be-
> yond it, which the subjects develop for one of the
> inmates. This inmate, for reasons that are not rele-
> vant here, prefers to withhold his name.
>
> Without his influence, it is safe to say that many
> cases reported at Valley Hospital would have ended
> in failure.

Rick had read the article in Rome. Unable to leave his
European commitments, he had cabled his New York
editor, asking him to set up an interview. The editor's
note, and a brief letter from Moore himself, completed
the dossier he had just taken from his attaché case. Valley

Hospital, it seemed, had no wish for publicity of any kind. The article in the *Journal* had been addressed to the medical profession only.

The *Record* had suggested that its star columnist pursue the matter at local level, using Bob Partridge as intermediary. . . . Rick looked up to find that Carol was standing in the aisle. He rose to make room for her at the window seat, leaving the attaché case open between them.

"Any luck with your calls?"

"Hal has finished his business in New York," she said. "He's flying down this noon. And Uncle Walter is sending his car to the airport. I asked him to come too, but he couldn't get away. I wanted to introduce you."

"I'm told your uncle avoids the press. In his way, he's as gun-shy as Dr. Peter Moore."

"I still hoped you could meet unofficially. At least he could explain why you'll never get to Valley Hospital."

Rick placed the attaché case on Carol's lap. "Read these notes through," he said. "Until you do, I won't say a word. And fasten your seat belt. We're about to be airborne."

Watching while she read, he saw her eyes widen at the finale to Moore's article. Her perusal of the *Record's* office memoranda produced a brisk nod of approval. When she returned the case, he tossed it to the overhead rack with a chuckle.

"Much as I'd enjoy holding hands again," he said, "I'm glad to see you managed this takeoff without it."

Carol stared down at the checkerboard of the Carolinas, twenty thousand feet below them. "If this is your idea of therapy, I'll endorse it," she said. "Those notes made revealing reading. They should convince you I'm right."

"Right about what? That Dr. Peter Moore is a high priest of medicine—and, like so many holy men, on the impractical side?"

"Isn't that his privilege?"

"Not if he's found a new way to heal the sick. Such discoveries belong to the world."

"Not until he's ready to share them."

"Tell me this much, Carol. Did he use this treatment when you were a patient?"

"I can't answer," she said quickly—but he was certain, from her taut voice, that he had hit the mark.

"You were pronounced cured eight years ago," he said. "Since that date, Dr. Moore has claimed many similar cures. It's time the public was informed——"

"Science is a long process of trial and error," said Carol. "Ehrlich needed five years to establish the properties of salvarsan. Can't you allow Dr. Moore his own period of testing—when his province is the human mind?"

"What's the inmate's name? The one whose thought transference is part of the therapy?"

"You must see I can't reveal it."

"I won't rest until I have the answer."

"Dr. Moore will never see reporters. And I'm moving to another seat—unless you stop asking me to violate a confidence."

"Who asked you to cover up? Moore—this patient—or someone else?"

Carol rose from the seat, with a red flag at each cheek. "Won't you believe I'm protecting a friend from needless suffering?"

"I'm trying hard," he said. "It'd be a lot easier, if you'd give me the man's name."

Her cheeks still flaming, Carol left him without another word. He made no move to follow her as she moved forward, to take a vacant seat behind the pilot's cabin. Twice in the next hour (watching her fingers tense on the seat arm, knowing she was still fighting the private devils of fear), the need to rise and comfort her was hard to control. But he knew he had burned his bridges: there could be no retreating now, no yielding to sentiment. For better or worse, he was committed to solving the mystery of Valley Hospital.

In Carolina, the gusty February day had held more than a hint of winter. In Central City, the air seemed balmy as May. As the plane door swung wide, Rick was conscious of the aromatic breath of pines, of a wide, tan river, of live oaks heavy with Spanish moss beside a traffic-filled highway. This, he sensed instantly, was the real Deep South, as removed from the Old Dominion of his youth as a cracker drawl. . . . He did not need the glimpse of a wedge of tall buildings on the horizon's rim to see it was also the New South—brash and bustling (for all that deceptive air of repose) and intolerant of any notion that clashed with its own.

Carol was the first passenger to leave the plane. Rick forced himself to keep his distance as she followed her bags across the tarmac and entered a chauffeur-driven limousine. Then, lifting his attaché case from the rack, he stepped down to Southern earth, and moved toward the line of waiting taxis.

"Howdy, Mr. Jordan."

He turned in mild annoyance toward the voice: accustomed as he was to recognition, he had hoped to reach a taxi unheralded. The man who faced him at the barrier was stoop-shouldered, china-bald, and faintly rumpled. He seemed to doze on his feet as he leaned against the gate.

"Don't worry—I won't ask for your autograph. Bob Partridge sent me to welcome you to God's country. My name's Judd. Theobald Judd."

The name was familiar. Rick extended his hand, and tried to pin down the memory. "Sorry you had to be troubled; I could have taken a cab."

"Easier to use my station wagon," said Judd. "If you'll give me your ticket, I'll collect your bags."

"Let me handle that, at least. How's Bob these days?"

"Still rooting for Utopia," said Judd. "And still on the warpath. I'm to deliver you at the shop. Where are you staying—the Cavalier?"

A moment later, when he had climbed into a decrepit station wagon and noted the battery of cameras in the rear seat, Rick understood why his companion wore a Rolleiflex at his neck, as naturally as most men would sport a muffler. He spoke the name aloud, as recollection struck a tardy chime.

"Theo Judd! The 1960 Pulitzer, wasn't it?"

"Nineteen sixty-one," said Judd, with a bobbing motion of the head that was oddly bashful. "I'm one of Bob's picture crew, when I'm not his trouble-shooter."

Rick could see the photograph in his mind's eye, along with the searing caption. Judd's camera had broken a state scandal wide open, pinpointing an actual payoff in gangland, in a fashion not even the machine could dispute. As a result, the *Times-News* had known its day of glory in Sunday supplements. . . . Judd's sleepy exterior, thought Rick (like the battered car he was driving), was only camouflage.

"We'll go by the River Road," said the photographer. "It's slower than the expressway, but you'll get a better idea of the town. How long since you've been here?"

"Nearly three years. This is my second look at Central City."

"You'll find we've grown," said Judd. "That's the Case Tool Works on your right: twenty thousand men, working under one roof. And there's the North City High School— padlocked since September, like the whole state. Is that what you're gunning for, by any chance?"

"This time, I'm after different game. What can you tell me about Valley Hospital?"

The photographer snorted, without looking up from his driving. "Only that it's out of bounds."

"Outside the city limits, you mean?"

"In a manner of speaking. One of those places we don't go until we're asked. Like the state prison farm, or Bowie

Stead's stag dinners. I don't think a reporter has set foot in Valley since it opened—and that was ten years ago."

"Wasn't it worth a try?"

"Not in Central City, Mr. Jordan. We all know Bowie milked the taxpayers for plenty, when he ran up those lovely buildings. There was a real hoopla when the place opened—and that was curtains. If graft was news in this state, we'd have to print a two-hundred-page edition to cover all of it."

Rick did not pursue the topic: the cynical dismissal was hardly reassuring. It was evident he had picked up a lead the local paper had missed—thanks to the massive, winnowing thoroughness of a metropolitan daily like the *Record*. Bob Partridge, who seldom flubbed a story, had merely lumped Dr. Peter Moore's hospital with the vast mushroom of corruption that spread like an umbrella above Central City. . . . The oversight was not to his discredit—nor to Theo Jüdd's. The most seasoned reporter, working at State House level, could turn over just so many stones.

"Bob was hoping you'd come down to do a column on the school closings," said Judd. He had swung away from the river, to enter a traffic-clogged commercial artery. Ahead, the looming office buildings of Central City rose clifflike against the sun. "I'll drop you first at the office, then take your bags to the Cavalier. The boss is primed with a fight talk to get you started."

"Not on integration," Rick said firmly. "I've already put my views on the line—as Bob well knows."

"I've read your stuff on Little Rock, and the Virginia smoke screens," said the photographer. "If you don't mind the observation, that was some time ago——"

"Has the situation really changed?"

"In Bob's opinion," said Judd, "Little Rock was just a skirmish before the main event." He tramped on the gas, shooting ahead of a trailer truck, to beat a long line of cars to the light. "It's his hunch the real war will start right here. Don't let the quiet deceive you."

They had entered the inevitable Negro section that clings (like jungle moss) to the fringe of every Southern city. This colored town, Rick saw, was no worse than others—no more jumbled than most, despite its squalor. The bleached houses gave off a dry, acrid reek of poverty his trained nostrils recognized instantly, but there was no real overtone of despair. Resignation was the dominant note, from the crone chewing her snuff stick in a doorway to the children at play in the shade of a mulberry tree. . . . In his youth, he had taken that resignation for granted. Driving through the Negro quarter of Danville, he had seldom troubled to glance into the dark faces that had stared up so blankly at his passing. The picture was unchanged today—and he made the admission freely. Here in the South, one took the changeless for granted.

"Locust Street is still our dividing line," said Judd. "Minute that light changes, we'll be out of Coon Hollow."

"Is that what Central City calls it?"

"We don't mince words here, Mr. Jordan. And I'll tell you more. They've three schools in the Hollow—all of 'em wide open. No question of race-mixing *there*. Bob says it's to rub people's noses in the fact that colored folks who know their place can still get educated—to a point. It's only troublemakers who get locked out——"

"Along with a few thousand white children."

"Nearly twenty thousand, in Central City alone. Leastways, that's our Governor's notion. So far, he's made it stick in most people's craws. They're beginning to gag, now their kids have been moping or raising hell for over six months."

"What comes next?"

Theo Judd shook his head vigorously. "That's Bob's baby, not mine—and he's been raising it, ever since '54. All I can do is point my camera and hope for the worst."

"Don't you mean the best?"

"The worst picture often makes the best news."

The car was cutting through a workingman's suburb—long rows of bungalows, each with its plot of sun-bitten grass, its carport, and its backyard truck garden. Here there was no trace of the bitter poverty that had marked the Hollow. Yet, oddly enough, these houses seemed just as drab as the Negro shanties—and, despite their smug prosperity, just as faceless. Seen en masse, the area reminded Rick of the trailer camps that stretched for miles along tourist highways in Florida.

"You might call it a company village," said Judd. "Sleeps and wakes when the Case whistles blow. Eats high off the hog today—and God help it when the whistle stops. That's when they'll start burning crosses in the Hollow——"

The wheels turned; the station wagon entered a broad, tree-shaded avenue that curved to embrace a college campus, and one of the largest playing fields Rick had ever seen. "Here's Fraternity Row, and our State University. You'll have to go to Texas to find a bigger football field——"

"Didn't the team lose a Bowl invitation—because the charter forbids it to compete with Negroes?"

"Your memory's first-rate, Mr. Jordan. We're headed for Crestwood now—our best residential district. Cheer up; the Cook's Tour is almost over."

"Did Bob order it, by any chance?"

"It was my own idea," said the photographer. "I wanted you to have a picture, before we reached home plate. See that skyscraper dead ahead? It's the Case Building. One on the left is the Dixie Trust. The Union Depot's between 'em. State House is on the next hill. You can't see it from here—which is just as well. It's Bowie Stead's idea of heaven, so it's on the garish side."

"Thanks for the briefing. No matter what Bob tells me, I'll be prepared."

3

Bob Partridge (owner, publisher, and managing editor of the Central City *Times-News*) was sturdy, broad-shouldered, and so short of leg as to seem almost squat. Thanks to the impact of his personality, most people remembered him as a colossus. At forty-five, he had long since gone gray—but the white cockscomb above his snapping blue eyes was only an amusing grotesque. One knew by instinct that Bob would never really age. The shout he flung at Rick Jordan, the moment Rick had settled in his office, was resonant as a college cheer.

"Damn Valley Hospital, boy! And damn headshrinker Moore! Don't waste a thought on him. I'm offering you an inside track, on the best story you'll ever write."

"There's a story in Dr. Moore too, Bob."

"Granted. A rose on a dunghill is always good copy. You can compose that prose poem later. *My* story is popping right now."

"If I listen, will you help me to set up an interview?"

"It won't be easy, Rick. Theo's told you that Moore's asylum is out of bounds."

"What's that supposed to mean to a reporter?"

"Like most of the loony bins you've visited, Valley's a dumping ground. A port of missing men. If Moore keeps things on an even keel there, and the Health Department can line enough pockets, everyone's satisfied to leave him be."

"Doesn't the setup make you curious?"

"Not when there's a bigger problem to solve—the destiny of this whole damned state. What's more important—

to track down a mad dog who's at large, or to visit a few hundred who are locked up?"

"A single mad dog—or a pack?"

"Call it a rabid pack with a ringleader. Damn you boy—why won't you catch fire?"

"I might, if you'd give me some facts."

Bob Partridge strode to the window that looked down on Central City's business district, and shook his fist at an invisible enemy. Familiar as he was with the gesture, and the verbal fireworks that were part of it, Rick knew this was no idle ranting.

"You must take the first big fact on faith," said the editor. "Even a transplanted Southerner will find it hard to believe. Our great Governor Bowie Stead has got this state sewed up tighter than most South American dictatorships. That's why you'll get nowhere with Moore, if the Health Bureau says no——"

"Things can't be that bad."

Bob's fist smashed down on a filing cabinet, so savagely it rang like a jungle tomtom. "Rick, you must live with this situation to see the point. It began when the civil rights hassle split us down the middle. Year by year, it's been getting worse. Talk about dictators and demagogues! Even I can't take some of the names that are coming up for election—and not just in our piney-wood counties. Back in the fifties, if these same fellows had filed as candidates, they'd have been hooted out of town. Now they're sweeping every primary——"

"In Central City too?"

"We've kept our city hall clean, thank God—and our city police. It's another story at the State House, now that people with moderate views are afraid to vote."

"I'm aware that few Negroes go to the polls here. Have they taken away the white franchise too?"

"It isn't a question of taking away," said Bob. "*Staying* away is a better word. Why not—when there's no real option for the intelligent voter? Decent men are unwilling to buck Stead and company. So it's a choice between

some gallus-snapper who believes only the white man is
descended from Adam, or a real leftist who'd smash our
whole system overnight. The voter who skips a primary in
such a situation is helping the state machine, as surely as
though he pulled the lever."

"Some people have spoken out."

"Not in the Deep South."

"Not even when the schools close and kids run
wild?"

"Not even then. John Public shuts his mouth and keeps
it shut. If he doesn't, he'll find dynamite in his garage."

"Have they threatened you again?"

"So often I've stopped counting," said the editor. "Forget about me, Rick. What really matters are the millions
of decent Southerners—men who know the Negro must
have his rights, if we're to hit our true potential. We've
got to reach those millions, if this thing's to be
stopped."

"I won't argue that, Bob."

"We were making progress—until the Supreme Court
jumped the gun in '54, and turned the whole desegregation problem into a political football. As a result, we've
not only lost the timing of our social evolution: we're
losing decent government. We're surrendered the destiny
of our children to men who are worse than bigots. You've
seen the same breed operate abroad. They can take over
the whole country, unless they're exposed for what they
are."

"Surely the trouble hasn't gone that far."

"It has in our State House, Rick—and the illness is
spreading. What argument can we offer for world peace,
when thirteen million of our citizens can't feel secure
because of their color? When other citizens, who happen
to be white, are blowing up churches and schools—and
the homes of people who oppose them? Foreigners are
already saying we're no better than the junta that runs
Russia——"

"Save it for an editorial," said Rick. "*I* don't need convincing."

"Be honest, boy," said Partridge. "You think I'm a do-gooder who's lost his mind. Like everyone else, you're sick of old wives' tales. Shall I shut up now—before I really bore you?"

"Stop being a fool, Bob. I believe every word."

"Prove it, then. Dig into this mess all the way. When you have the facts, do a special telecast on the state."

"That's asking a great deal. My program's off the air."

"You can get network time simply by asking. Remember what it was like here in '54? We were a great city in the making, progressive at all levels, a center of education for the whole South. Left alone, we'd have licked our race tensions the slow and easy way. We were ready for school integration, until Stead's gang began preaching to the woolhats——"

"As a blind, you mean?"

"Of course the school issue is a blind. Even a shyster like Bowie Stead knows the Constitution is the law. What they're shooting for is absolute control. And after that——"

"Slow down, Bob! Let me catch up."

"Remember my metaphor of the mad dog—and the wolf pack? Think it through, boy. You've got your answer."

"I find that hard to buy," said Rick. "I'm not being stubborn about the telecast—please believe me. But the whole idea of an American dictator, even at state level, is too fantastic."

"Take my word, this new campaign is well organized—and masterminded."

"By a single man?"

"By a leader, using the methods of the super-hoodlum. The campaign is regional right now—but it can spread. Don't think ours is the only area with problems. Suppose a man on horseback really takes over the state machine? In time, he'll sell his ideas beyond our borders. Give him solid power—and a real lever, like a war scare, or a countrywide depression. He could write his own ticket. Maybe even name our next President——"

"Huey Long is dead and buried, Bob."

"Even in the 1930's, Huey came awful close. This fellow has resources Long never dreamed of."

"Any candidates for your mastermind?"

"It isn't Stead. Bowie's an old-fashioned mugwump who does what he's told. Our man's an organizer behind the scenes. Someone with unlimited funds, who's used to making people jump. Completely ruthless, more than a little mad——"

"Admit that covers a lot of ground."

"The list isn't too long. You could name him, if you'd come into this all the way. Take off his wraps, Rick—and give him both barrels on your next *Profile for Tomorrow*. It's all I ask."

"What would a single telecast accomplish?"

"Don't be so modest. The *Times-News* reaches a half-million readers. Most of 'em don't get past the headlines and the comics. Your *Profiles* have an audience of forty million. People who know you're unbiased, that you deal with facts——"

"I can't even consider the idea, without a name to build around. You must see that."

"Give the project a week. If we don't turn up a worthwhile lead, you can call it quits."

"How could I begin, without giving myself away?"

"You came here to interview Dr. Moore. Follow through on that line. Bang your head against the State House wall: watch the Stead commandos in action. Maybe you'll see who throws the switch."

"It won't be that easy, Bob."

"Every would-be tyrant has his weak spot—his Achilles heel. Find that weak spot, and we'll bring him to earth."

"It's a tall assignment."

"For a tall man," said Bob Partridge. "Tell me you'll

take it, and I'll sleep easier tonight—with or without dynamite."

"Suppose they put a stick under my bed?"

"It's a risk you'll run, of course."

Rick breathed deep, then held out his hand. "I'll try it," he said. "For a week, at least—and always providing I can cover Valley Hospital, if they let me inside. I slept with my last bomb in Berlin. It's time I tested my nerves again."

The editor seized his hand and pressed it fervently. "When will you start—tomorrow?"

Rick laughed. "You *are* getting old, Bob—if you'll let me sleep on this. You spoke of a pattern just now. Can you fill it in?"

"Not all the way," the editor admitted. "But it's getting clearer every day. You know about the newest bombings, of course?"

"Who doesn't?"

"They follow a definite timetable in this state, as though they were pinpointed on the map. All of 'em precede or follow bombings elsewhere. Here in Central City the police have collared a few suspects. Some of them have talked. So far, no one of importance has been implicated: we aren't even sure where the explosives come from. Most of the culprits are hit and run. The sort who preach doom from the nearest soapbox. Or sell hate sheets that smear Catholics and Jews as well as Negroes. Obviously, they're skirmishers who don't even know the name of their general."

"You can count on the local police?"

"Almost completely, so far. Of course Stead controls the state troopers, and most of the county sheriffs."

"What about the troubles outside the state? Do you think they're plotted from the same headquarters?"

"It figures, Rick—it really does. If they're spontaneous, why do they never overlap? And why else would the various state machines correlate their publicity? Hate merchants always work on the installment plan."

"Any rumbles from the Klan?"

"It never counted here—even in the twenties. Blowhards for the most part, who were satisfied with robbing hen roosts. The leftovers, such as they are, have been absorbed into the Knights of Freedom. You might call it the aftermath of the KKK."

"It hasn't made too many headlines, so far."

"The Knights are still a new outfit. Ten thousand, maybe, in the whole state—but they're growing. They've a double-barreled slogan: *Keep the South Pure*—and *Peace without Violence*. They hold rallies at the University stadium that sound like an open lodge meeting. But they wear the same nightshirts, and they burn the same crosses. That's part of the plot, of course. It's my hunch their Grand Leader and our mastermind are the same man. Whoever's giving orders, they put on a damned impressive show—by mob standards."

"Twentieth-century chivalry—and power on leash?"

"And no violence. Right now, we get that from our motorcycle clubs."

"I've read about them too."

"They're nothing new, of course. We've had cycle clubs for years, all over the South. In this state, we've branches in every county—all of 'em organized like circus riders. Naturally, they wear a sort of uniform—cowboy boots, skin-tight jeans, crash helmet. Most of 'em couldn't afford the helmet, let alone a machine. They're on someone's payroll."

"Has there been a marked increase in crime?"

"No more than you'd expect, with gangs of teen-agers owning the roads, and no schools to use up their high spirits. That's also part of the grand design. Peace and prosperity on surface—the mailed fist underneath, for anyone who talks back. Each Knights of Freedom cell has a hard-rock core: I can prove they're armed to the teeth. So are the instructors who train the cycle clubs. That's what hurts me most. All the undirected passions of the average boy, tied up in one package for purely evil ends——"

"Like Hitler's S.S. guards?"

"There are other parallels. Check 'em on your own, Rick. Don't accuse me of forcing history to repeat itself."

"Let's get back to my cover—as they say in Army G-2. Should I head for Valley Hospital and crash the door? Or is the smarter to get lost in the State Capitol?"

"We'll start your cover right here," said the editor. "Your visit with me will be all over town. Theo's spreading the word from the Press Club bar. We're running a front-page story on your arrival—including your plan to interview Dr. Moore. If they really mean to keep you out, they'll have time to throw up barricades."

"Suppose I get red-carpet treatment?"

"You will—to a point. The first man to see tomorrow is Dr. Matt Penfield, our State Director of Hospitals. He's a political appointee—less than a year in office, a real double-talker. He'll be your first sounding board. If he balks, you can be sure the road blocks are up. If he gives you a snow job, take down the details. I'll translate later."

"One thing more, Bob. Where does Hal Stacey fit into the Central City story?"

For the first time, Partridge looked startled. "Is Hal Stacey fouling up my backyard? That's bad news to me."

"I flew down from New York with his fiancée. He's taking the next plane."

"Don't tell me Hal's in Central City permanently. He's never anywhere for long."

"His fiancée tells me he's working for Case Construction."

The editor was really frowning now. Bob Partridge was seldom puzzled by the behavior of his fellow-humans. At such moments, he resembled a small boy with a case of sulks.

"This could be an angle," he said. "It won't be the first time Hal's played on both sides. If he's working for Case, he could be shilling for Bowie Stead too. I wouldn't put it past him."

"Nor would I," said Rick. "I'm sure of this much: he's eager to know what I'm after here. Of course that's always Hal's way. There isn't a smoother brain-picker."

"Who's the lady he's planning to marry?"

"Her name is Carol King. She's Case's niece—one of his industrial designers."

"I know Miss King well. She's a damned fine woman. Much too sensible to fall in love with Hal."

"Since when has a woman in love been sensible?"

"I'll get a line on Hal before we talk again."

"No one plays tighter poker than Stacey," Rick warned.

"I'll put Theo Judd on it. Being in the same trade, he may pick up something. Besides, he's an old friend of Carol's. Helped with her models, when she was first starting at Case——"

"Tell him to keep my name out of it," said Rick. "I asked a few questions too many on the plane."

"About Valley Hospital?"

"How did you guess?"

"She was there as a patient, for almost a year. In the Case Pavilion. In her book, Peter Moore is first cousin to the saints—and deserves his privacy. Theo himself tried to wangle an interview a few years ago, and she came down on him like a ton of bricks."

"My case is hopeless then. I've already told her I mean to blast my way in."

"Keep on saying that, boy. It's your cover—remember?"

Rick got to his feet. It had been a revealing half-hour, though hardly a comforting one. Outside the city room hummed with a special rhythm that meant a deadline was approaching. While the two men shook hands a second time in the open door, a copy boy rushed in with galleys. Bob grinned as he read them through.

"I see by tomorrow's paper that a distinguished newshawk is in our midst," he said. "A fellow named Rick Jordan. Seems he's hell-bent to do a piece on our number-one mental hospital. Like to read our interview?"

"I'll trust you there," said Rick. "Just kill the adjective."

"Sorry—it's already on the press. See you deserve it when you go to work tomorrow. By the way, I'm giving you Theo Judd as a man Friday. Don't hesitate to use him."

"I won't need a photographer at the moment."

"Theo's not just a photographer. He's also a first-rate leg-man—and he knows the short cuts."

A line of reporters waited at the door: there was a murmur of interest as eyes identified Rick Jordan, but he was only vaguely conscious of the scrutiny as he moved on. Bob Partridge had laid a heavy task on his shoulders, and he was beginning to regret his easy acceptance. So far, he could devise no way to lift it.

If what Bob said was true, he had chanced on the story of the year—perhaps even the decade. So far, it was based on conjecture—but he could trust Bob's judgment, as surely as he trusted his own. It was a solemn moment and a chilling one—and he needed solitude to organize his thoughts. Once he had slept on an assignment, however difficult, he could rely on his subconscious to prepare the right attack.

At his hotel, a bellboy was ready with his bags. After he had registered, he strolled to the entrance of the café-bar—and drew back at once, glad of the protection offered by the ornate grillwork. Hal Stacey was just surrendering his hat to the checkroom: Carol King stood inside, chatting with the maître d'hôtel while she awaited her escort. Both were in evening dress, and both were obviously on the town. . . . Following his bags to the elevator, Rick could not suppress a pang of envy: he

could not deny that Hal and Carol made a handsome
pair.

Even if he had not quarreled with Carol on the plane,
he could not have intruded on another date with her
fiancé. The enigma of her anger remained—like a grain
of sand in the cogs of a well-oiled machine. The solution
must wait. Bob had supplied a partial answer, but her
motives lay deeper.

In his room, he unpacked and lay for a half-hour in a
scalding tub before he sought his bed. Feeling his eyelids
grow heavy before his head could touch the pillow, he
pictured Hal and Carol dancing in the café fourteen
stories below. It was not a happy image. Yet, oddly
enough (since he was a man who had had little truck with
rapture), he could say in all honesty that he was close to
content. Ways and means to separate Carol from the
camera reporter could still be found, before it was too
late. With luck, he might even prove that he was her
friend.

Meanwhile, he was facing what might prove the task of
his career—and it was the work he loved.

Rick wakened to a dull rumble that might have been
thunder: even in sleep, he knew better. The second blast
shook the structure of the hotel. It found him completely
awake, dressing with all the speed of a volunteer fireman,
almost before he could remember where he was.
Newsmen, like poets, are born and not made—and he had
responded to that familiar herald of disaster by instinct.

He was knotting his tie at the mirror before he was
fully awake. There was still no lost motion when he dialed
the *Times-News*.

"Another bombing, Mr. Jorden," said the night city
editor. "We just got the flash from our district man. This
time, it's a Catholic day school. Our Lady of Mercy Convent, on the North Side. Whole place is already on
fire."

His second call, to the night desk of the New York

Record, brought Jim Nichols to the phone. Jim (a friend of rewrite days) sounded only faintly surprised.

"In harness so soon, Rick? I thought this was a busman's holiday."

"I'm calling from Central City. A Catholic school has just been bombed, and I'm ready to cover. Do we have a stringer here?"

"Not at the moment," said Nichols. "We pick up our stuff from the *Times-News.* It's a break having you there. Sure you want to handle it alone?"

"This could be a feature, Jim. Bob Partridge says these blasts are pinpointed. I'm beginning to think he's right."

"File the first story, and we'll fly someone down tomorrow for the follow-up. Can you make the late city?"

Rick glanced at his watch: to his surprise, he found it was only midnight. He had slept barely three hours, yet he felt completely rested. "With luck, I'll be on the wires in an hour."

"Luck's usually with you, fellow," said Nichols. "I'll keep a front-page spot."

In the lobby, Rick paused to ring Theo Judd's number— and, when it failed to answer, assumed he was also en route to the convent. When he was in his taxi, the full import of Nichols' last words struck home. It was true that luck had always perched on his shoulder. Tonight, every instinct he possessed insisted he was en route to big news. This was no isolated incident in the long chronicle of man's inhumanity to man—but a deliberate act, as coldly planned as a move in chess.

Memory ticked off the roll call, while the taxi sped down a short cut to the North Side. The first bomb in the current salvo (and this, too, was part of the pattern) had destroyed the home of a Negro minister in a city five hundred miles distant: the man had been a leader of his race, prominent in the fight against segregation. The next had blasted the synagogue of a Northern rabbi who had spoken against racial discrimination. Last week, a mysterious fire had demolished the print shop of a militant weekly that had attacked the censorship activities of a right-wing group, in a town just over the state line.

Now in Central City itself, Catholics were the target. He knew without asking that the convent of Our Lady of Mercy, like so many other Catholic schools, did not discriminate in the admission of students to its classrooms.

4

CENTRAL CITY was already a metropolis in size if not in spirit: Rick fumed in the back seat of the taxi for a good twenty minutes before it reached the scene of the bombing.

Here, as he had feared, he found the way blocked by a cordon of patrol cars. Uniformed men were everywhere. Their picturesque garb (knee-high boots, whipcord breeches, gray-white tunics and cowboy sombreros) identified them as county patrolmen. Evidently, North Side was just over the city line—outside the jurisdiction of the city police.

Even at this distance he could see the school building had been partially demolished. Though fire spouted from the gutted walls, the danger was under control, judging by the welter of hoses that filled the street, and the steam that rose from all sides, as a half-dozen nozzles inundated the flames. The fire department, it seemed, had arrived with commendable dispatch. It was hard to understand the cordon of troopers. The school stood apart from the nearest residential district, and only a handful of spectators had gathered to watch the firemen at work.

Waving his police card, and hoping he would be mistaken for a local reporter, Rick raced toward the nearest of the engines, only to have his approach barred by a six-foot trooper, a good block from the school.

"Stay where you are, mister."

"I'm Richard Jordan, of the New York *Record.*"

"I don't give a damn where you're from. Nobody gets any closer till the sheriff gives the word."

45

"What's his name? I'd like to talk to him."

"He's too busy——"

"Having trouble, Rick?"

He turned in relief; the lanky form at his elbow was Theo Judd. "This man won't believe I'm a reporter. Will you tell him my police card's real?"

"I know who you are, mister," said the trooper. "I got a TV set at home. I still won't let you through. And that goes double for *Times-News* snoops—with or without cameras."

The photographer plucked at Rick's sleeve. "Follow me," he whispered. "We'll try another angle."

"What gives here?" Rick demanded as they moved away. "Don't they let the press cover a fire until it's over?"

"Not if it's in the county. Sheriff Colt is a crony of the Governor's; the county police are well drilled for these shows. He's up there right now, risking his life among the embers—to make sure no real clues are left behind."

"You mean the sheriff knew of the bombing beforehand?"

"Doubled in spades," said Theo. "Follow me—and move fast. I see a friend in need."

Two minutes later a bill had changed hands and they were on their way to the fire chief's car, parked on a concrete apron that separated the parish school from the convent proper. It was now evident that the fire-fighters had gained the upper hand. Save for a corner of the shattered building, where a red geyser spouted skyward, the blaze had been reduced to embers. The helmeted, water-soaked man who stood on the front bumper of a car to survey the operation seemed anything but happy at the result.

"This is Chief Porter, Rick," said Theo. "Does Rick Jordan need an introduction, Harry?"

The chief pushed back his helmet, and wiped a streaming brow. "The television man, is it? I heard you were in town."

"What happened here?"

"Blew out a whole wall of the school, and most of the roof. Delayed-action fuse, and just enough incendiary to wipe out the proof."

Theo, mounting the car bumper in turn, lifted his Rolleiflex to snap the first of several shots. "Same old routine, Harry? No evidence?"

"They do these jobs by the book," said the chief. "You know that by now. It could just as well have happened tomorrow—my kids go to that school."

"Any advance notice, this time?"

"The usual blind phone call—saying a school would be bombed. Who thought it'd be this one? The Sisters never hurt nobody."

"Apparently they hurt the men who set the bomb," said Rick.

"How come, Mr. Jordan?"

"By being what they are—and opening their doors to anyone who wanted an education."

"Reckon that's the size of it," said the chief. "There *were* a few Nigra children in the middle grades. Not more'n a dozen, at the most, but——"

"This place won't open again until fall," said Theo. "If it does, most folks will be afraid to send their children. Can we get any closer?"

"I'll take you myself," said the chief.

"The sheriff's men tried to keep us from getting this far," Rick warned.

Porter swore a blistering oath. "If Colt had his way, the place would have burned to the ground. Next time those troopers put an oar into my business, there'll be broken heads."

Shepherded by the chief, the two newsmen moved toward the ruins of the school. A heavy-set man in the uniform of a trooper, and wearing a gold badge of office, was guiding a party along the fire ropes. Rick was hardly surprised to see Hal Stacey in their midst—still in evening clothes, the shutter of his Leica clicking busily.

"Looks like the criminal left no prints," said Theo. "Hal wouldn't be wasting film, unless Colt gave the word."

The sheriff, hearing his name, dropped the role of guide to storm toward the arrivals. "Who the hell let you in here, Judd?" he roared.

"Something you don't want us to see, sheriff?" Theo asked mildly. "May I present a fellow-newsman, Rick Jordan? He's covering our latest atrocity for the New York *Record*."

"Get out, both of you!"

Hal Stacey moved forward and touched Colt's arm. "You've given me a first view, sheriff," he said. "I don't think it's fair to exclude my colleagues." He shook hands with Theo Judd, and bestowed a solemn wink on Rick as he introduced him. "The sheriff is only trying to find out how this came about."

Colt's jowls had darkened at what could only have been a reprimand: for the moment, Rick was puzzled that he had taken it so readily. "Just don't get underfoot while I show the Mayor's committee around," he growled. "I know how you fellows operate."

Rick did not press his advantage as the inspection party moved on. "Is this really a Mayor's committee?" he whispered to Judd.

"Sure is. All of 'em are fire buffs; they have special badges. If you ask me, Colt's sweating blood tonight, for fear they'll turn something up."

"How could Hal get here so quickly?"

"Probably has a police radio in his car. Looks like he was driving Carol home from some shindig when the news came through."

For the first time, Rick saw that Carol King was in the group circling the fire ropes. Like Hal, she was in evening dress—and wore a hooded cape to protect her from the mixture of steam and smoke that swirled above the ruined building. When their eyes met, he saw she was aware of his presence, and deeply disturbed by what she had seen here. He acknowledged her glance with a bow, and spoke formally, aware of the curious glances of the fire buffs.

"Good evening, Miss King. We seem to meet in strange places."

Carol nodded coolly, but did not speak. He could have sworn that there was a plea in that glance. Hal Stacey's fiancée (he thought swiftly) had received a rude shock tonight.

Hal, his last flash bulb exploded, jumped nimbly over the fire rope. "Can I fill you in, Theo?" he asked.

Rick and the *Times-News* man exchanged glances. It was not in character for Hal Stacey to share the details of a story. Apparently this was a spur of the moment decision, to continue the illusion that the three newsmen were really friends.

"It'd be a help," said Rick. "We had some trouble convincing the sheriff's men I was a reporter."

Again, Hal Stacey spoke quickly, before Colt could rumble into speech. "Fifty sticks of dynamite—perhaps more—were placed in a basement locker room, along this facing wall. They were detonated by a clock that operated a battery switch." At Hal's nod, a trooper came forward, carrying what seemed to be a disemboweled alarm clock, snarled in a festoon of wires. Watching Colt narrowly, Rick saw he was purple with wrath as the mechanism was offered for inspection. Hal Stacey (it as past all doubting now) was giving the orders here. It could mean only that his place in the state machine was openly acknowledged by the sheriff.

"It's all the fire spared us," Hal explained, with the air of a man who has done his duty—and deplores the smallness of the result. "A high-school boy could have done the job, without cutting a class."

Theo Judd's Rolleiflex had already put the infernal machine on film. "Are you calling it the work of high-school boys, Hal?"

Stacey lowered his voice a trifle. "I'm not here, officially, Theo, as you're well aware. I'm only taking flashlights to oblige a friend."

"Skip your friends for now," said the *Times-News* man. "Is this job getting the juvenile delinquent label? That's what they called it last week, when the Greenville print shop burned. In your place, I'd show more variety. Won't do to bore your readers————"

Hal's tone was still patient. "I said a high-school boy *could* have done the job. That isn't a specific charge————"

Rick addressed the sheriff for the first time. "May I have your opinion, sir?"

Colt's eyes sought Hal's. "No comment, until my investigation's over."

"Mr. Stacey has just said this clock is your only evidence."

"Maybe so. I hope to turn up more later."

Rick saw that the man had been rocked by the indirect questioning, and pushed his advantage. "Isn't it true there was a warning?"

"So the fire chief said. His department gets buzzed most every night, and so does mine. Crackpots that hang up before we can trace the call."

"Would you call this the work of crackpots?"

" 'Course I wouldn't," said Colt heavily. "This is an expert's job."

"An expert acting on orders?"

"I don't know what that means, Jordan.".…

"Surely you've some opinion," said Rick. "A convent school wouldn't be bombed for no reason."

"All right, mister." The sheriff's voice was just short of a bellow. "Print this in New York, and see how your readers like it. Chief Porter's phone call wasn't the first tip-off that this school would be blown apart. *I* warned the Sisters there'd be trouble, but they wouldn't listen."

"When did you issue this warning, sheriff?"

"A week ago. I told 'em if they didn't get rid of them burrheads————" Choking on his own anger, Colt forced himself to speak calmly. "Any Southerner will tell you why it happened. Go downtown tomorrow, and ask the first man you meet. I'm making no statement now."

"Was this the only school in the area that accepted both white and Negro pupils?"

"Didn't I tell you that?"

"Can you explain how the bomber slipped past your guards?"

Colt snapped at the bait. "Who said anything about guards? I got better use for my troopers. D'you take me for a damn fool?"

"The temptation's strong," said Rick, with the same quiet courtesy. "I'll resist it, until you give me a straight answer."

He let the remark sink into silence, watching warily as the tension built in the brute in uniform, who faced him with both fists clenched. He saw that Carol King now stood a little apart from the others. She had put out her hand to touch the undamaged wall of the school, as though she had need of support. Even in the glow of dying embers, her cheeks were paper-white: the eyes she turned toward Hal Stacey were dark pools of doubting.

"This is a big county, Rick," said Hal. "How could the sheriff find men to guard all the schools?"

"He said he'd warned the Sisters a week ago. Doesn't he mean he *told* them it would happen?"

"You Yankee snoop—that's enough!"

Theo raised his camera as the sheriff charged forward, and fired a flash bulb. The click of the shutter stopped Colt in his tracks. Rick could imagine the picture perfectly—the beefy face suffused with rage, the fist lifted to strike, the small, baffled eyes glaring straight at Judd's lens.

"Don't try to smash another camera," Theo drawled. "I know my rights—and so does Mr. Jordan. That was a charming pose, Colt. Your public will love it, when they see it in the *Times-News* tomorrow. I might even give it to the wire services—if you think it'll help you in the next primary."

"Gentlemen, gentlemen!" Hal Stacey's voice had never been smoother, but Rick caught the note of anxiety beneath. "Sheriff Colt is disturbed tonight—and with reason. Rick, I'm sure there's nothing personal in this questioning——"

Rick accepted the olive branch without hesitation. Now that Colt had blurted out the truth (the damning admission that he had been given advance notice of the bombing), there was no need to goad him further. "I'm glad to apologize, if I sounded personal," he said, "Nothing was further from my thoughts. All I'm really asking is why this particular school was bombed."

"I've answered that," said Colt. His voice was still a growl, but he was walking warily now. "Because they put niggers in the classrooms with white children. That spells dynamite in my language. This ain't our first bombing—and it won't be the last. The Sisters should have listened when I warned 'em."

"The Sisters serve God first, sheriff. I'm afraid you can't ask them to share your viewpoint. Or expect them to have much instinct for politics." Rick had spoken with the utmost courtesy. His words were addressed to Hal Stacey (and the white-faced girl who stood behind him), not to the man in uniform.

"Politics had nothing to do with it," said Colt. "Black's black, and white's white. Both have their place."

"An equal place before the law, I hope—in theory, at least?"

" 'Course they'll get the same chance, so long as they don't mix," said Colt heavily. "If I catch the men who set this blast, I'll give 'em hell——"

"Open quote," said Theo Judd. *"I am making every effort to apprehend these vandals. We are following several clues, and my office will make a statement tomorrow.* Close quote. Will you buy that for size, Colt?"

Once again, the sheriff's fist lifted—and the *Times-News* cameraman raised his tiny Rolleiflex like a shield. There was no click of the shutter this time: Hal had already stepped between the two men to make the dismissal final.

"This is hardly an occasion for wit, Theo," he said. "We all know the sheriff is making every effort to close the case promptly——"

"Isn't that what I just said? I'm only quoting the statement he made after the synagogue bombing——"

Colt stood his ground, with a fist on each hip. Remembering his last *corrida* in Madrid, Rick could think only of an oversized bull, fixed by a last flourish of the matador's cape, and too bemused to charge again.

"Print what you like," Colt said. "I know what I meant: I got witnesses. Just get the hell out—both of you. I may really lose my temper."

"Good night, sheriff," said Theo. "And thanks again for everything." He took Rick's arm, and steered him into the darkness. Colt, satisfied that his defiance had restored his damaged authority, had already stumped into the ruins, with Hal Stacey behind him.

"If you ask me, Colt served our purpose nicely," said Theo. "You haven't too much time, if you want to file for New York——"

"May I have a lift to town, Theo?"

Plotting the dispatch he would soon be sending to the *Record,* Rick had half-forgotten Carol King. Now, as she hurried to join them, he could see she had recovered her poise, though her voice was still high and strained.

"There's nothing I enjoy more than chauffeuring a pretty girl after midnight," said Theo. "Sure Hal won't object?"

"Hal will be busy here for quite a while."

"I can believe that," said the *Times-News* man dryly. "Take her arm, Rick. My station wagon's a block away, and we've editions to catch."

If he had expected revelations on the drive to the city, Rick was soon disappointed: Carol King, seated on the wide front seat between them, did not speak a dozen words. He had only an occasional glimpse of her face in profile, as a passing street lamp threw it into relief in the darkness. And yet, despite her silences (and her air of withdrawal), he was conscious of a new tension between them, a current as tangible as though an electric wire had joined their bodies. He had proof of its reality when the car stopped before an apartment building in midtown, and he stepped out to escort her to the lobby door.

"Thank you, Rick," she said—and held out her hand. "That was a revealing experience. I'm glad it's behind me—but it had its value."

"I'm afraid I don't understand, Carol——"

"I can't explain now," she said quickly. "But I do admire courage—even if I'm not free to endorse its objective." She was gone on that before he could speak again. He stood for a moment beneath the fanlighted doorway, staring blankly as the slender figure crossed the lobby and stepped into a waiting elevator.

Theo, who had witnessed the exchange, was grinning broadly when Rick returned to the car. "You made your point with the sheriff tonight," he said. "I'm glad to see you hit Carol just as hard. She needed that sort of body blow."

"Surely she knows the score."

"Plenty of folks know the score," said Theo. "Damn few of 'em are ready to add it up. Let's say that Carol King is suffering from a bad case of divided loyalties— and let it go at that."

"Is this the first time she's suspected Hal?"

"I'm sure of it. It wasn't just Colt—giving the show away. What she couldn't take was the boy friend, doing a job of covering up." Theo Judd laughed aloud, and swung the station wagon into the back alley that gave to the *Times-News* loading platform. "A few more revelations in that vein, and she may hand Stacey his walking papers. That would be good news for any society editor."

When he returned to his hotel, after putting his dispatch on the New York wire, Rick tumbled into bed to sleep the sleep of the just. Carol's enigmatic good-by had given him no real cause to hope—yet he dared to hope nonetheless. The sheriff's blunder (while it had named no names) had convinced him that Bob's hunch was right. Somewhere in Central City, last night's bombing had been plotted in advance, as part of a grand design. The plotters could be exposed in time, no matter how clever their disguise. Even if their leader had headquarters elsewhere, the trail could be opened. All that was needed was a blend of patience and luck—or so he told himself, while his euphoria lasted.

Waking in midmorning, he could see that burst of optimism in its true colors, but there was no chance for a letdown. The *Times-News* had been thrust into the service slot in his door. The fat black headline that greeted him was proof enough that last night's strategy had paid dividends:

SHERIFF COLT CONFESSES
EXPECTING SCHOOL BLAST
YET GAVE NO PROTECTION

The lead story had been run without a byline: Theo Judd had dictated it verbatim to a rewrite man. Rick (with the memory of his own hastily typed story fresh in mind) could only marvel at its accuracy. The cameraman, it seemed, had a photographic memory as well as a rare skill with a Rolleiflex. Every word the embattled Colt had uttered was faithfully set down—and the portrait of entrenched evil was all the more searing for its deadpan realism. The three-column cut of the sheriff about to go berserk, fist raised and face distorted into a demon's mask of hate, made a perfect capstone to the news.

Beside the photo was Bob Partridge's front-page editorial, written at top speed in the early morning hours. It was in his best polemical style, burning as brimstone:

The dragon's teeth of racial hatred and injustice, as every Southerner knows, have been sown prodigally throughout the region we call the Deep South. Last night the whirlwind was repeated one more time, when terrorists detonated some fifty sticks of dynamite, in the basement of an old building used by the Catholic Sisters of Mercy as a convent school on the North Side. As a result, the building was all but ruined. It is doubtful that it will ever be reopened as a school. Only prompt action by an efficient fire department kept the damage from spreading.

It would, perhaps, be futile to hope that this latest bombing, which shook so many of our citizens in their beds, could also shake the consciences of the men in high places who are, in the final analysis, responsible for its occurrence.

It is too much to hope that these same men, since they aid and abet smaller men in their return to savagery, should have a change of heart.

But it is not too much to hope that decent citizens all over the South will open their eyes at last and face the facts.

Her in Central City, in the State House and elsewhere, it is the men of ill will who call the tune today. Until the men of good will awaken to the true character of the politicians they have placed in charge of their government, until they rise in their righteous wrath and cast these villains out, our future will be dark indeed.

Today, from the front page of this newspaper, the face of bigotry stares out at you in a photograph that speaks more eloquently than words. Beside it is the news story of last night's bombing, the chapter-and-verse proof of the shame that had come to Central

County, where the elected protector of the peace admits he had advance warning of the event, yet made no move to prevent it.

The attempt of an entrenched minority to bludgeon a people into submission to evil—whether in the name of fascism, Communism, or such antiquated nostrums as states' rights—has the same face. It was an identical blend of intolerance and lust for power that caused a man who preached peace and love to be crucified on a hill outside Jerusalem. Have we the right to expect that these United States (a democracy in name if not in fact) can escape a like fate?

The page of newsprint still burned Rick's fingers as he picked up the phone to order breakfast. Bob had written at a non-stop tempo, pouring out his hopes and fears with no thought of personal consequence. It was typical of the man that he could rise above the shoddy facts, using them as a reason to preach the brotherhood of man. Yet Rick could not help wondering how well those ringing words had served the cause of truth. The dragon's teeth had still been sown, the men of ill will were still in power. . . . Editorials of this stripe could earn every honor in journalism. In the end they might also earn the writer an assassin's bullet.

The phone rang, a moment after Rick had given his order to room service. It was Theo Judd, sounding as cheerful as a two-year-old.

"Did you see Colt's picture?"

"You deserve a medal for that one, Theo. And another for that story you dictated. Why didn't you tell me you had total recall?"

"That's a trade secret. Of course, Colt's picture would have been even better if I'd caught him in the act of slugging you. I couldn't take that risk: he's already broken too many jaws."

"How's Bob this morning?"

"Still turning handsprings at the way you conned the enemy into speaking up. He wants to see you later today, when you have a moment."

"Any line on the bombers?"

"Not a shred—and there won't be. Are you still covering for the *Record?*"

"They're flying a man in this morning. As of now, I'm a free agent. I'm still trying to crack Valley Hospital, remember?"

"I've done some legwork there, Rick. Saw Doc Penfield at the State House an hour ago. He'll talk to you if you'll drop by his office——"

"Does that mean I'll get a gate pass?"

"I'm afraid Valley itself is strictly taboo, along with the head swami. But you can go over the records to your heart's content. The state archivist is an old friend of mine. He's setting up the files and the microfilm——"

Twenty-four hours ago, Rick would have fumed at this automatic road block. Today, with other goals in prospect, he was almost glad that access to Valley Hospital had now been denied him officially. There was larger game in Central City—if he could get it in his sights.

"I suppose it's still good form to insist on meeting Moore? Demand to see the Governor, if need be——"

Theo Judd chuckled. "Doc Penfield will be hurt if you don't throw your weight around. He's quite conscious of his importance."

"Give me an hour to get breakfast and rehearse my tirade; then I'm your man."

The phone rang again as it touched its cradle. This time, the voice was Carol King's.

"Did I call too early? I know newspapermen always sleep until noon." Today, her voice was entirely friendly—and he had no real reason to suspect its timbre. Still, he was careful to keep his own tone non-committal. In the clear light of day, it was hard to forget that Carol was still Hal Stacey's fiancée. Or that, at best, she had done no more than declare a truce when they parted last midnight.

"I've been up for hours," he lied. "I've a busy day ahead, trying to break into Valley Hospital, via your Mental Health Department."

"I expected that, Rick—and I won't scold you for it now. Will you come to my apartment for cocktails? Theo can bring you."

He hesitated deliberately, to make his point. "Does this mean we've buried the hatchet?"

"Did we ever really quarrel?" she said. "If I behaved badly on the plane, I'm sorry. Even at the time, if you'll remember, I admitted you had a job to do."

"I'm still doing my job, Carol."

"I can't blame you for that," she said. "And I won't tell you again that you're wasting your time. I'll give you a cocktail at six, to console you."

"It's a bargain, then—and I'll be glad to come. Is it a large party?"

"No more than twenty. There are several people I'd like to have you meet."

"With or without arguments?"

"I think you'll find us fairly civilized," said Carol. "Naturally, I can make no promises. Bring Theo, if you feel you need a buffer."

When he had hung up, Rick weighed the talk carefully, and could find no flaw in her model-hostess manner. It was reasonable to assume that Hal Stacey had suggested the invitation, for reasons of his own. Yet it was hard to accuse Carol of guile, nor could he believe that her desire to present him to Central City society was anything but genuine. He was still pondering the contradictions in her manner (as opposed to her stated viewpoint) when Theo called from the lobby.

The photographer was non-committal on the cocktail invitation. "I'm glad you accepted," he said. "You'll meet a cross section of our upper crust—if that's the way to describe 'em. Thanks to her job, and her uncle, Carol knows practically everybody. What's more, she *likes* nearly everyone—including the stand-patters. She's a damned nice girl."

"Will her uncle be there?"

"It's highly unlikely. He's been an almost complete hermit since his wife died. Thinks the world of his niece—but lets her lead her own life, now she's safely over her breakdown."

"What sort of fellow is he?"

"One of the great men of the South. He's spent millions on education, hospitals, and research, and refused to take personal credit. There's no doubt he's a genius in his field. Some people say he's an unhappy man because his marriage is childless—but that's only hearsay. My guess is that he's one of those old-line gentleman who doesn't feel at home in this century, and prefers to hold aloof."

"Have you ever seen him?"

"Only twice. Once at the dedication of the Case Pavilion at Valley Hospital. And again, when they laid the cornerstone for the University amphitheater. Even then, he refused to be photographed. I needn't tell you he never grants interviews——"

"Just like Dr. Peter Moore?"

"Now you mention it, they're two of a kind in that. Take my advice, Rick, and don't try to persuade Carol to introduce you. He'll give you no help in this dragon hunt—I'd stake my life on that. People like Walter Case are simply above the battle."

At the Capitol, Rick was ushered into Dr. Matt Penfield's office with no wait whatever—an ominous sign that the departmental defenses were in order. The Mental Health Commissioner was a bluff and hearty physician who seemed almost boyishly eager to prove he had nothing to conceal. It was soon apparent that he had not read Dr. Moore's article in the *American Journal of Psychiatry,* the one slender clue on which Rick had based his try for an interview. Rick did not emphasize it as the argument thickened. It seemed best to let Penfield speak his piece.

"Dr. Moore is doing a magnificent job, Mr. Jordan. But I needn't tell you heading a state mental hospital is a touch-and-go affair. He prefers to practice his therapy in his own way, with no visitors."

"Don't you want a little real publicity for the best hospital in the whole state system? Perhaps even in the South?"

"Not if it means losing Dr. Moore. He'd resign at once, if I permitted you to descend on him with your cameras——"

"I wasn't thinking of a telecast, Dr. Penfield. Only a talk with the man himself—and a column on the work he's doing."

"I'm afraid you're being unduly modest, Mr. Jordan. Your column is syndicated all over America. Once you turned the spotlight on Valley, there'd be demands from other sources, including the national picture magazines."

"Wouldn't he relent, if you spoke a word in my behalf?"

"Frankly, it's a risk I'm not prepared to take."

It was time for Rick's own set speech, and he uttered it, as furiously as he could manage.

"Are you aware, Dr. Penfield, that I've done some fifteen columns on mental health in America? This is the first time I've been refused the fullest co-operation. How can you possibly justify such an attitude?"

The Health Commissioner took refuge in dignity. "Our state hospital system is an open book, Mr. Jordan. You have only to call at our achives to read it through."

"Statistics aren't news. I want to see the man who made them."

"In this case, it's impossible."

"Even if I went to the Governor?"

"Governor Stead will be delighted to meet you, Mr.

Jordan. He's flying back from Atlanta at this very moment. If you like, I'll set up an appointment for noon."

It was a neat withdrawal—and Rick could not help admiring Penfield's footwork. "If you'll excuse the rudeness," he said, "I insist on meeting Governor Stead. Perhaps he'll realize the New York *Record* refuses to be muzzled."

"You'll find our Governor a reasonable man, Mr. Jordan, as well as a charming one. Meanwhile, if you'd care to go over our files——"

In the vast, air-conditioned arcana of the State Archives Building, Rick spent a conscientious hour with the records, including the cost sheets for each mental hospital in the state, lists of both white and colored inmates—and the pathetic graphs showing the meager percentage of the cured, as opposed to the thousands for whom admission to hospitals of this sort was equivalent to life imprisonment. Most of the facts and figures were only a chilling repeat performance of his nationwide investigation on mental health—including the incredible crowding, and the shockingly inadequate funds that could do little more than provide domiciliary care for all stages of the insane.

In the case of Valley Hospital, there had been some attempt to gloss over the statistics, if only to justify the taxpayers' expenditure. Due notice was given to the frequent and generous contributions of the Case Construction Company—which not only supported a wing for private patients, but had also supplied recreational facilities for the inmates, including a baseball diamond and an auditorium where frequent plays and concerts were given. Curiously enough, the usual graph detailing the percentage of cures (which had been so startling a part of Dr. Moore's own report to the medical profession) was missing from the file on Valley. Noting the omission in his own dossier, if only for the benefit of the clerk who had assisted his research, Rick did not protest it. The clock had warned him that it was time for his appointment with the Governor—and he could not afford to waste ammunition.

The gubernatorial sanctum in the State House was in the best tradition, including ankle-deep carpets, life-size portraits of three Confederate generals who had joined forces to keep the Yankee armies out of Central City until the final months of the Civil War, and a massive mahogany desk, back-stopped by crossed standards bearing the American and the state flags. The figure in the swivel chair behind the desk was no less traditional. Bowie Stead was the picture of the Southern governor—from white lion's mane to varnished boots. His booming welcome was part of the man, along with the iron-firm handshake, and the bovine eyes that radiated innocence and good-fellowship, as predictably as twin neon signs. Like his name, the Governor was part of his milieu. He could have gone into the waxworks museum whole on the roof, without touching the inch-long ash on his cigar, or changing a hair of the luxuriant mustache.

"Mr. Jordan, your visit to Central City is an honor long overdue. I wish it could have occurred at a happier time."

"If you're referring to last night's bombing, sir——" Rick had not missed the neatly folded newspaper on the desk: it was a copy of the special airplane edition of the New York *Record*.

"I deplore such outrages, sir, with all my heart and soul." Stead gestured the folded copy of the *Record*, in gentle reproof. "What I deplore still more are accounts like this—based on emotion rather than reason."

"I was a reporter last night, doing a spot-news job," said Rick. "Surely the story is accurate——"

"If you'd come to me, Mr. Jordan, I could have set you right in short order."

"You were out of town, sir. There was no time to get a statement."

"That bombing was an inevitable product of race-mixing. Why didn't you say that the Sisters ignored Sheriff Colt's warning? Or that their school was condemned long ago as a firetrap?"

"Governor Stead, last night's news was the actual bombing. Such details can come later. The big point, after all, is to name the bomber."

"Young man, I'll tell you who the bomber was. It was the federal government and its Supreme Court. A like fate awaits every such structure in the South—so long as its owner persists in denying the states their God-given right to educate their young as they see fit."

It was the beginning of a five-minute harangue, and Rick took it in silence—disengaging his mind neatly from the speaker. It was a trick he had perfected long since, when a prospective news source turned out to be rhetoric, and nothing more. From the moment he had laid eyes on Bowie Stead, he had realized the Governor was more caricature than man—a marionette who lived only when the strings were pulled offstage.

"Mr. Jordan, I am not an ordained minister, but I'm familiar with the Word of God. It's not only sheer nonsense to say that the black man is the equal of the white. It's contrary to Holy Writ. How can you ask that he enter our schools, to compete with our children—when the Bible states clearly that he was born to be a hewer of wood and a drawer of water at the well?"

"If you'll pardon the observation, Governor, that story in the *Record* makes no editorial comment. Last night, I reported the facts as I saw them. Actually, as Dr. Penfield must have told you, I'm here on quite another mission——"

"Did Penfield send you to my office? A thousand apologies. I thought you'd come to interview me."

"The *Record* has a staff man here now, to do a followup on the bombing. If you'd care to make a statement——"

Stead was scrabbling through a welter of memoranda on his desk. When he came up with an interoffice memo, he studied it for a portentous moment before he rumbled into speech again.

"I'm afraid I've nothing to say to the Northern press, sir. I am also afraid we must deny your request to visit Valley Hospital. Didn't Dr. Penfield tell you why?"

Fifteen minutes later, Rick made good his escape to the fresh air of the rotunda. Here (settling on a marble bench beneath a frowning bust of John Calhoun) he was uncertain whether he should laugh aloud—or shake his fist at an antagonist no less frightening because he had refused, so far, to take definite shape. In the end, composing his senses as best he could, he went to bolt a hasty lunch among the clerks who thronged the Capitol cafeteria, then returned to the Archives Building to resume the slogging farce of note-taking for an article that would (in all probability) never see print.

One thing was certain: the State House in Central City, with Bowie Stead as its focal point, was a wind machine that only sudden death could silence. Another fact was unmistakable: the notebook—which Rick had been careful to leave in plain view on the work table—had been checked over thoroughly in his absence.

He had left the trap deliberately. In a way, he was glad his enemies, whoever they might be, had snapped at the bait. At the same time, he could not ignore the prickles of fear that ran like needles down his spine. The last time his notes had been ransacked had been at the Hotel Metropole in Moscow, just two months ago: there was no escaping the parallel. . . . At least it was proof positive that his cover story was accepted. For today, he had no choice but to continue this meaningless note-taking—though he was certain Carol King was right. Valley Hospital, and the mystery man who presided there, were immune from direct assault.

In the late afternoon, feeling that he had pushed his play-acting beyond the call of duty, Rick closed his notebook and taxied to the *Times-News*. Bob Partridge, looking none the worse for a night without sleep, received him almost gaily in his office.

"I'd send you a medal, if I had one to spare," he said. "Throwing Colt off balance last night was a stroke of genius: the switchboard's been jumping ever since."

"Any reaction from Colt himself?"

"The usual threat of a libel suit. He knows better than to bring one, of course. How was your day at our noble State Capitol?"

Bob listened intently while Rick described his visits with Dr. Penfield and the Governor, and the tampering with his notes. "Don't be discouraged," he said. "I know it was a numbing experience, but the side effect should be valuable. D'you want a look at the opposition press—or have you swallowed enough blarney for one day?"

"Hand it over. I might as well hit bottom."

The Central City *Sun,* Rick saw, was one of those afternoon journals whose front page never spoke when it could scream. Today, its banner head was typical:

GOVERNOR STEAD SAYS CHURCH AUTHORITIES BROUGHT ON BOMBING BY RACIAL MIXING

BULLETIN!

Interviewed this morning as he was leaving the Southern Governors' conference in Atlanta, Gov. Bowie Stead stated unequivocally that last night's bombing of the Catholic parish school at the Convent of Our Lady of Mercy was "another inevitable by-product of race-mixing."

"Repeated warnings, by Sheriff Colt and others, were ignored by the Sisters," he said. "The school, condemned months ago as a firetrap, was actually bombed by the federal government and the Supreme

Court. So will all such structures throughout the South, if their owners persist in defying the God-given rights of the states."

"Stead quoted that to me this morning," said Rick.

"Don't blame Bowie too much. He hasn't many thoughts; he makes the few he has go a long way."

Rick skimmed down the page. Three other Governors had been pressed for opinions at the Atlanta conference. One had said that the parish school should have been closed by law, to head off the violence he, too, called "inevitable." Another, citing similar troubles in his own bailiwick (which had been caused by "Harlem agitators masquerading as the black man's friend"), felt the problem could be solved overnight, if "foreigners" were required to show their credentials before crossing a state line. Legislation to this effect was now on the floor of his own State Senate: he recommended that Bowie Stead go and do likewise. . . . The third, contenting himself with a more fatalistic view, said merely that the newest Central City bombing was the logical preliminary of a terrorist campaign, which would abate only when the Supreme Court was forbidden, by Congressional fiat, from meddling in the affairs of the states.

"Do you believe me now, when I say the script was written in advance?" asked Partridge. "And don't say it can't happen here. It already has."

"To my ear, it sounds like Stacey prose."

"I don't doubt that Hal composed some of it," said Partridge. "Theo spotted him this morning, slipping into the State House by the back door. It won't be the first time he's worked on more than one payroll."

"What's my next move, Bob?"

"At the moment, I'm devoid of ideas," said the editor. "Play it by ear for a day or so. Your cover's established: you should be able to move freely. Theo tells me you're both invited to Carol King's for cocktails. You may find a lead there——"

"D'you think it's safe to go?"

"Nothing's safe in war, Rick. Of course, your enlistment's up in a week. I won't keep you here a minute longer, if you haven't hit on something tangible." The editor glanced at the clock. "You haven't too much time, if you want to change. Just don't give Carol's friends a chance to talk behind your back."

5

AN HOUR LATER, with both shoulders planted firmly on Carol King's mantelpiece and Carol's cocktail party roaring full blast on three sides, Rick felt some of his apprehension fade away. The lessened tension, he hoped, was not due to one carefully nursed highball. Nor could he ascribe it to the friendliness of the groups that had converged upon him to ask his opinion on every subject from Russia to religion. From his cub days, he had learned to discount the false euphoria of alcohol; from his first appearance on a television screen, when his company had been sought by all and sundry, he had learned the dialectic of the cocktail hour, until he could speak it ad lib. . . . This evening he could say, in all honesty, that he was enjoying Carol King's friends for their own sake.

He had met two engineers from Case Construction— one just returned from the Argentine, the other deep in blueprints for a community center in the West. Both had seemed men of tomorrow, clear-headed, sharp-spoken, and certain of their destiny. He had talked awhile with Carol's assistant, a plump girl whose Boston accent contrasted pleasantly with the easy Southern drawls. He had met bankers and doctors and lawyers, and clubwomen of every age and shape. He had discussed the future of education with a professor of sociology from the University, and the future of the drama with the Little Theater coach on that same campus.

In each exchange, he had sensed an acceptance he knew was genuine. It was hard to believe that Bob (as a parting shot) had warned him to stand with his back to the wall and volunteer no information whatever. Or that Theo Judd (still hanging warily at the corner of the mantel) had been told to guard his flank at all moments.

It was only now, as the groupings shifted and he was given a short breather, that he understood the reason for his false sense of immunity. It was true that the conversation had seemed general, the arguments spirited—but talk had remained within safe limits No word had been spoken of the political corruption at Central City's vitals. There had been not even a passing reference to the school bombing—nor had the unsolved dilemma behind it been given so much as a name.

Carol herself had paused to chat with him brightly on his arrival—but their talk had been on the safest of topics, the lessons he had learned from his recent Eurasian tour and the prospects for his next series of broadcasts. Hal Stacey, moving from group to group like a sure-footed pixie, had given him an occasional anxious glance—but even Hal seemed convinced that the evening would pass off without fireworks. He was now deep in talk with the Mayor of Central City, a roly-poly man who resembled a clean-shaven Santa Claus. . . . Significantly, he was the only announced politician in the room. Rick had only stared when Theo had whispered (in an earlier aside) that two of the lawyers he had met, and at least one banker, were members of the local White Citizens' Council, and that the Little Theater director was a Grand Master in the Knights of Freedom.

Theo slid smoothly along the fire screen to join him, and Rick felt his shoulders tense even before the photographer could speak.

"Get your guard up, Rick. Here comes trouble."

"From which side?"

"See that rooster in the tweed coat who's talking to Carol? His name is Clay Webster, and he's ready for battle. *General* Webster, I should say—though how he earned his star is beyond me——"

Combing his memory quickly, Rick recalled that the testy ancient (who seemed to creak visibly as he bore down upon the mantel) had once tried to lead a third-party group of extreme right-wingers out of a national convention—a move the party stalwarts had smothered, along with General Webster's own brand of *fin-de-siècle* oratory. He looked for a retreat, but it was too late. The General had already planted himself before the fire screen, with one arthritic finger pointed between Rick's eyes.

"Introductions unnecessary, young man! This is a meeting too long deferred——"

"The pleasure's mine, General——"

"It isn't mine, I assure you, Mr. Rick Jordan. But I wanted to see with my own eyes a man who still has the gall to defend the Supreme Court."

"You might start with John Marshall, sir—and work down to your namesake."

"Those were the great courts, the real courts." The General's voice had risen to a forensic thunder, clamping silence on the room. "As you well know, I refer to the present—to this damned Republican court that's trying to run our government."

"I think you'll find the majority of the present court was appointed by your own party, General. You *are* a Democrat, I presume?"

The General's complexion, normally claret, had gone to rich purple as someone tittered in the background. "Never mind my politics, Mr. Jordan: I'm all too aware of yours. D'you dare to defend the court here in the South, after its miserable record over the last decade?"

"I've no need to defend anyone, sir. As a reporter, I'm without affiliations."

"Yet you support the court's usurpation of power!"

"I'm not aware that Congress has been deprived of its powers."

"Mr. Jordan, have you read the United States Constitution?"

"Carefully, sir. Especially the Fourteenth Amendment, which the Supreme Court felt duty-bound to enforce. In my opinion, such enforcement was long overdue. After all, someone must protect the rights of people who can't always vote because their skin is black———"

Webster's bellow was topped by Theo's good-humored shout. "Turn off the record, General, and I'll buy you a drink. That's Rick's round, and you know it———"

"Not while there's breath in my body, Judd!"

As though by prearranged signal, the crowd regrouped again, forming a solid phalanx between Rick and his would-be baiter. Carol, who had witnessed the exchange from the foyer, made her way to his side.

"I'm sorry, Rick. I couldn't head him off———"

Rick managed a grin, and accepted a drink from a passing tray. "Don't apologize, please. I'm a sitting target this afternoon—I expected pot shots a lot sooner."

"I wanted you to see we *could* be civilized here, in spite of last night," she said. "Now this happens. I'm truly ashamed———"

"Why did you invite him?"

"He's an old friend of my uncle's; he'd have been hurt if I'd forgotten. Besides—in spite of that New England echo—his family founded Central City. You know what that means socially, in this part of the world."

"There's no need to apologize," he told her. "By this time, I'm used to crossing swords with people who are— shall we say, a bit dogmatic? Come to think of it, I was just as dogmatic as the General. I should be asking you to forgive me."

He had hoped to ease her apparent tension by this avowal, but Carol continued to look round the room with anxious eyes. "Don't hate us, Rick," she said. "We can't help being what we are. As a Southerner, you must admit that———"

"I'll admit it freely. Is that the only reason I'm invited?"

"Believe me, I've another purpose—a much better

one." She turned aside for a moment to whisper with her assistant. "Uncle Walter is waiting in my study now. Would you like to slip away and meet him?"

"Walter Case—in person?"

"You'll find he's quite real," she said. "I don't want to seem mysterious—but we must go in at once. He's one of those busy people who rations his time."

"Did you arrange this at his request?"....

"I did indeed," said Carol. She took his hand firmly, leading him down a short corridor that separated her studio living room from the rest of her apartment, waving off all pleas for conversation en route. Startled as he was, Rick had just time to catch Hal Stacey's eye before the door closed. Judging by Hal's smug expression, the camera reporter was aware of Carol's move.

The study was part workroom and part cheerful den. Sketches and photographs of Case Construction's handiwork filled each wall, and a pine-knot fire danced in the hearth. At first glance, the room seemed empty. Then Rick was aware of a wreath of tobacco smoke, rising from the tall-backed armchair that faced the fire. From the doorway, he could see only a short, plump hand on the armrest: at that distance, it seemed oddly lifeless. It was clear that Walter Case was in no hurry to acknowledge their presence. Even when Carol spoke his name, he did not stir.

"Is Mr. Jordan alone, my dear?"

"Of course, Uncle Walter. No one knows you're here—besides Ellen and Hal Stacey."

"Come in, please. And close the door." The voice was precise, and deeply resonant, as though a giant spoke from the armchair. When Case rose at last, Rick was startled to observe that he was only a fraction over five feet tall—a stumpy man who held himself proudly erect as he crossed the room. His face was firm-jawed, with heavy, almost sensual lips and eyes that seemed half asleep in their sparrow pouches. Thanks to a bang of

mouse-gray hair that fell across his brow, his resemblance
to one of the Caesars was startling. (Augustus, thought
Rick—or even Claudius.) Yet, as his niece had just said,
Walter Case was entirely real. So was the glow of welcome in those pale eyes, and the iron-firm handshake.
Rick found that he had responded instantly to the man's
warmth—and warned himself to keep up his guard.

"Do you mind meeting like this, Jordan? Without warning, as it were."

"I'm aware of the privilege, Mr. Case. Will this be an
interview for the *Record?*"

"My reason for calling you in is quite personal." Case
turned to his niece. "I've been here over two minutes, my
dear. Couldn't you bring your guest in sooner?"

"I'm sorry, Uncle. I had to detach him from General
Webster."

The heavy lips parted in a porcelain grin—and the
resemblance to Caesar vanished. Rick took in the change
with a certain relief. Here, it seemed, was another queru-
lous executive, whose power in his own empire was absolute—who could hardly be blamed for fancying his
slightest whim was law.

"Clay Webster still feels he must live up to his famous
namesake," said the industrialist. "It's too bad he has
nothing whatever to say." Again, he turned to Carol.
"Forgive my rudeness, but would you mind leaving us?
You know I hate wasting time."

"All too well, Uncle Walter."

Neither of the men stirred until Carol left the room.
Case continued to study Rick with the same alert courtesy—but there was a special probe in the slightly protu-
berant eyes. Rick had undergone such scrutiny before, in
a score of executive suites: he found he could endure it
easily. He was careful to hold his tongue. Experience told
him that Case would make the first move.

"You'll find that armchair comfortable," said Case.
"I'll sit at the desk. Perhaps you'll join me in a prime
Havana."

"I'll smoke my own, thank you," Rick leaned forward, to pass a match across the cigar Case had just taken from its aluminum cylinder.

"I've been wanting to meet you for some time, Jordan. D'you find it odd that our paths should cross in this fashion?"

"I'm grateful to Carol for arranging it, sir."

"Stacey suggested I talk to you. To my mind, the timing is appropriate."

"In what way—since I'm not to be granted an interview?"

Case ignored the question, with perfect politeness. "I seldom watch television," he said. "And I've little time to read newspapers. But I've seen most of your *Profiles,* and read your columns. You aren't at all what I expected."

"In what way have I failed?"

"I'd hardly call you a failure, Jordan. It's the man who surprised me, not his works. A television screen has a way of magnifying a personality—even distorting it. I expected you to be pontifical. Impressed by our own importance. Ready to magnify it still more——"

"You'll find me quite life-sized, Mr. Case."

"I can see that now. You're far too intelligent to be deceived by the rituals of success. Let me venture another estimate. You are completely dedicated to your work— and proud of the fame it's brought you. Are you sure you haven't abused it?"

Rick stiffened in the armchair. He had not expected the attack so soon. "Because I report events as I see them?"

"I am speaking of your dedication, Jordan. Few men are truly dedicated. It gives them a special aura, which others feel and respect, often without knowing why. Surely you're aware this is the secret of your power—your ability to make millions believe what you say."

"You feel I've misused that ability?"

"Let us waste no time on politeness," said Walter Case. "Your attitude on racial equality is an illustration. I consider your views wrongheaded, and against the public interest. Southern whites will never agree that the Negro deserves his privileges. Everything in our heritage denies it."

Again, Rick was jolted by the unfairness of the attack. Even as he answered it, his voice was harsher than he wished. "Don't you mean everything you've been *told* was your heritage?"

"I'm aware of no such distinction."

"It exists, Mr. Case—and it's important. Folk taboos are one thing—facts are another. When the Negro is given an even economic break, when he can really educate his children, there are no practical limits to his abilities. Any anthropologist will tell you the brain is there. It's just that it's been starved, held down——"

"I'm familiar with that argument. It's only the opening wedge for mongrelization. Would you receive a black man in your home?"

"As a journalist, I know most of our prominent Negroes. Many are my friends. I've visited their homes, and invited them to mine—and I'll do no name-dropping to make my point."

"Just what is your point, Jordan?"

"Such men are a credit to America. They're a proof to other countries that we're still a land of opportunity. Naturally, I don't admire *all* Negroes. Some I actively dislike. There are scoundrels and rabble-rousers on both sides. Not all our cowards and terrorists are white—like the men who bombed your parish school."

"I expected precisely this reply." Case's voice had lost none of its politeness. "A Yankee could hardly say less."

"It may surprise you to hear I was born a Virginian."

"I'm familiar with your background, Jordan: I had you thoroughly checked. Perhaps I know you better than you know yourself. Let me put my conclusions in the simplest terms. You were brainwashed by the one-worlders years ago—and you're too stubborn to admit your error. Look at your country as it is today, not as you'd like it to be. You'll see you're on the wrong side. No civilization in history has survived when idealists controlled the government. Take the Greeks———"

"Or the Romans, Mr. Case?" Despite his slowly rising anger, Rick found he could take a perverse enjoyment in the argument. "They were the most practical people in their day—with a genius for planning other nations' destinies. When their hour struck, they fell apart fast enough."

"Only because they were destroyed by an even stronger force, the barbarian invasions." Case had risen—and, with shoulders braced, he did his best to tower. The bored, slightly amused eyes blazed with a fanatic fire—a revealing flash that vanished in an instant. He was smiling again when he moved to Carol's drawing board, took a sheet of drafting paper, and began making diagrams with a T-square.

"Don't let my enthusiasm disturb you," he said. "History is one of my few passions outside working hours. I've made its conquerors my speciality. Whatever their visions, however warped their ends, their means were always practical."

"Like yours, sir?"

"Perhaps you meant that as a slur, Jordan. I'll take it as a compliment. My staff will tell you I seldom rough it. My flair is planning—and finding the right man to implement those plans. Believe me, there is little such men can't have, if they serve me well."

"Suppose they fail?"

"There's no such word at Cast Construction—not at staff level. I buy strength, and use it to its limits. So far, I've rarely been disappointed."

"How do you define strength, Mr. Case?"

"I'm a plain man. To me, strength means getting your own way—no matter what the opposition, or the cost."

"Will you admit there are degrees of strength? That some of them are evil?"

"Evil is another word I've never seen defined to my satisfaction. Has any leader used his strength for noble ends? Isn't his sole purpose his own advancement? I call it the basic law of existence."

"Jungle existence, perhaps. Not civilized living."

Case kept his eyes on the T-square—but Rick saw the fire leap again behind the lowered lids. "How do you separate jungle law from what you call civilized existence? I've seen little of the latter in my own business dealings. My own life's been threatened—often enough so that I have a pistol permit, and carry one, night and day. A man like yourself, who covers the world's trouble spots, must have observed still more. How much milk of human kindness were you offered on your last call at the Kremlin? Or today—when you saw Bowie Stead?"

The coolness of the comparison took Rick's breath. "You *are* well informed on my activities," he said. "May I ask why?"

"First let me ask a question of my own," said Case. "You knew in advance you'd hit a stone wall at the Capitol. Why did you bruise yourself needlessly?"

"If you mean Valley Hospital——?"

Case's eyes lifted: they were hard as stone. "What else would I mean?"

"I'm convinced there's a story in Dr. Peter Moore. I intend to pin it down."

"Believe me, you'll never meet. Nor is there any reason why you should. Moore is a scientist—as dedicated as yourself. His experiments in healing are his own concern. He wishes no interference from outside. This includes spying by the press."

"Honest reporting is not spying, Mr. Case. If Moore's work is of real value, the public should know of it."

"The public's a great booby, Jordan: already, it knows far too much for its own peace of mind. Only this afternoon, I was discussing Dr. Moore with your colleague Stacey. *He* agreed to stay clear when I explained the situation. Can't you be as reasonable?"

Recalling Hal Stacey's nose for news, Rick choked down a disclaimer: just in time, he had remembered the camera reporter was on the Case payroll. Beginning to sense the industrialist's purpose, he kept his face bland as the older man threw down the T-square and moved to the desk again.

"Let me set you right on certain basic facts," said Case. His quiet voice was an odd contrast to the portentous words. "The future of our Negro population is only one of them."

"So we're back to the racial question?"

"In a way. This time, I'm concerned with a more general threat—the destruction of states' rights by our Supreme Court. The desegregation ruling is a glaring example. The coddling of home-grown Communists is another. I won't repeat the list. I'm merely reminding you that the men who founded this country guaranteed certain rights to each of our states. Among them, you must agree, is the right to manage internal affairs. The keeping of the peace at local level. The rearing of our children according to local customs. The management of minorities——"

"Only when such management doesn't conflict with personal freedom."

Case shrugged.. "If a man can't abide by his state's customs, let him move elsewhere."

"You're forgetting one essential element, sir. Democracy depends on individual liberty, not local privilege. Every states'-right movement in America, including the Civil War, has sacrificed the first to preserve the second."

"What privileges do you resent in Central City?"

Rick gripped the chair arms, and met the agate-cold stare. "Two examples will do, Mr. Case. The privilege of white terrorists to destroy a schoolhouse, because they don't like the color of the pupils. The privilege of a machine-made politician to keep a reporter from the truth."

Case smiled faintly. "Which do you resent more? The

bombing of a school, or the fact you were snubbed at the Capitol?"

"That's a debater's question. I don't think it requires an answer."

"Jordan, when you entered this room, I was prepared to offer you an important place on my staff. I'm still prepared—if you'll abandon your absurd notions."

"What kind of post, Mr. Case?"

"The same post your friend Stacey occupies—improving public relations. The circulation of news on Case Construction. The spread of my ideas."

"How could I do such work and honor my present contracts?"

"I know what your yearly earnings are, to the last dollar. Come into my organization, prepared to back my principles. I'll double your income."

Rick cut in sharply. "No press agent's worth that much, Mr. Case."

"I'll do better. Speak out for states' rights on your next telecast, and I'll pay you in stock. It'll cut your federal tax in half."

A great light broke through the helpless haze in Rick's mind: the purpose of Walter Case was now crystal clear. It was his first real contact with an atavism no culture could stamp out entirely—the king-maker who used money as a club to change enemies to friends, the monster cynic who was convinced that each man (even as Hal Stacey) had his price. Reason was wasted in such a presence. If Rick lingered a moment more in Carol King's study, it was only to see how far Carol's uncle would go.

"Explain one thing more, sir. You say you've gone thoroughly into my record. How could you believe that money would change my tune?"

Case took out another prime Havana. His voice was mild again, his glance benign. "I owed it to myself to make the effort. First-rate brains are rare these days. I hoped against hope that yours were for sale."

"Will you respect my reasons for declining your offer?"

"I'm afraid that's beyond my powers: tolerance is not among my weaknesses. You're making a serious mistake in refusing me. Are you aware of that?"

"Isn't the right to differ a blessing of democracy?"

"As a working journalist, you can't deny that democracy is a word, and nothing more. A myth that's praised each Fourth of July—and never really practiced."

"No system of government is perfect: it's the idea that matters. Either the individual is served by his government —or we've lost to the Soviets before the first rocket is fired."

"Then your answer remains no?"

"Sorry, Mr. Case. I'm still naive enough to prefer imperfect liberty to American-brand fascism."

"Is that your label for our states'-rights movement?"

"I feel it's accurate. Don't you agree?"

"A zealot can be a dangerous man, Jordan. Particularly if his zeal is misdirected."

"He can also be valuable, if he warns his fellow-citizens in time." Rick pulled up quickly, aware that he was shouting in a vacuum. He still felt the need of stating his credo, if only to prove he did not fear that fanatic stare. "Let me restate my position. As you remarked, I've a large audience—one that trusts me. I've worked hard to deserve that trust. I can't betray it."

"Is that your last word?"

"Surely we've no more to say to one another."

"You've been frank with me, Jordan. Now I'll be frank with you. I'm not quite sure why you're in Central City. Perhaps you still have hopes of interviewing Dr. Moore. Perhaps you intend to join forces with Partridge to make the black man king. Whatever your purpose, it cannot be served by remaining."

"Is this your way of saying, *Yankee, go home?*"

"As of now, you are not wanted in Central City. If states' rights were a reality, you could be removed by force. Unfortunately, the best I can do at present is issue a warning. The sooner you return to New York, the safer it will be for you."

"Is this a threat?"

"The word is *warn*. Good day, Jordan. May I wish you a pleasant flight North?"

It was a dismissal, issued in the fewest words by a man who wasted neither words nor time. The fact that Walter Case had spoken in the most courteous of tones did not lessen the impact. The impulse to pick up the gauntlet he had just cast down was strong, but Rick resisted it. Men of this stripe invariably had the last word: their mouths, like their strange lusting after power, could be stopped only by death. . . . Without speaking, he turned on his heel and left the study.

From the threshold of the studio, Rick saw that Carol's cocktail party had broken up: the guests who remained were clustered in a tight group at the bar. His first impulse was to go without a word, boorish as such action would have been. He stood his ground when Carol detached herself from the group and hurried toward him, with Hal Stacey a step behind.

"What happened, Rick?" she asked anxiously. "Did he make you an offer?"

"Isn't that why you arranged the meeting?"

"He told me he wanted your advice on a series of articles. I saw no harm in that."

"I'm afraid your uncle's plans were a bit more extensive, Carol."

Hal tossed an arm around Rick's shoulder. "Speak up, fellow! Are we on the same payroll—or aren't we?"

"I turned him down, Hal. You know why."

"People don't turn down Walter Case. Not when he really opens his checkbook——"

Rick tossed off the camera reporter's arm. "If you'll excuse me, Carol, I've a date at the *Times-News*." He turned gratefully: Theo Judd was at his elbow with a double Scotch. No one spoke while he drained it. He could understand the concern in Carol's eyes when he saw his image in the mantel mirror—but he made no attempt to relax his black-browed frown.

"Please don't talk over my head," she said at last. "What did Uncle Walter want?"

Rick hesitated. Unsure of the depth of Carol's loyalty to the industrialist, he could hardly tell her everything. It was still vital to his self-respect that he explain his position clearly.

"Mr. Case felt that one press agent, however brilliant, was not enough to explain his thoughts to the public," he said carefully. "He asked me to give up my present commitments, and become his second mouthpiece. Naturally, I refused."

Carol's face had fallen: at the moment, he could rejoice in her surprise. "I wish I'd known that sooner, Rick. Really, I had no notion——"

"I'm sure you didn't, now."

"What else did he say?"

"You'll be glad to learn he backs your stand on Valley Hospital—and Dr. Peter Moore. He forbade me to set foot there."

"Uncle Walter *forbade* you?"

"He also suggested I leave Central City by the next plane, since I was distinctly *persona non grata*——" Rick bit off the rest in time: he had told Carol more than enough.

Hal broke in at last. "What'd you expect, fellow? It's been a long time since anyone said no to Walter Case. If you ask me, you got off damned lightly——"

Rick turned to his hostess. "What do *you* think, Carol?"

"You can hardly ask the man's niece to take sides," said Hal quickly. He took Carol's arm, and turned her toward the study door. "Go smooth him down, my dear, before he explodes——"

Carol shook off his hand, and turned to Rick with a

pleading gesture. "Hal's right, I suppose," she said quietly. "He *is* a bit of a tyrant—and he's easily offended. Most men are, when they are used to getting their own way. Perhaps I should have warned you——"

"No warning was needed," said Rick. "I've met Walter Case before, in every corner of the world. The model doesn't change, Carol."

"I won't apologize, then," she said—and moved toward the study door. "Good-by, Rick, and thanks for coming."

Their hands touched briefly—but there was time for a last exchange of glances before she went through the study door. Her eyes, he saw, were filled with the same blank doubting he had noted at the school fire, when he had accused Sheriff Colt.

"Of all the grandstand plays——!" said Hal Stacey.

Rick turned on him, with something like relief: it was good to have a target for his wrath. "Save it, Hal—or I'll ram it down your throat."

"So you turned down a million-dollar contract," said the camera reporter. "That's your affair, of course. But why pose as Galahad for Carol? After all, the man's her *uncle*——"

"You know what Case wanted. He talked with you beforehand. Did you think I'd accept?"

"Don't ask me to unscramble your motives, Rick. We work on different wave lengths."

"Case advised me to leave the state at once, if I valued my life."

"Now you're grandstanding for Theo——"

"You know what Case is—and what he's after. Why not admit it?"

"This is still a free country——"

"Not if he has his way!"

"A millionaire's a citizen too, Rick. He has a right to his views."

"Do you endorse them?"

"Of course," said Hal. "I can recognize other men's viewpoints, and respect them——"

"You respect a fast buck too, Stacey," said Theo Judd. "Don't waste a punch on him, Rick: you'll only break a hand on his armor. Let's hit the road."

The photographer (as Rick had already learned) had one attribute rare in mortals—the ability to remain silent until an opinion was called for. He did not speak again until they stood on the sidewalk outside the apartment.

"D'you want to see Bob? Or was that an excuse to leave?"

"I can't get to Bob soon enough, Theo. What do you make of this business?"

"Frankly, I'm on my beam ends," said Theo. "I'd heard that Case was a hard boss, but a fair one. I'd never dreamed he'd try to bully a New York newspaperman— much less buy one. He can't be so far outside reality."

"It's the one angle I can't figure out," said Rick. "The rest jells, but not that."

"The meeting made sense, then?"

"It made plenty of sense—once you translated Case's language."

Theo knitted his brows, but did not pursue the topic. "One thing I'm sure of," he said, "Carol's in the clear— even if she does work for Case. Put yourself in her place. She *had* to bring you two together, since the old man asked for it."

"I'm not blaming Carol," said Rick. "I'm just sorry I couldn't do more to—enlighten her."

They had moved down the sidewalk while they talked. Theo had parked his station wagon beside the loading platform of a department store. A light rain was falling, and Rick turned up his coat collar: he was still only vaguely conscious of externals, thanks to the sudden, tumultuous inspiration that had crowded to the forefront of his brain. Standing by while the photographer fumbled for his keys, he did not even look up when the two figures descended from the platform and approached the car. It was only when one of them spoke that he noticed the motorcycles canted on the pavement beyond—and realized that their own arrival had, in some way, been anticipated.

"Hey, mister! Don't you know better than to park your heap in a loading zone?"

The speaker, Rick saw, was a boy of eighteen, six feet or more in height, with football shoulders. His companion was only slightly smaller. Both were identically dressed, in black leather windbreakers, boots and breeches. Their crash helmets hung on their shoulders at matching angles and the white scarves at their throats might have been knotted by the same hand. At another time and place, this bizarre costume might have brought an indulgent smile. Tonight, in the rainy dark, without another soul in view, they seemed menacing enough.

"Can't you talk, mister?" asked the smaller youth.

Theo, giving the questions no notice whatever, found the right key at last, and turned the lock of his car door. Rick moved a step closer by instinct: the photographer's nonchalance had not deceived him. The pair were obvious members of one of the motorcycle brigades Bob Partridge had damned so eloquently. He had looked into the faces of too many juvenile hoodlums to underrate their threat.

"I spoke to you, mister," drawled the tall youth. "Ain't you got no politeness?"

Theo turned at last, with a foot already in the door. "Look, son—this is a press car. The sign's on the window. Even if your school's padlocked, I know you can read."

"He talks after all," said the smaller boy. "What d'you know?"

"He won't talk for long," said the other. He collared Theo with the words, dragging him from car to pavement. With the move, the second boy took a step closer—and each lifted a free fist from the pockets of their windbreakers. Even in the bad light, Rick could recognize the shape of the ugly, lead-weighted blackjacks.

With Theo in the grip of one thug, there was no time

for argument. The bludgeon descended before he could grapple with Theo's assailant, catching the photographer at the temple with a sickening thud, and dropping him in his tracks. When the cyclist's arm lifted to give Rick the second blow he moved in, using a trick he'd learned years ago from a judo master in Japan. Seizing the arm as it flailed downward, and diving beneath it, he used it as a fulcrum to lift the boy's body to his shoulder—and sent him crashing across the hood of the car, so violently that the ex-fullback tumbled to the street beyond.

He turned to grapple with his smaller assailant, but the second youth was cat-quick. Rick saw the blackjack descending from his blind side, and knew there was no way to avoid it. A second later, he heard a sharp, cracking sound—and realized it was the impact of lead against his own skull.

A red light exploded before his eyes, and he knew he was falling into darkness—powerless to stay the fall, or to ward off the punishing impact of boots against his ribs. Then the blackout closed in completely.

6

RICK WAS CONSCIOUS of a sharp sting behind one ear and
the smell of antiseptic. He opened his eyes, but the light
sent a wave of pain through his head and he shut them
quickly.

"Don't try to move, Mr. Jordan. You'll be all right in a
bit."

The voice was briskly professional. There was a wise,
firm pressure of fingers above his hairline—and a deeper
pain that told him sutures were being placed in the wound
the cyclist's blackjack had made. Feeling his head clear
with the reassuring words, he risked opening his eyes a
second time. He was in the white-tiled emergency room of
a hospital. A nurse stood beside him, in the act of taking
his pulse; a doctor, visible only as a white-uniformed
figure, hovered above his head.

"That does it, I think," the doctor said. "It should heal
in a few days. I'll put on a little collodion dressing and
you'll never know you were hurt." The voice became a
face now, tanned and alert, with horn-rims that seemed
enormous at this close view. "Dr. Fowler, Mr. Jordan—
assistant resident at Central City General."

"How did this happen?"

"Apparently a couple of our local hoodlums worked
you over. It's getting so a man can't be safe on the streets,
with all these high-school punks at large."

"What about Theo Judd?"

"He's going to be all right too. Neither wound was
serious—and you were brought in promptly, thanks to
Mr. Walter Case."

"Did *Case* bring us to the hospital?"

"You were attacked outside his niece's apartment. The report says they found you lying in the street and put you in his limousine." Dr. Fowler's hand touched Rick's shoulder—a kind, unhurried pressure. "Miss Logan will take you to your room now."

The stretcher rolled from emergency room to hallway. Nurse Logan, who seemed to float beside Rick like a disembodied spirit, had already rung for an elevator.

"Am I booked here as a patient?"

"Mr. Partridge took care of that, sir. The admitting clerk phoned the *Times-News.*"

His room, he discovered, was on the top floor of the private pavilion, a pastel heaven with a private balcony overlooking the river. Bob was seated there, glaring at a half-smoked cigar. He lifted a hand in greeting, but stayed clear of the room until Rick had been transferred to the bed.

"Are you able to talk, boy?"

"The doctor thinks so. How's Theo?"

"Theo's doing well enough," said the editor. "At his age, he should know better than to tangle with teen-age goons. So, for that matter, should you."

"You heard what happened, then?"

"Case's office phoned the paper, to say he'd brought you here. I've also talked to Miss King. What's your version of the brawl?"

"Let's skip the brawl for now," said Rick. "This isn't the first time I've been hurt on a story. The big point is, I've found our man."

"What man?"

"Our Huey Long. Or, rather, the fellow who's beginning operations where Huey left off. I was 90 per cent sure when I left Carol's party. Now I'm positive." Despite a splitting headache, Rick found he could laugh at Bob's blank stare. "Wake up, Partridge! Where's that celebrated nose for news?"

"Are you sure you weren't clobbered harder than you realize?"

"I tell you I've pinned down your mastermind—your kingmaker. His name is Walter Case."

"I'm afraid you're punch-drunk."

"No you aren't, Bob. You know I'm right."

The editor of the *Times-News* sat down heavily beside the bed. "Can you prove this?"

"Not yet—but I'll stake my head on it." Rick touched his bandaged ear tenderly. "In a way, I already have."

"Walter Case has never been active in politics."

"Of course he hasn't—openly. That's part of the smoke screen."

"Just what happened at Carol's apartment? Start at the beginning, and don't leave anything out."

Bob listened in brooding silence, while Rick described the people he had met, his passage-at-arms with General Webster, and the interview in the study.

"Are you telling me Case tried to bribe you to join his team?"

"How else would you describe it? Naturally, he didn't expect me to consider the offer, much less accept. The whole thing was planned beforehand, to scare me out of Central City. The interview first. Then the beating."

"But he brought you here in his car!"

"Naturally. So I'd have no way to accusing him."

Bob had not stirred in his chair. Again, his baffled astonishment gave him the look of a small boy, sulking over a problem beyond his ken. "Rick, I'll be frank. I wouldn't even consider this, if I didn't know you so well. Or, rather, your record for playing hunches."

"This is more than a hunch. Case is our man. He spelled out his whole credo. It dovetails with the picture you drew yesterday——"

"Only in outline. You haven't a single solid fact to go on. Or a single lead."

"What about Valley Hospital—and Dr. Peter Moore?"

"How do they fit in?"

"Something exists in that hospital that won't bear the light of day. It could be the key to our enigma—to Walter Case himself. Why else would he use such strong methods to warn me off?"

"If you ask me, no warning's needed. Valley Hospital's closed to the press. Not even Houdini could pick the lock."

"I still say that Case is the sort of operator who makes doubly sure of everything. That's why he ordered the blackjacks, even before he set eyes on me. Now he's taken my measure at Carol's, he's probably tagged me as another of those Northern liberals. He hopes I'll stay clear, now I've felt the mailed fist. What's more, I intend to prove he's right."

"You mean you're skedaddling?"

"Tomorrow, if I can make it. Nothing's easier to fake than the aftereffects of concussion. My headache's real now. Tomorrow, it's going to be worse; I'm insisting on flying back to my own doctor, for further examination. Later, the *Record* will run a story, announcing my convalescence in Switzerland. Later still, I'll resume my column: I've a backlog of stuff with European datelines. Operation Blackjack will have served its purpose."

The editor leaned forward. The small boy's frown had been replaced by a happy grin. "I'm beginning to get your drift, Rick."

"The front door at Valley Hospital may be burglarproof. But there's bound to be a side entrance—one marked *Personnel*. I worked six weeks as a ward attendant in California, while I was chasing copy for my series. If Valley will hire me, we'll call this job a postgraduate course."

"What about that television mug?"

"Give me a week under a sun lamp, and a little fake scar tissue. Once I've raised a beatnik beard and sideburns, my own editor wouldn't know me."

Bob nodded slowly. "You can probably swing it, Rick.

Every state hospital has a fast turnover: Valley's no exception. It's still a risky thing."

"Because of tonight? Don't think I scare that easily."

"Next time, they won't stop with a curbside workout—" The editor bit off his foreboding and rose to take his leave. "Damn it, Rick, I'm not sold on your theory. Those cycle clubs still beat up citizens for fun. We've reopened a dozen cases, all over the state——"

"This beating was done on order, Bob. We'll try proving that tomorrow. Meanwhile, you can feature my injury for what it's worth."

"The story's being written now."

"And dig up all you can on Case's background. You might also tell Dr. Fowler I'd like the next bulletin on Theo."

"Don't worry about Judd," said the editor. "They're sending him home tomorrow. His skull is thicker than yours, if that's possible."

Rick slept through the night and far into the morning, thanks to the demerol administered by Dr. Fowler. He had complained of a severe headache at the time, to prepare for the symptoms he planned to develop—and he complained again, when the assistant resident made his rounds at noon. As a result, he was wheeled into X-ray, with orders that the plates be rushed. Actually, his head was clear as a bell when the orderly returned him to his room. Save for the pain at his temple, it was hard to believe that he had received an injury that might have been fatal.

To his surprise, he saw a great burst of roses on the dresser. Carol King, who had been seated on the balcony, rose to greet him.

"Guests aren't struck down on my doorstep every day," she said. "As you'll observe, I've brought a peace offering."

"Please don't feel responsible, Carol. I'm afraid Theo and I were both a bit careless."

"He tells me those young monsters were waiting to attack you."

"That's my opinion too."

"We've had far too much violence of this kind since the schools closed. Do you think they recognized you, and followed you from the hotel?"

"Let's leave it at that, since we can't prove otherwise."

"How is your head, Rick?"

"It still aches badly," he lied. "The diagnosis is a small concussion. Nothing time won't cure."

Carol shivered at the words. "Thank Heaven, Uncle Walter's chauffeur drove up when he did. At least we got you here in record time."

"Thank him for that, when you see him again," said Rick gravely. "He managed things well."

Again, she regarded him with troubled eyes, and seemed on the point of speaking her own mind. "Will it help—if I say I'm sorry you couldn't hit it off?"

"For your sake, Carol, I wish we spoke the same tongue. I'm afraid we never can."

"What will you do now?"

"Return to New York—the moment I'm able."

"What about Valley Hospital?"

He managed a grin. "Counting yourself, at least four people have warned me I wouldn't be welcome. The thought has finally registered."

"I came here today to withdraw my objection."

He studied her narrowly, but she met his gaze without flinching. "May I ask what prompted your change of heart?"

"As I told you on the phone, I had my own reasons for protecting Dr. Moore—as well as a certain patient at Valley. Today, I found those reasons no longer exist."

"Perhaps you'd better tell this from the beginning, Carol."

"I drove out to the hospital this morning, for a talk with

Dr. Moore. He's willing to see you, if the Health Commissioner will permit it."

"Because you persuaded him?"

"I used no persuasion. When I was a patient there, they said Seth was insane. Incurably so. Dr. Moore wanted no outsiders asking questions——" It was Carol's turn to smile. "You're right, of course. I must begin at the beginning."

"Who is Seth?"

"Seth Randall—a Negro musician. Ten years ago, when he was admitted to Valley, he was on his way to a career as a concert pianist. He hasn't lost that, of course. Dr. Moore has insisted he keep up his practice: it was part of his therapy." Again she paused, in some confusion. "I'm sure that I'm telling this badly. It's impossible to *explain* Seth, until you've talked to him."

"He must be a hopeless case, if he's been locked up for ten years."

"We all thought that when I had my—breakdown. Today, he's completely cured, yet he prefers to stay at Valley. Of course, there's always the chance that his illness may recur—but Dr. Moore would release him, if his relatives asked for it."

"There's nothing odd about his remaining. Many a mental patient clings to the shelter of a hospital wall, long after his disturbance has passed."

"It goes deeper with Seth. He's assisted Dr. Moore, almost from the start. Now, even though he's well, he prefers to go on helping."

"In what way?"

"I'm not sure I can describe it," said Carol. "It's something you must go through to understand."

"Don't forget I've had clinical experience too," he said, doing his best to hold down the tide of excitement that swept him.

"When I began as a private patient at Valley," said Carol, "Dr. Moore took personal charge of my case. He's a fine psychiatrist in his own right, as you must know. At first, he gave me no obvious treatment—beyond listening to my story. He showed me where I was wrong in some of the assumptions I'd made. And yet, for a long while, neither of us could reach my disturbance, or change it."

Carol paused briefly; Rick could see, by her frown, that she was trying hard to tell her story clearly. "One morning, he brought Seth Randall to see me. We talked all that day—and for several days thereafter. It wasn't long before I saw my disturbance for what it really was. Within a month I'd forgotten my melancholia and my self-pity, and begun turning back to life. Eventually, Dr. Moore pronounced me cured."

"Because of Randall?"

"Dr. Moore called it thought transference. Is that too hard to grasp?"

"By no means. It's a standard method in applied psychiatry."

"Rick, if I tried to describe those talks with Seth, I'm afraid you'd laugh at me. It wasn't what he *said*. It was all kind and gentle—and commonplace. I suppose he was still insane at the time—though you'd never guess it. But no matter how we began, I'd find myself unburdening my deepest troubles before we ended. Somehow, he'd take over the burden. Or if I just needed to—*think* my way out of some fear, he'd go to the piano and help with his playing. Is that too fanciful to suit you?"

"Far from it, Carol. Music's another standard therapy in mental illness. What did he play?" ....

"He has the whole literature of the piano at his fingertips. I've heard most of the great performers—but Seth Randall has something extra not even they could give. Sometimes, he'd play compositions of his own: tone poems, he called them. Or he'd just improvise—until I was ready to talk again."

"I gather you weren't the only one he's worked with."

"Far from it. In the last ten years, he's helped scores of patients to find themselves again. That's why he feels it's his duty to remain. Even today, he sleeps in the wards, with the Negro inmates——"

Rick broke in sharply. "According to the article, Dr. Moore preferred to keep his work anonymous. I can see why now. As you just remarked, a thing of this sort is hard to explain to the layman. Wrong publicity would do more harm than good."

"That's what I thought—when we discussed this on the plane. Now I know you better, I'm sure you'd tell the Seth Randall story fairly."

"I'm afraid the Seth Randall story isn't too important," he said. "Such transferences are more usual than you realize."

"You mean you aren't interested in writing it now?"

He knew she was staring at him incredulously, and made a great effort to keep his faintly bored mask intact. "I appreciate your change of heart," he said. "But there's no story for me at Valley after all. Even if I could get past the door—which is still impossible."

"Surely they'd give you permission at the State House, if they knew Dr. Moore was willing."

"Your uncle refused permission too," he reminded her.

"Only for my sake, Rick. If I went to him and explained——"

"Walter Case and I are on opposite sides," he said quickly. "I'm in no position to ask favors. Especially through his niece."

Carol had been seated in the visitor's chair, with both hands clasped. She tossed them apart now, with a sudden gesture of dismissal, and got to her feet. Though she did not look at him directly, he saw the light in her eyes was close to contempt. *She thinks you're afraid,* he told himself. *She believes you've given up, without fighting back.* Since this was just the impression he wished to convey, he could hardly destroy it with the truth.

"You won't let me help you, then?"

"Sorry—I feel I've intruded quite enough. As I say,

this power Seth Randall possesses isn't the earth-shaking news you imagine. Why should I fight the entire state machine—and your uncle—to get an interview, when I don't feel he's worth a column?"

"At least you've learned what you came for," she said slowly. "I'm glad I was of that much service."

"Thank you for your frankness, Carol. And thanks again for the roses."

"This is good-by, then?"

"I'm afraid so. I can't get back to New York too soon."

He made a gesture of farewell from the hospital bed— and the hand she gave him was cold and unresponsive. For a moment more, she stood beside the bed, as though there was still an unanswered question between them— but her voice was even colder than her manner when she spoke again.

"Good-by, Rick."

She left the room without meeting his eye, her chin at an angle that could only be called defiant. Knowing how deeply his dismissal had hurt, he was tempted to call her back—to confess his real plans for Valley Hospital, even to enlist her aid, as an observer in her uncle's camp. . . . The sentimental impulse died painlessly. This, after all, was not a good-by, but the beginning of a campaign. For the present, it would have been folly to trust Carol King all the way.

He reached for the phone, and called the *Times-News*.

Sitting in the same visitor's chair (like a chunky Chinese idol), Bob Partridge heard him through. The bogus detachment did not deceive Rick for a moment. He knew the editor was now quite as excited as he.

"So you know the name of Peter Moore's assistant," said Bob. "How does that make the job easier?"

"His record may tell us all we need to know. Did you see if Seth Randall has a clipping file, as I asked?"

"Theo's working on that now, but he isn't too hopeful."

"I'll admit it could still be blind," said Rick. "Perhaps Randall is staying with Dr. Moore because he wants to. Case may really think I'll upset Moore's *modus operandi,* if I get inside those hospital walls. The fact remains, every bit of evidence we've turned up—scant though it is—points to a deeper motive. Something a lot more sinister than a crazy Negro who's cured himself and learned to cure others. Or the forgotten history of a girl's nervous breakdown——"

The editor spoke heavily. "You've still no evidence to prove Walter Case is involved."

"Didn't he order me to stay out of Valley?"

"Only at the end of your argument—when he was convinced you were his enemy. For all you know, he wasn't even trying to cover Carol. He may dislike you so violently that he's convinced *any* news story you wrote about his state would be bad publicity. Even if you interviewed the dog catcher."

"You don't think he's our man, then?"

"I need convincing, Rick—a solid clincher. I dug into Case's record last night, from every angle I could think of—and it's clean as they come. He's a conservative, I'll grant you, like most of our top industralists. For example, at one of his few public appearances, a dinner at the local Engineers' Club eight years ago, he said he'd prefer a government of, by, and for gentlemen. If you could have such a government in an imperfect world——"

"How was he on McCarthy?"

"Negative—so far as I could gather. Now and then, I'm sure, he's put up silent money for right-wing candidates. He supported Clay Webster's third-party movement for a while, until he discovered the General was a hopeless idiot. But even that's hearsay: I can't pin it down. There's no open evidence that he's helped Bowie Stead——"

"Naturally. He's too clever."

"I can name most of Bowie's backers—and their contributions."

"Men like Case always work through others. It's part of their system. That's why he's willing to hire Hal Stacey as a front. Hal's a past master at creating dust storms to cover an employer's true motives."

"Damn it, Rick! Suppose I could prove Case is backing Stead all the way. Does that mean he wants anything for himself? Hundreds of our finest businessmen support the machine: they honestly believe the way things have been run here, for the past hundred years, is the best way. You can't persecute Case for his convictions, just because he's living in the wrong century——"

"I tell you the man's a fascist."

"That's only a label."

"Every word he uttered yesterday in Carol's study fits the pattern. All his life, he's been an absolute monarch—in an industrial empire where his nod meant life or death. Now he's decided to expand. He's preparing to ride the same wave that always takes dictators to power. He's sure of his backing and his issues. So sure that he can order me out of his state, as arrogantly as though I were a spy in enemy country. What more do we need?"

"Something we can print," said Bob Partridge. He turned as the bedside phone rang, and picked it up. "That's for me. I told Theo to call me here."

Rick lay back on his pillow and watched hopefully, while the editor of the *Times-News* took the photographer's message. When Bob gestured impatiently for paper and pencil, he thrust the attaché case across the bed. The call was a longish one, and Bob had made extensive notes before he hung up.

"I'll eat my words," he said. "There *was* a story on Randall, after all. Two, in fact—both of 'em in the *Times-News* just under ten years ago. Theo tracked 'em down after a morning's digging."

"Never mind the background, Bob. What'd they say?"

The editor spread his notes: his eyes were blazing now. "Seth Randall had just turned twenty when he was locked up. He was studying piano in New York. Gave several concerts at student level—and seemed headed for a big success. No background to speak of: both his parents were small-time storekeepers in the colored section of Eldon, a turpentine town thirty miles from here. Apparently, he was one of those natural-born prodigies, with a screw loose——"

"Stick to the facts, Bob. Leave out the comment."

"Randall was on his way home for a holiday, when he learned that his father had died in an auto crash. He phoned his mother from Central City, and she confirmed the story: when she was questioned later, she said he went clean out of his mind while they were talking. Next thing he did was to buy an ice pick in a local hardware store, and drop out of sight. Two days later, he was seen wandering on the road outside the Case Tractor Works. The guards at the gate figured he was just another vagrant, and sent him on his way with a routine warning. A little later, according to Randall, he rode into the plant in an empty freight car, and spent the night in a storeroom. That night—according to the story he told at his arraignment—his father's ghost visited him in a dream, and ordered him to kill the first white man he saw. As luck would have it, that white man was Walter Case himself. He'd come to the plant on a surprise inspection tour, with only his chauffeur-bodyguard——"

Partridge turned a page of notes, and looked hard at Rick before he continued his résumé. "It's an interesting sidelight, but the bodyguard was Harold Colt—the present sheriff of Central County. He was a first-class hero. When Randall charged Case with the ice pick, he took it in his own chest instead——"

"Don't tell me that's the end of the story?"

The editor of the *Times-News* shrugged. "Randall didn't even make the front page. It was the year the river jumped the levee. Most of downtown was under water that day: it was all we could do to print a special disaster edition. Randall's attack came under the heading of county news. It was covered by our district man, including the hearing that came afterward. According to his report, Randall stuck to his story. From first to last, it spelled out insanity, both to the judge and the doctor who examined him."

"Did Case agree?"

"So it seems. The second news story is dated ten days later. No one pressed for an indictment—conviction would have meant twenty years to life, for attempted murder. Instead, the Case lawyers waived all legal action. The judge handed down a suspended sentence, directing that Randall be sent to the violent ward at Valley Hospital. The mother signed commitment papers. There the trial really ends."

"Did it satisfy you at the time, Bob?"

"I'll level with you on that," said the editor. "I don't even remember the occurrence, nor does Theo. Why should we? An insane Negro goes berserk—attacks a leading citizen, and wounds his bodyguard instead. That was story number one. Worth a front-page spread, with pictures, on a dull Monday—but not with the Catalpa River on a rampage. Ten days later, that same leading citizen makes news again, when he magnanimously waives all legal action, agrees with the judge's ruling of insanity—and stands aside to permit the crazy man's next-of-kin to sign his commitment papers. What could be more logical?"

"Does it seem logical now?"

"I can hardly go to Case—or Sheriff Colt—and demand a playback, ten years after the events."

"Where's the reporter who covered the story?"

"He was just out of college, Rick. He was drafted a year later, and died in Korea."

"The judge and the doctor must be on tap. You can get statements from them—and from Randall's mother, if she's still living."

"We'll have to do it quietly," said Bob. "If there's more here than meets the eye, we can't give ourselves away."

"There's no if about it now, Bob."

Their eyes met and held. "It seems you're right," the editor admitted. "I still feel like a blind man, hunting for a black hat in the dark."

"That's why I'm losing no time crashing the gate at Valley," said Rick. "I can't even wait for a complete briefing on Randall."

Partridge nodded. "Theo will supply that. And we'll put friend Walter on a twenty-four-hour stakeout. Not that I'll expect it to show much result."

"Nor will I. The hospital's our news source now. We must get Seth's story on the line. Then we'll know what to dig for in Central City."

"Will you need much time to change into an orderly?"

"Give me ten days to be sure."

"How do we keep in touch?"

"I'll rent a room outside the hospital. We can arrange our phone contacts later."

"Don't call me at home," said the editor. "I'm sure that wire's tapped."

"I'll work through the paper."

"Fair enough, Rick. And don't slip on that disguise. I won't remind you that last night's love tap was only a sample. When can you leave here?"

"I'm taking the night plane. After I've griped once more about my headache."

"You'd better sign out against the advice of the physician. It'll look better that way."

"That's my idea too," said Rick. "In your place, I'd go back to the paper, and start hunting the black hat you just mentioned. If it doesn't fit Case's Roman brow, I'll never play a hunch again."

7

THE VINTAGE DODGE, despite its rust-pitted chassis, ran like a sewing machine. On the long viaduct that led to the river bridge, it had dueled with Cadillac and trailer truck on equal terms; it had zoomed into the dual highway beyond, just as the light was changing. Now, cruising at sixty-five, it was one with the traffic stream, a vagabond that would eat no man's dust.

The driver belonged to this segment of the American road. He would have belonged, just as naturally, had the dual highway wound through the mesas of the Southwest or the cranberry bogs of Cape Cod. The fact that this particular turnpike linked the Webster Memorial Bridge and the Deep South capital named Central City was incidental. The man was mahogany-tanned. The mustache and the tuft of beard at his chin were both luxuriant; the too-long sideburns and the tumbled, jet-black hair above them suggested Spanish blood—but the face was American Gothic, blurred by a scar that ran from the left eye to the jawline and spoiled its hard symmetry.

There was nothing dour in the hardness. The mouth beneath that flowing mustache was relaxed and good-humored: the steady dark eyes invited friendship. Only the faded jeans, the high-heeled boots, and the California plates suggested that Dick Sloane had just crossed a continent—and might cruise even farther before he settled down.

His license stated that he was thirty-eight, and that San Francisco had been his birthplace. In his wallet, he carried identity cards from an airplane factory in Los Angeles and an auto plant in Sacramento. In the zippered pocket of his windbreaker were three letters of reference—one from a rancher in the Sonoma Valley, two from state mental hospitals, recommending his skill as an attendant in both open and violent wards. Like Dick Sloane's car and his sunburned visage, they suggested he was a rolling stone but not a tramp, an individual who worked or loafed as the spirit dictated, an adventurer who could protect himself from all the snares of man.

There was nothing about car or driver to suggest that Dick Sloane was really Richard Jordan. Or that the vintage Dodge had left a Cincinnati garage only yesterday, to launch him on the longest gamble of his career.

The ten days Rick had allowed his metamorphosis had grown to three full weeks before he had dared to begin this lone journey South. Impatient though he was to depart, he had found the interlude useful.

His head wound had proved more severe than a first prognosis indicated: he had used the time of his convalescence to perfect his disguise. A sun lamp in his apartment had laid on the Indian-dark tan in short order; a plastic surgeon had helped him to design his scar, using a waterproof make-up that could be applied in a moment; the beard and mustache had needed all of twenty-one days to attain their present fullness. . . . Finally (and this was most important) his mind had needed those three weeks to grasp the full dimensions of the threat he had vowed to root out and expose.

It had been meticulous research. Rick had begun it in his apartment; later, when his wound healed, he had combed through clippings and microfilm at the *Record*. He had talked with fellow-reporters, who had covered events in Little Rock, the Tennessee riots, the Virginia boycotts; he had measured the fumbling attempts at integration in Miami and other centers.

His spadework had uncovered nothing new. Like many

Americans, he had grown weary of a nine-year pattern of resistance that seldom varied, of suit and countersuit that seemed to lead nowhere. The news stories he reread now seemed cut from the same stencil—but the cumulative weight of the evidence was staggering. He had closed the last file folder, wondering if this discordant symphony of rebellion was the work of a single brain.

It was, of course, beyond belief that Walter Case was behind it all. The method, and the madness, were ready-made for his use.

In state after state, political combines dedicated to white supremacy were now established—a position of power so firm that it might take a generation to dislodge them. The credo of these machines was purely selfish: the perpetuation of their own status. Defiance of federal rulings, and the denial of the Negro's rights, were mere rallying points where all factions could agree. All of these regimes had employed violence to enforce their will—though the leaders were the first to deplore its use, to blame its origin on others.

Too often (as the record showed) law-enforcement officers had stood idly by while the terrorists went about their work. There had been an inevitable rise of crime, an appalling growth in the ranks of juvenile delinquents. Most tragic of all, in Rick's view, was the fact that a difficult (but by no means insoluble) problem had been perverted past all reason; as the long erosion continued, he saw that a part of his Southern heritage had been ground under, by the very men who had sworn to uphold it. Hate of the Negro, as of today, was the slogan—and the schoolyard was the battleground. With each head-on collision, relations between the races (kept on a relatively peaceful basis for the last half-century) had been heated to fever pitch.

In such an environment, the voice of reason was long since stilled—or, if it spoke at all, dared only to whisper. Today, for every Bob Partridge, a dozen Southern editors held their peace. For every honest police officer, there were ten Sheriff Colts. Rick had closed the balance sheet, half-convinced that he had chosen a task beyond his powers.

Central City and its state, he concluded, were no worse than others that bordered it. True reform was impossible while the present politicians retained office—and an apathetic public refused to face hard facts squarely. As a transplanted Virginian, Rick could understand the reluctance of many Northern friends to accept the true picture: to them, it seemed an invention of extremists. Men like Walter Case, in their view, were only annoying eccentrics, latter-day Bourbons who still had a right to their views, even though they had turned their backs on the realities of their century.

What if Bob Partridge was right—and Case was only another stubborn businessman, bored with his trade and dreaming of an off-center Utopia with himself as king? The hoodlums' appearance could have been coincidental; the fact that a crazed Negro had once attacked Case (and gone to an asylum as a result) was hardly proof, per se, that the industrialist was evil. Other states had their White Citizens' Councils, their absurdly robed brotherhoods, their crash-helmeted cyclists. Even if Case had contributed to them all, it was still a voter's privilege. . . .

Thinking of those motorcycle brigades, Rick was conscious of a steady whine of sirens. A glance at the rearview mirror warned him that one such group was behind him now, whisking like careless dragonflies through traffic to re-form in the first clear stretch. He counted ten cyclists in all, each of them in identical black. Once their formation was complete, they roared on as precisely as a wedge of jet bombers. Already, they were less than two hundred yards distant, and gaining fast.

Two vehicles were still between—huge trailer trucks in the act of passing one another, refusing to be hurried by the wail of the sirens. The delay gave Rick time to tramp on the gas and increase his lead to a good half-mile. He breathed a sigh of relief when he saw that his turnoff (the

feeder road that led south to Eldon and Valley Stream)
was just beyond.

The relief was short-lived. Two minutes after he had
turned south, he heard the sirens a second time. The
phalanx of flying steel (augmented by another group that
had evidently made contact at the crossroads) was bearing down again, at a speed that made escape impossible.

While the terror lasted, he was ready to admit defeat.
Walter Case had informers everywhere: it seemed all too
evident that he had been warned of Rick's ruse, and had
sent his reception committee to the state line. Yet even as
he fought that fear, Rick knew a show of panic would be
fatal, that he must fit his disguise. His California plates,
and his obvious skill at the wheel, suggested he was not
only an outlander, but a bit of a daredevil—a driver who
had won other duels with death, and was prepared to
duel again.

For the next three miles, he could do no more than
cling to the pavement. The road, a two-lane highway,
crossed a swamp that had almost inundated its sides after
a heavy rain. Both these shoulders, as a result, were
water-soaked sponges—and, since Rick dared not cut
down his speed, there was no way to avoid his pursuers
without drowning in gumbo.

Beyond, the road lifted in a long, easy curve to higher
ground. Rick saw that a half-dozen motorists, warned by
the sirens, had pulled out to leave the concrete open. As
the Dodge swooped from swamp to pine barrens, the
twenty-odd cyclists (who had hung playfully on his taillight for the last mile) increased their speed. Half the
troop moved on to take the lane ahead while the rest
hung behind. Three of the number, obeying a shouted
command, swung recklessly into the left-hand lane to
keep pace with him, lest he turn into a side road.

Before they could breast the next rise, the maneuver
was complete. Yielding to another shouted order, Rick
had straddled the center line. He was now flanked by

cyclists on either side. Others choked both lanes behind
him, and filled the lanes ahead; the leaders, leaning hard
on their sirens, drove in triangle formation, at a speed
that never dropped below eighty miles an hour.

The formation called for bumper-to-bumper precision,
so he had little chance to take in details. The black-clad
figures seemed identical: he would never have recognized
them at a second meeting. The inscription on each windbreaker informed him (with more flourish than grammar)
that this troop was known as the *Eldon Elites*. Remembering that the town of that name was only a short
distance ahead, he could hope they would part company
at the city line.

Already, he saw that this was only a routine test of
nerves. The Dodge had been picked at random to prove
the troop's skill—and it had closed in with no motive,
beyond the natural urge of the young to make sport of
their elders. What disturbed him most, in this wild race,
was the smoothness of the cyclists' discipline, their casual
willingness to take impossible chances. Twice in the next
ten minutes, the steel wedge narrowed to avoid stalled
cars; once it parted and re-formed, when a sign warned of
construction ahead. There was no cutdown of speed. The
intent young faces that surrounded him, (featureless as
zombies under the crash helmets) showed no trace of
fear.

His bizarre captivity ended as suddenly as it had begun, just as a stretch of farmland gave way to the first
suburban bungalows of Eldon. Obeying the lifted gauntlet
of their leader, the troop peeled off in single file, to stream
from highway to side road. The last rider in line, a youth
no more than sixteen, flipped a salute as he passed—this
too, Rick gathered, was part of the ritual.

"So long, Pop! You got nerve!"

There was a gas station at the side road. When the
hammering of his pulses had eased, Rick retraced his
route, and swung in beside the pump.

From this vantage point, he saw that the troop had deployed on a wide field beyond, to mingle with other groups. There were now perhaps a hundred cyclists in all; at the moment, most of them were wolfing box lunches dispensed from a parked truck. Early arrivals were practicing formation driving on a cinder track that circled the field. At the distance, there was nothing remotely sinister about this mass play. Even the mechanics in dungarees who were directing the rides, or helping others to tune up their motors, seemed a natural addition, like Scoutmasters at a jamboree.

Rick grinned at the attendant who had approached to fill his tank. It was his first chance to use the Western drawl that belonged with his license plates.

"What goes over there, pardner? Circus come to town?"

"Them's the *Eldon Elites*. Ain't you heard of our cycle clubs out your way?"

"Sure. We got our share of 'em out West—but nothin' like this. I saw the first big troop yesterday, across the Mississippi. Seems like the farther south you drive the worse they get."

The attendant leaned an elbow on the car door. "What d'you mean, *worse?* Kids need somethin' to take up the slack, when our schools ain't open."

Rick made his drawl even broader. "You got a good argument there, pardner: where I hail from, we've no nigs to keep in line. Who pays for those motor bikes? They look damned expensive."

"You're right they cost money, mister. Can't rightly say who foots the bill. 'Tain't our Citizens' Council—they don't have that kind of cash. Some say our cycle clubs are backed by the Knights."

"Knights of Pythias?"

"I'm talkin' about the Knights of *Freedom*. You might call it a fairly new outfit. Leastways, we only organized after this new nigger trouble started in the schools. The best men in this state are behind it. We got just one aim—to teach patriotism. The good old American brand."

"Do you belong, pardner? Or is that question out of line?"

" 'Course not. The Knights have their secrets, same as any lodge—but we're open and aboveboard. Our Eldon cells hold weekly conclaves right there on Jackson Field. Anyone's invited to watch—and anyone can join who agrees with our principles. Most folks do hereabouts, times bein' what they are."

"I saw a photo of your last state rally, in the Frisco papers," said Rick. "You looked mighty like the old Ku Kluxers—but I hear your aims are different."

"The Klan's a dead letter down here, mister. *We* preach white supremacy without violence. And, believe you me, it needs preachin'."

"Out on the Coast, we have the same trouble with the chinks and the *pachuchos*—the ornery Mexicans who think they're white."

"Glad to hear some foreigners speak our language." The attendant accepted payment for the gas, and a fifty-cent tip, with a smile that was almost friendly.

Lunching at the Busy Bee Café in Eldon, and making the most of a few shopping chores, Rick heard several variations on the theme. One of the merchants with whom he chatted advertised his Citizens' Council affiliation openly, on a sign beside his cash register. Another announced, without prompting, that he had helped organize the first Knights' cell in town, and hoped to be elected a Grand Master at the next state conclave. At the café, Rick's waitress informed him that one of her two beaux was a squad leader in the *Eldon Elites*. The other was a Horseman in the Knights, a cavalry troop complete with shields and lances that held jousting matches each week on Jackson Field. She was torn between the cyclist (who was the handsomer of the two), and the Horseman (who owned the best mortuary in Eldon and could afford marriage).

Most numbing of all was the final word Rick received, when he drank a glass of beer in a saloon on the southern outskirts.

"You're a stranger here," said the bartender. "I can't expect you to see what we're up against. But the day them Washington shysters tried to open our schools to niggers was the day I dug into my granddad's trunk and got out his confederate money. That was back in 1954: I still think I did right to save it."

"Don't tell me you'd start another Civil War before you'll integrate?"

"I ain't jokin', mister—so you better not laugh."

"I believe you," said Rick. "And I agree—it's no laughing matter."

His heart was heavy when he drove south again. Eldon, he reflected, was typical of its kind—a town of twenty thousand, dependent for existence on lumber and turpentine. At the moment, these industries were booming—but prosperity had brought no tolerance in its wake. Like too many other towns from Little Rock to Tallahassee, Eldon had simply closed its eyes to its peculiar dilemma—refusing to admit, even for the sake of argument, that true prosperity could come only with equal opportunity for all its citizens.

Obviously, the last opinion he had heard in Eldon came from a fogged brain—yet it would be unfair to call any of these people bad. The echoes of their ignorance were no less dismal. It was not that they had spoken with a single voice: he had expected that. It was the fact that they seemed to utter these dogmas from closed minds, like children repeating a lesson learned word by word.

Just north of Valley Stream (the village that gave Dr. Moore's hospital its name) Rick parked beside another filling station and entered the phone booth that stood outside. Midafternoon was one of the hours he had fixed for calls to the *Times-News*. There would be no opportunity to call from the hospital itself: for the present, pay stations of this sort were his only safe outlet.

Bob Partridge came to the phone, as he had hoped: the editor could speak frankly from his closed office.

"Dick Sloane, here. How are you, sir?"

"I've kept busy, Dick. Where are you calling from?"

"The Gulf Filling Station, just outside Valley Stream."

"Get your job yet?"

"I'm on my way to apply now. Thought I'd see if you had any news."

"Theo turned up some information on your friend Walter. Not that it tells us anything we didn't know—but it does round out the picture. Can you take notes?"

"Fire away."

Rick took down Bob's report word for word. Since he was working under wraps, Theo Judd had needed the three weeks to put together the story of Seth's trial. Certain papers had been lost in the State House archives (whether deliberately or through carelessness Theo could not say). The judge who had sat on the case had been unavailable for direct comment, and the psychiatrist who had called Seth insane was traveling abroad. . . . In the end, working through friends and keeping his own reasons for inquiry secret, Theo had spelled out a legal routine that reflected small credit on the Central City courts.

Seth Randall had been tried before a judge whose record as an accommodator of the Stead machine had been spotless. His lawyer had been appointed by the court—and, since the defendant was obviously out of his mind, the appointee had been chosen from a list the judge himself recommended. In these circumstances, the trial had been only a formality. The medical report had been signed by two physicians: one, the prison doctor; the other an ambitious young medico fresh from a big-name clinic in New York, who had been given a profitable appointment shortly thereafter. He was now chief of the Welfare Department's Medical Section at the State House, a position whose take, in legitimate graft alone, ran into five figures.

The defendant had thrown himself on the mercy of the

court. He had made no objection when the judge had ordered commitment to Valley Hospital, with a suspended sentence of attempted murder. Seth Randall's mother, his only living relative, had signed the commitment papers. Since that time, she had lived on quietly at Eldon, earning her living as a laundress and a general storekeeper.

"You might check on that end later," said Bob. "I doubt if she'll talk, but one never knows."

"I just drove through Eldon. It isn't the best climate for frank discussion."

"I can believe that, Sloane." The editor seemed anxious to quit the phone: they had agreed that long conferences via this medium, even with proper safeguards, might prove dangerous. "Anything more I should know at this end?"

"Not at the moment. Next time, I'll call Theo, to keep our signals mixed."

"I've ordered a round-the-clock stakeout on friend Walter—since the *Record's* footing the bill. By the way, I hear their best columnist is in Switzerland."

Rick chuckled. "He went abroad to convalesce, after a head wound he received in your fair city." His New York editors had planted the fiction that he had left the country for a rest. When his column resumed publication, it would bear a European dateline.

When he hung up, he realized Bob Partridge had told him nothing new. It was now an established fact that a Negro named Seth Randall had been railroaded to the living death of a state mental hospital: Walter Case's reason for the commitment remained dark as ever. The mystery was no less compelling for the murk that surrounded it. Hemmed though he was by hostile strangers, positive that his first wrong move would be his last, Dick Sloane of California was humming as he entered his car for the last lap of his journey.

Valley Stream, he found, was no more than an overgrown hamlet, surrounding a farmers' market and a gristmill beside the railroad. Valley Hospital was already in view on the ridge beyond. He had expected something imposing from his reports. Even so, he was startled by the neo-Grecian façades that rose in stern (and somehow forlorn) majesty against a westering sky. Now, more than ever, it was evident that the all-powerful state machine had intended Valley to serve as a showcase.

The hospital road wound up the side of the bluff, with a sheer drop from the beginning of the grounds, where steel-mesh walls rose like a man-made cobweb. Below the main gate was a visitors' parking lot, crowded with cars: evidently Rick had arrived at an hour when relatives of patients were permitted a brief, carefully supervised reunion. He did not make the mistake of adding his own car to the others. Instead, he drove boldly toward the gate, until a guard put out a hand to stop him.

"I'm looking for a job. How are chances?"

The guard seemed to take the query in stride, a reaction which lifted the visitor's hopes. "Got your references with you?"

"I've worked in other places, on the Coast."

"Take the gate marked *Personnel* in the second wall. Employment office's on the side of the main building."

Thanking the man as he shifted into low for the steep climb ahead, Rick chuckled inwardly at the simplicity of his ruse. A direct approach to Dr. Peter Moore had drawn an instant blank. Now, with only a dozen routine words, he was inside the doctor's domain.

At this nearer view, Valley Hospital seemed no less immaculate—but the nature of those massed white buildings could hardly be mistaken, even without the second wall. It was true that the screens on each window had no visible bars—and the attendants strolling from ward to ward might have been hospital orderlies anywhere. Perhaps it was that aloofness from the world that spelled out the difference. Or the silence that brooded over each rooftree—which was, in its way, more chilling than all the moanings of the damned.

There were three gates in the second fence. One opened to the private pavilion, a handsome, pillared mansion with two wide wings, so skillfully camouflaged in its azalea beds that it could have passed for the overgrown dwelling of a Southern squire. The second gate gave access to the hospital proper—a half-dozen businesslike white rectangles, whose grim purpose was muted by identical porticos and massive doorways. A third gate, wide enough to admit auto traffic, was marked *Personnel*: it opened direct to a graveled turnaround before Valley Hospital's administration building, a foursquare structure that made no attempt to disguise its function. Rick noted with approval that every wall shone with fresh paint; the lawns were smooth as billiard tables and the paths freshly raked. Already, it was evident that Dr. Peter Moore's domain was well policed. Experience told Rick that most of these routine tasks had been done by inmates, a standard practice in state-owned hospitals to cut down on salaried staff and thus lower unit costs.

A guard sat at the second entrance, his chair tilted against the sunny side of his booth. Evidently, he had been informed of Rick's talk at the main gate, for the Dodge was thumbed on without question. Parking at the employees' door, Rick made a second welcome discovery. Out of some twenty cars, sixteen bore doctor's plates. Allowing for visitors, this meant that Valley's professional staff was far above average, with at least two men for each of the six wards. Walter Case (or, rather, the political directorate Case controlled) had been generous in its appropriations—no matter how sadly other state hospitals might lag behind.

The employment office, he found, opened from an immaculate marble rotunda. There was a barrier across its width, and the gray-haired woman who presided there was the sort of Cerberus he remembered from similar adventures.

"I'm looking for a job, ma'am. How are chances?" Using the same words he had addressed to the guard, he

was careful to keep the light behind him. Until he had
settled into his alter ago, he would continue to fear that
each glance had bored through, to find the real man
beneath.

The female Cerberus pushed a form across the barrier,
and nodded to the lectern that stood across the room.
"Fill this out—then bring it back, with your references."

He was careful to labor over the form before he completed it, in a somewhat cramped hand: the facts of his
alter ago, backed by the references he attached to the
sheet, were beginning to take on a separate reality. Clicking his high-heeled boots on the linoleum, he permitted
himself a slight swagger as he handed the papers to the
guardian—and took out a pocket comb to groom his
sideburns while she read them through.

"Richard Sloane. Aren't you part Spanish—I mean
Mexican?"

"Like it says on the form, one of my grandmothers was
from B.A. I'm no *pachucho,* if that's what you mean. My
dad was a California rancher."

"Apparently you've had real experience in hospitals."

"I've been round the circuit, ma'am."

"Come this way, please. Mr. Wright will talk to you:
he's our personnel director."

The anteroom to which he was conducted was bare,
save for a table and two chairs. Rick sat down, aware that
the man in the office beyond (who seemed to be reading
every syllable of the form) was studying him openly. He
was white-haired and over sixty—but still ruddy with
health. When he entered the anteroom, his catlike walk
suggested he had been an athlete in his day, perhaps even
a boxer.

"This is quite a background, Sloane. Is your certificate
from Oakland still valid?"

"Sure is, Mr. Wright. I worked there last year."

"What made you apply at Valley?"

Rick shrugged. "Like I told the lady, I've seen 'em all. You looked clean from the road."

Wright smiled faintly. "You'll find we're better run than most. Any objection to night work?"

"A new man always draws night duty, doesn't he? I can sleep any time."

"It says here you've worked in locked wards."

"I can handle myself, Mr. Wright."

"We tolerate no rough stuff here. That includes soap socks."

"I never used one in my life." Rick had spoken truly. A cake of laundry soap, enclosed in a sock, could deliver a stunning blow, without leaving a trace. He had preferred to rely on judo when dealing with an excited patient.

Wright opened a stamp pad on the table. "You'll get fifty a week and two meals. Can you manage on that?"

"I always have."

The stamp banged down on the form. "When can you start?"

"Tonight—if I can locate a room in the village."

"We've a dormitory. It'll save rent."

"Eight hours behind bars is enough, Mr. Wright. I'll work better if I live outside."

"Mrs. Claiborne runs the best boardinghouse in Valley Stream; you'll find she's reasonable. It's on Front Street, across from the mill."

"When do I sign in here?"

"Eleven o'clock, in this building. Report to the head attendant—in the Chief Nurse's office. You'll pass it as you go out. By the way, shave off that goatee before you go on duty. It's too good a handle in an argument. What's it mean—that you're one of these cool musicians?"

"Music's one of my hobbies."

"Stop at the director's office upstairs—Dr. Peter Moore. He likes to see new men."

In his wildest dreams, Rick had not expected to meet Moore so easily. Now the chance had fallen in his lap, in his first ten minutes at Valley, he was unprepared to exploit it. Climbing the stair on lagging feet, he knew he must go on being Richard Sloane, as best he could. So far, the performance had been convincing.

He had pictured the director of Valley Hospital as a blend of Freud and witch doctor. Peter Moore turned out to be a quiet, birdlike man; his sanctum resembled a sitting room more than an office, with only the massed diplomas and the long, horsehair couch to remind the visitor of his trade. He seemed hesitant at first, almost bashful: before they could exchange a dozen words, Rick found it was unwise to trust first impressions. The man was a born healer. Serenity enveloped him in waves, like an invisible aura.

Moore's questions (when he reviewed them later) were no different from those he had been asked downstairs. Yet Wright had been grimly cynical—and nothing more. The director of Valley seemed genuinely concerned with his new employee's past and future. There was no trace of the analyst in his manner: it was the talk of friend to friend.

"What are your plans, Dick? Do you mind if I use your first name?"

"Not at all, sir. I won't deny I'm a rolling stone. My record proves it."

"No pressing urge to settle down?"

"Not until I've seen everything, Doctor. I'll earn my keep here. I'm a damned sharp attendant. I've yet to see a ward I can't keep shipshape."

"You'll get a chance to prove that tonight." The director made a notation on a calendar. "I'm putting you down for 3–1. That's Ward One, in Building Number Three. I should warn you that it contains our most troublesome patients."

"You mean it's the birdcage?"

Moore nodded. "Precisely—the violent ward. I'll put another man on duty with you. An attendant named Jed Bragg. You'll be in charge—but he'll help if anything unforeseen develops. Of course, if you'd prefer a less trying start——"

"I've handled birdcages before, sir. If you like, I'll take it alone."

"That won't be necessary tonight. I don't doubt your competence, but I'd like you to observe our methods firsthand. Not that they're too different from most hospitals—but we do have special techniques for our disturbed patients." The director returned the letters of introduction, and tucked Rick's entrance form into a manila envelope. "It says here that your hobby is music. Does that explain the goatee?"

"Mr. Wright warned me to remove it."

"Do you play a particular instrument?"

"I was a fair guitarist, not too long ago."

"For money, or for pleasure?"

"A little of both, sir. When I worked in Oakland, I was side man for several Frisco combos." Again, he had spoken a half-truth. At Chapel Hill, he had played in dance orchestras for extra cash.

"You'll find we have a complete library of records in the recreation room," said the director. "They come from a friend in Central City. A Miss King—the niece of Walter Case, the construction man."

"I'll look forward to hearing them, sir."

"We use music a great deal in our therapy; it's an integral part of the system." Dr. Moore rose from his armchair, and shook hands warmly. "Paul Rountree is our chief attendant. He'll introduce you to Jed tonight, when you go on duty. You'll find him a pleasant young man, a bit on the garrulous side. Don't be surprised if he's inventive about his forebears——"

"I've known my share of Southerners, Doctor."

"Jed claims to be a direct descendant of Braxton Bragg, the Confederate general. It's pure fiction, of course—but such delusions aren't uncommon. In his case, the fantasy is essential to his well-being. So long as he believes *one* of his forebears was famous, he'll find life worth living."

"I understand, Doctor. The illusion's more real than reality——" Rick stopped himself in time. A hospital attendant named Dick Sloane, whose education had stopped at high-school level, would hardly be quoting Plato.

"Precisely, Dick," said Peter Moore. "Make your illusion live, and you're a happy man."

In the rotunda again, Rick paused to draw breath. All things considered, he thought, it had been a rewarding day—though that brush with philosophy had been a near thing. His fingers caressed the goat's tuft at his chin. It had been the high point of his new personality, and he would part with it reluctantly—but it was no longer needed. Dick Sloane of California had been accepted at his face value: the illusion and the reality had merged. Rick Jordan could even feel a twinge of shame at the ease of that acceptance.

At the rooming house on Front Street, Mrs. Claiborne had welcomed him cordially enough when he produced a month's rent in advance. After he had shaved off his goatee (and trimmed his too-exuberant mustache) he had turned in and slept soundly for six hours. It was a discipline he had perfected long ago, an essential to any journalist who must keep odd hours. He was careful to arrive early at the hospital. Parking for the second time in the employees' lot, ringing the night bell outside the rotunda, he felt he was already in the groove.

The headquarters of the Chief Nurse was a double room: on the half-open door, a plaque spelled out the name of Paul Rountree. Entering without knocking, Rick crossed the darkened outer office, vacated at this hour by the daytime nurses' brigade. The cubicle at the far end was half filled by a tun-shaped man who seemed about to burst the seams of a spotless white uniform. A ledger lay open before him: he scarcely looked up, as Rick made his way among the desks and filing cabinets.

"Mr. Rountree?"

"Come in, Sloane. Aren't you a little prompt?"

"I thought I'd need time to get a uniform. I've brought my own shoes."

"Locker room's down the hall," said Rountree. "You'll find a pile of clean suits on a hamper. Pick out one that fits, and stow your other gear. I'll take you to your ward when you're ready. Bragg's there now."

The locker room, Rick discovered, was as immaculate as the head attendant—and so was the stack of freshly starched uniforms. Surveying himself in the wall mirror after he had donned the first one that fitted, he decided his appearance was convincing. He pulled back from his inspection in time when he heard the head attendant lumber in his direction, rattling his key chain as he moved.

"Wright tells me you've handled violent wards before."

"I've worked all kinds. This is my first job in the South."

"3–1 has white and colored sections, like every floor. The chartroom's between the two wards."

The head attendant moved fast despite his bulk: they needed only a moment to reach the portico of Building Three, where a single night light burned. Here, Rountree paused to detach a key from his ring and handed it to Rick.

"This door opens into a corridor that leads to the control room," he said. "I'll let you carry on from here."

Realizing that this was his first testing, Rick turned the key in the lock, stood back to let the attendant precede him, then locked the door behind them both—a routine security precaution in every violent ward. The corridor, illumined by a series of caged bulbs, bisected the building, and led direct to a second door, where Rick repeated his maneuver with the master key. They now stood in a small office, sparsely furnished with a desk, a wall phone, and an office intercom box. Against the wall was a filing cabinet: this, Rountree explained, contained the case histories of every patient on the ward. Beside the outside door, matching portals in the facing walls bore the inevitable *White* and *Colored* placards. There was a stench in the room that not even the softly humming air-conditioner could dispel. Less marked here than usual, it was the hallmark of every mental hospital Rick had visited.

Rountree glanced at the night book that lay open on the desk. "Bragg's checking the white section at the moment," he said. "We'll have a look at the coloreds, just to give you a start."

"Do I keep this key?"

"Day and night. Don't lose sight of it for a moment."

The chartroom gave direct access to a cell-lined corridor. Each door had a lock and a grilled window; at Rountree's nod, Rick studied the inmates as they passed through. Most of them were sleeping: a few roamed their cubicles like caged animals. In one cell, a huge Negro, fists anchored to the outer windowsill, was cursing in an almost soundless whisper. This, the head attendant explained, was Cooter Coe, a recent arrival. Cooter was an upstate farmer. He had killed his wife and son in a fit of maniacal rage; the State Psychiatric Board had committed him to Valley after a routine hearing.

"He's our newest hardrock at the moment," said Rountree. "Most of these men have been locked up for years. As you see, they're quiet enough tonight."

They moved on to the dayroom, which filled the midsection of the ward. Beside it was a long sleeping porch, containing some thirty cots, each occupied by a sleeping man. These, the attendant said, were less violent cases: all of them had responded to therapy, and would be sent to open wards if their improvement continued. As before, Rick was surprised by the almost perfect repose. Here and there, a man tossed and muttered. For the most part, they slept as deeply as children.

"I thought these patients were criminally insane, Mr. Rountree."

"Most of them were our worst hardrocks, a few months ago."

"By that you mean hopeless cases? Like lifers in other prisons?"

"Dr. Moore doesn't like that word 'hopeless.' Quite often, his optimism pays off. As I just told you, these black boys will go into non-violent wards in another fortnight. Only the ones who really backslide will be locked up again."

"Are they under sedation?"

"Not on the porch. A few in solitary are on tranquilizers."

"You must have a tough ward boss," said Rick. He had encountered this deceptive quiet before—in hospitals where a particular patient (because of physical strength or lack of feeling) was allowed to play the tyrant to keep his fellow-inmates cowed.

"We've nothing of that sort here," said Rountree sharply. "Get one thing straight right now, Sloane. We use force at Valley only as a last resort."

"How do you keep order, then?"

"You'll see how, when you've been here awhile."

The head attendant's tone discouraged further talk, and they returned to the office in silence. Here, a small, fox-faced man in hospital white was taking his ease, with his feet on the desk and a paperback mystery open on his lap. This, Rick guessed, was Jed Bragg. He held out a hand when Rountree made the introduction.

"Glad to have you aboard, Sloane," said Bragg. "I'll be happier still tomorrow, when I go on day duty. What's the routine, Paul? Shall I take him through the white ward—or has he seen enough?"

"Let him do a bed check at three," said the head attendant. "And remember this, Bragg. If I catch you sleeping in that chair one more time, it's curtains."

When Rountree had left them, Bragg ran through the daybook for Rick's benefit, describing typical inmates and giving a rule-of-thumb account of procedure. For all his sly air, and his evident enjoyment of goldbricking, he was obviously capable (Rick concluded that Rountree's parting remark had been more joke than warning). Even when Bragg seemed to half-doze in his chair, he could feel the men's shoe-button eyes upon him, and warned himself to proceed warily. Tonight was his trial run—in more than one sense. To justify his credentials, he knew he must keep his manner casual, and avoid pointed questions.

"Is the ward always quiet?"

"Not always," said Bragg. "Whenever there's a turnover, the new patients make the others restless. The big buck in 217 hasn't started howling, so far. If he does, one of the medics will give him a shot. Use that wall phone, if there's something you can't handle. Paul will come running."

"Who uses the intercom?"

"It has outlets in both wards—and a connection with the Nurses' Room. Throw the switch when you make your rounds. It can be mighty useful if you're cornered."

Rick nodded, as he tested the switch on the box. It was an efficient system, permitting a single attendant to handle seventy patients without too much personal risk.

"Do the doctors stop by after dark?"

"The night man will be along before morning. I think we've drawn Dr. Morton on this shift. He's a good Joe. You'll learn how to humor the fussy ones. We keep a taut ship here, as they say in the Navy. By and large, it's a happy one."

"Were you Navy in the war?"

"Wing commander on a carrier," said Bragg. "First time any of my family fought on the Yankee side. I suppose they've told you that General Braxton Bragg was my great-great-uncle?"

After that lead, Rick found he could keep up the conversation with an occasional monosyllable. In the next hour (after a branch-by-branch inventory of the Bragg family tree) he learned that the attendant had made a fortune in Texas oil, and lost it in a single poker game, that he had been a carnival stunt man and a Hollywood actor. His present job, said Bragg, was only a stopgap, until the death of his grandfather made him a millionaire for a second time. . . . Later, Rick would be told that Jed's exploits—if laid end to end—would cover the best part of two centuries. Like all free-wheeling liars, the fox-faced man was never content to keep his stories simple.

"How long were you a croupier at Monte Carlo?"

"Just six months," said Bragg. "Long enough to get another stake. I blew that one in Tangier—in just three days. Ever been to Tangier?"

"Once, long ago."

"There's a sin trap to end all binges. I got out of hock by running guns to Algeria———"

Curiously enough, though it was impossible to separate the real Jed Bragg from the fictional picaroon, the attendant proved to be as shrewd as he was capable. Trained as he was to absorb the stories of other men's lives, Rick hoped he had been a model listener, as Jed continued to pour out his fancies. At another level, he felt he had passed muster when he made the rounds of the white ward at midnight, and helped Jed to separate a babbling octogenarian from a mysteriously acquired penknife—so deftly that the scuffle did not even waken the occupants of adjoining cells. . . . He was sure of his place an hour later, when the cursing of Cooter Coe (the Negro murderer in 217) had begun to stir the ward to restlessness, and Jed stood back to permit him to enter the cell.

Dr. Morton (the staffer who had drawn the midnight-to-dawn shift) waited in the corridor with a fifty-milligram ampule of chlorpromazine, ready for an intramuscular injection. Rick moved in slowly, keeping up a flow of soothing words. Cooter was crouched far back in the cell, his eyes glowing with suspicion and hate: in the half-light, he seemed huge as a heavyweight boxer, and twice as menacing. A sudden move, of course, would be fatal—yet the man must somehow be quieted before the needle's plunge.

For an instant (as he felt his skin prickle under that baleful stare) Rick could wish that regulations at Valley permitted strait jackets—or even the soap sock he had so virtuously abjured in his interview with Wright. "Don't be afraid, Cooter," he whispered. "Dr. Morton wants to help you. We *all* want to help——"

"Keep out, white man! *Keep out, damn you——!*"

The words were hot with rage, but Rick had caught a slight wavering in that febrile glare, and knew he was winning the battle of looks. He did not relax the stream of words as he moved closer, step by cautious step.

"Time for bed, Cooter. You need to rest——"

He was beside the mattress now—bolted to the floor with a canvas cover, as was customary in the violent wards. When the cursing died, he put out his hand as though in casual greeting. Automatically, Cooter's own hand rose to meet it. Still avoiding sudden motion, he exerted a gentle pressure, drawing the man from floor to mattress.

"Dr. Morton has medicine to help you sleep, Cooter. Don't you want to sleep awhile?"

His hands were soothing the Negro's shoulders now, persuading him to yield. The doctor, moving on tiptoe, raised the ampule. Cooter gave a reflex jerk under the needle—but Rick's hands had already begun to knead the shoulder muscles, willing them to relax.

"Easy does it. You're getting sleepy, aren't you?"

He could feel resistance lessen as the needle was withdrawn, and knew that Cooter's eyes had closed, as obediently as a child's. Nodding to the doctor, he moved to lock the door.

"That was a neat boarding party," said Bragg. "If I'd run it myself, it couldn't have been neater."

"Does this mean I get the job?" Rick cast a puzzled glance into the Negro ward, and closed the chartroom door. There had been vague stirrings in the cells, while he assisted the doctor. He had heard no sound from the sleeping porch, though several patients had lifted their heads to watch the white-clad figures at work.

"If it weren't for Rountree," said Bragg, "I'd let you take over until morning."

"Will he give me the ward tomorrow?"

"You're damned right he will, if my report means anything. I liked the cut of your jib, Sloane—the minute you came alongside."

"We're shipmates, then?"

"Until we move on to better things," Bragg settled in the chair, with a cavernous yawn. "I'm at Mrs. Claiborne's too, you know. Like to come to the firehouse for Saturday poker?"

"How big is the game?"

"Hell, Dick—it's just five-and-ten, but we have fun. We might drive into Eldon afterward, and do some tomcatting." Bragg winked broadly, and leaned toward the air-conditioner to light a forbidden cigarette. "You ain't married, by any chance?"

"I seldom marry, Jed."

"My sentiments too. It's funny, when you think of it—but I never got out West. Is it true you have niggers and people in the same school?"

The question was revealing. Jed, for all his untrammeled imagination, had probably never left the borders of his own state.

"We had a few, I guess," Rick said carefully. "I never noticed."

"Don't they fight the white folks?"

"I don't remember fighting a dinge. Most of my fights were with greasers."

"Wasn't there lots of intermarrying—and you-know-what?"

"Not when I was in school."

"Maybe you paid it no mind, Dick. Only yesterday, a fellow on the Central City radio was saying we'd *all* be part nigger, if we didn't keep the South pure——"

"Keep the South pure?" Just in time, Rick remembered this was a slogan of the Knights of Freedom.

"Ain't that what America means to a white man?" asked Jed. "Us on top—and the rest underneath? How else can you enjoy life?"

"Now you mention it, things weren't too different in Frisco," said Rick. "Our greasers and chinks ran in packs. So did the micks. The other kids made 'em."

The picture seemed to please Jed completely. In another moment, with the broadest of winks, he lapsed into a doze. On his side of the table, Rick lit a cigarette of his own, and warned himself to watch his own flights of fancy. It would never do to be tagged as an integrationist, his first night at Valley.

When the shift ended, and Rick had gone his sleepy way to the rooming house on Front Street, he knew he had passed his first test. The real testing came twenty-four hours later, when he was in charge of the ward. Like most crises, it arrived without warning.

He had come to 3–1 on the dot to relieve the night attendant; he had done his best to seem unconcerned as he settled for his vigil. On the stroke of twelve, he had made the rounds, finding both wards as quiet as before. Even the dark destroyer in 217, under fresh sedation, snored as lustily as the others. Back in the chartroom, he had just begun a check of case histories when the uproar started.

It began abruptly, as though a chorus of wildcats had opened up on cue. Knowing it was a planned rumble, initiated by the patients in the white ward, he ignored the racket for a moment, in the vain hope it would subside. When the bedlam increased, and the locked cells added their voices to the din, he saw he must take action.

He was tempted to phone Rountree—but it was his duty to stop the uproar himself, since it was a clear test of his authority. Failure would only make his life miserable hereafter. Rountree might even dismiss him, stopping his investigation dead. Remembering to flip the switch on the control box, he braced his shoulders and unlocked the chartroom door.

Ignoring the shouted imprecations from each cell, he strode to the dayroom of the white ward and turned on the overhead lights. As he had suspected, the whole sleeping porch was astir. Twenty men (grotesque phantoms in their hospital pajamas) stood with heads joined, howling in unison. Others, too timid to leave their cots, banged tin basins and books against the footboards. It was a spine-curling sight—and, though he knew most of these poor wretches were harmless, Rick felt the breath choke in his throat. Disarming a tottering ancient in this same ward, with Jed Bragg to help, had been one matter: he must handle this crisis alone.

Some of the patients had turned to face him. The concerted baying was laced with catcalls, telling him (all too plainly) that they had sensed his hesitation. His vital forces rose to the emergency, turning his voice into a parade-ground bellow that shocked the porch into silence.

"All right, men! You've had your fun—now break it up!" He let the silence hold, then spoke quite calmly. "I may be new here, but I know the score. You've ten seconds to get into bed—or the whole ward goes on report."

The quiet words, and the threat behind them, had instant effect. These thirty patients were on probation; all of them looked forward to moving into an open ward, to freedom of the grounds in daylight hours. Going on report meant a return to solitary, with all that discipline implied. Rick glanced pointedly at his wrist watch, but there was no need for further discipline. Heads hanging, the men had begun to return to their cots, looking for all the world like children who had been sent supperless to bed.

The porch was clear before his time limit—and, from where he stood, each bed seemed occupied. He moved to cut off the light switch in the dayroom—realizing, just as the ward was plunged in semidarkness, that the cot nearest the door still lacked a patient. It was too late to turn when he heard the step behind him. In another moment, two powerful hands had fastened on his throat.

It was a true stranglehold, and he knew he was fighting for his life. Flailing with both arms, bracing one foot on the doorjamb, he strove in vain to make contact with an enemy he could not even see. The struggle only increased the pitiless pressure. He knew a moment of pure panic as he felt his vision dim. More than once, he had seen men rendered unconscious by pressure above the carotid artery, and felt sure it was happening now.

With a last, despairing effort he managed to swivel his body a trifle—enough to get a hammerlock on his enemy's knee. Unfortunately, the attack had sapped his strength. The effort to use a judo pitch was beyond him.

He heard the soft voice as his senses tottered on the verge of blackout. At first, the speaker seemed to whisper at his ear. He could almost believe his attacker had spoken.

"No, Don—no! You must go to bed—like the others!"

The fingers released their pressure. Rick staggered against the wall, breathing in sobbing gasps. He saw his attacker clearly now, a blond giant whose great hands were slowly unflexing. A slender, dark-skinned man in a hospital robe was steering him toward the empty cot. The giant sank into his bed with a hangdog air and a great creaking of springs. When his eyes met Rick's, he managed a grin, and bobbed his head in a wordless plea for pardon.

"Mr. Sloane is in charge," said the newcomer. "He's here to prove he's your friend. *I'm* your friend. So are all the others. You know you're safe here—don't you, Don?"

The stranger had bent above the giant's cot, fixing him with compelling eyes. The other cots were still. Watching incredulously, Rick saw his attacker had already relaxed, closing his own eyes as though in slumber.

"No more tricks, Don—promise?"

"No more tricks—I promise." The giant's murmur seemed an echo in the silence. For a moment more, the newcomer stood above the cot without relaxing his vigilance. Then he moved to join Rick in the dayroom.

"You won't believe this, of course," he said. "But that was Don's idea of skylarking. It won't happen again, I assure you."

"How did you get here?"

"I'm from the other ward. I heard the noise on the control box, and thought you might need me."

The visitor moved toward the lighted rectangle of the chartroom door, giving Rick a clear view. At first glance, it was hard to believe his rescuer was a Negro: it was only when he stood beneath the light that Rick noted the cap of jet-black curls. The man's skin was a rich brown, his cameo-fine good looks softened just enough to make the racial pattern unmistakable. There was no trace of accent in his voice and his smile transcended color or creed.

"With your permission, I'll stay a moment more," he said. "Thanks to Don's foolishness, they could start up again. My name's Seth Randall."

8

ROUNTREE BURST into the chartroom, just as Rick and Seth Randall returned from the ward.

"Everything in control here?"

Seth spoke from the doorframe. "It was only a trial run, Mr. Rountree. It's over now."

The head attendant's frown relaxed. "I heard them howling on the nurses' intercom," he said. "Was it rough?"

Again, the Negro spoke for them both—and Rick saw that Rountree was taking his statement as face value. "Mr. Sloane handled it easily. I only looked in to be sure."

The head attendant settled on the corner of the office desk. His broad moon-face had creased in a grin: it was the first time Rick had seen him smile.

"I told you we kept order here, Sloane," he said. "Are you beginning to see how?"

"Not quite, sir."

"Seth here is one of our inmates. If Valley Hospital were a prison, I'd call him a trusty. Right now, he's sleeping in 3–1, to make sure these men on probation behave. He has his own key; that's how he joined you so quickly."

"Believe me," said Seth, "it was nothing Mr. Sloane couldn't manage."

Rick hesitated before he spoke. Rountree's keen eyes could hardly have missed the print on Don's fingers on his throat. "As baptisms by fire go," he said, "it wasn't too bad. I'll manage—now I know Seth's nearby."

132

The head attendant nodded vigorously. Incredible as it was, he seemed pleased by Rick's white lie. "Can you stay a bit longer, Seth—in case they start up again?"

"I've told Mr. Sloane I'd be glad to."

"Better get your guitar, if they want music."

"It's in the closet, Mr. Roundtree."

"In that case, I'll let you two get acquainted." The head attendant fixed Rick with a steady eye. "You're lucky to have Seth in your ward."

"I've already realized that, sir."

The Negro stood unstirring as Rountree left them. "Thanks, Mr. Sloane."

"It's you who should be thanked, Seth."

"Don is a child who doesn't know his strength. He meant to frighten you just now: it was his idea of a joke. He would never have *killed* you. Can you take such an opinion on faith?"

Rick tested the tender welts on his throat. "Is that why you shielded him?"

"A year ago, Don was considered a hopeless case. He was sent here after killing a stepfather who treated him like a beast of burden." Seth held up a pleading hand, before Rick could speak. "Yes, it's quite true. He *was* a homicidal maniac—for good cause. Since he's been at Valley, he feels sheltered for the first time. What's more important, he's begun to feel wanted. For the last two months, he's been almost happy, knowing he's working out of his illness. Sometimes, his happiness spills over into violence, as it did tonight. I can't excuse him. I'm only asking you to understand."

"Could he be sent back to the world?"

"Dr. Moore says that's too much to hope for. Don still has the mind of a child. He needs the group security only a hospital can give. But he can lead a useful life here, once he's been transferred to an open ward. Perhaps that doesn't seem much to you—occupational therapy, work on the hospital farm. But it's infinitely better than solitary."

"Did we save him from that, Seth?"

"We did indeed, Mr. Sloane."

"With the head attendant's blessing, I gather."

"Mr. Rountree trusts my judgment in these matters. So does Dr. Moore." Seth moved to the door of the white ward. As they talked, both of them had been conscious of a low moaning from the cells. "Some of the bad cases are still restless," he said. "I'm afraid they'll keep the sleeping porch awake. May I quiet them?"

"Of course. Can I give you a hand?"

Seth opened a wall closet and took out a guitar. "I think this should begin as a solo performance: they know my voice."

"You're going to *sing* to them?"

"If you're sure you don't mind." The Negro had tuned the strings while he spoke. Now, tossing a knee over a chairback, he struck the first chord—and nodded wordlessly toward both doors. As Rick turned the bolts and swung them wide, Seth began to hum softly. In another moment, he was singing in earnest.

It was a true voice rather than a great one—a pleasant, resonant baritone never meant for the concert stage. And yet, for no reason he could name, Rick found it wonderfully soothing.

> *Down in de valley,*
> *De valley so low,*
> *Hang yo' haid ovah,*
> *Heah de win' blow.*

There was no parody in the easy Negro accent. One felt this folk song had been learned at a mother's knee and tuned to the learner's heartstrings. When Seth Randall reached the third verse, the murmur in the cells had ceased.

> *If yo' doan' love me,*
> *Love who yo' please.*

Put yo' arms round me,
Give mah heart ease.

The Negro sang a dozen songs in all. Long before he finished, both white and colored wards had added a low, pulsing obligato—broken, now and again, by sobbing breaths, as half-forgotten melodies brought back the past. In the end, the sobs were lost in the rising tide of the melody, which changed in turn to the deep exhalations of sleep.

Humming the last tune *sotto voce,* Seth roamed both wards, letting his voice die as the final whimper faded. Rick did not stir from the chartroom. This was the singer's moment. He had no right to intrude on the spell that had dissolved the anguish of seventy forgotten men. It was only when the Negro returned, and placed the guitar in the cupboard, that he rose to bolt the doors.

"I stumbled on this cure for insomnia quite by accident," said Seth. "It never fails."

"I gather you're a natural musician." It was a banal compliment. Rick had used it deliberately, knowing he must be careful to cover information he already possessed.

The Negro smiled, and pointed to the filing cabinet. "If you'll look up my case later, you'll find I once studied at the Juilliard School."

"Voice?"

"I have no voice to speak of, Mr. Sloane. Just a barbershop baritone, with no projection. The piano is my real instrument. I learned a little guitar after I—after they brought me here."

"Your music explains a great deal, Seth."

"I can't deny I belonged with these men ten years ago. In some ways, I still do. At least, that's the State's opinion. Dr. Moore has asked the Psychiatric Board to review my case more than once. The appeal has never been answered."

"Are you telling me that *you* were a——?"

"A homicidal maniac? So the record states."

"But you aren't, Seth. You couldn't be——" Rick hoped his slight stammer was convincing.

"What, Mr. Sloane? A madman without hope? Or the sort of illiterate Southern Negro you'd expect to find in a locked ward?"

"Don't pretend to misunderstand me. Tonight, you've proved you're a remarkable individual on any count. Won't you tell me more about yourself?"

"The whole story is in the record," said Seth quietly. "And I'm not in the least remarkable—except that I do have a bent for music. If you wish, you can call me a man who's found his place by helping others. Perhaps our State Psychiatric Board is right. I won't deny I'm useful here."

"But your music——?"

"I have my music too. My courses were ended at Juilliard when I was committed: I haven't lost my touch. There's a concert grand in the auditorium. I work there each day, with Dr. Moore's approval."

"Do *you* feel you're cured, Seth?"

"Mr. Sloane, it's a long time since I've asked myself that question. If you don't mind, I won't answer it tonight."

The Negro was gone with that gentle rebuke. Rick was hardly aware of his departure, until he heard the click of the automatic lock on the door that led to the colored ward.

That night, he studied Seth Randall's chart carefully, if only to complete his own record. As he had expected, it told him nothing.

The patient had been admitted to Valley with a diagnosis of acute mania (homicidal and recurrent). The chart stated baldly that he had attempted to kill a white man, for no apparent reason. Commitment had been ordered by a county judge—without formal trial, and with the permission of "next-of-kin." The ruling had been approved by two physicians, appointed by the court. Significantly, no names were given.

At the hospital, Seth had undergone shock treatment. For "a period of years," he had had routine domiciliary care. Most surprising of all, there were no medical notations to suggest he was now completely cured. The chart was a one-way ticket to nowhere, signed in invisible ink by Walter Case—and Case's motive remained obscure as ever. It was already obvious that Seth, for all his open manner, would answer no direct questions. Nor could Rick show too much curiosity when he visited Dr. Moore in his office the following afternoon, on the latter's invitation.

"Paul Rountree tells me you've done well in 3–1, Dick. I asked you in to congratulate you."

"It might have been another story—if Seth hadn't lent a hand."

"Don't be too sure of that. From what *he* tells me, you were more than capable."

"Coming from Randall, sir, that's praise indeed. He's an amazing person."

"We're really fortunate to have him here."

"May I ask his exact status?"

"Seth's hard to explain to outsiders," said Dr. Moore. "For that reason, we like our new attendants to make his acquaintance—as it were—on their own. Last night's a good example. Suppose I'd told you in advance that one of our Negro inmates could sing a whole ward to sleep. Would you have believed me?"

"I'm afraid not, sir."

"How much do you know of applied psychiatry, Dick?"

"I've read a good deal of the literature, Doctor."

"Are you familiar with the phenomenon of transference?"

"Only as a layman."

"Let me define it, as best I can. Basically, it's a feeling of trust, almost a father-child relationship, which develops

between analyst and patient. Ideally, it reaches a point
where the sick person has absolute faith in the analyst's
ability to understand and help him. In Seth's case, we
discovered, almost by chance, that he possessed that power. The discovery came in the course of his own therapy.
In the end, by helping others, he helped himself as
well."

"Do you mean the helping was part of Seth's cure?"

"I can't name names, Dick. Nor can I go into details,
without betraying confidences. I will say this. Seth Randall was under a heavy burden of guilt when he came to
us. Judging his case on the evidence, I wasn't at all sure
the guilt was justified—or that the diagnosis of homicidal
mania, which was the basis of his commitment, was a fair
one."

"Is that another way of saying he wasn't really insane
when he came here?"

"*Insanity* is a word no psychiatrist uses clinically. All
we recognize are the various forms of mental illness.
Some, I'll grant you, are beyond help. Others respond to
treatment, if the doctor is patient. Still others might be
called temporary aberrations, which the patient himself
recognizes after the event. After I'd observed Seth for a
few months, I was sure that he belonged in this cate-
gory."

"What about the guilt complex?"

"That was self-imposed, after the event. His crime, in
the eyes of the law, was a serious one. Most Negroes in
the South who attacked a white man without apparent
provocation—and with intent to kill—would not have
gotten off this lightly."

"Did you discover his true motive?"

"I can't answer that, without violating professional eth-
ics. I will say that Seth was convinced the attack was the
one great mistake of his life. When he first came here,
he'd made up his mind to turn his commitment into a life
sentence. In my opinion, such atonement was too high a
price for a moment of blind rage. No one had died as a

result: there was no reason to reproach himself forever. If I could release him from his sense of guilt, I felt almost positive I could pronounce him cured. Therefore, I began using him as an agent in the transference therapy I've just described——"

"Let me make sure I understand, Doctor," said Rick. "Does this mean Seth could forget his own burden by taking on the burdens of other patients?"

"It was a gamble, I'll grant you," said Moore. "Many of us are locked in the prison of self—so securely that we've no wish to break out. Occasionally the psychiatrist finds a man like Seth Randall, who can open his heart to others, and discover his own soul by doing so." The director of Valley Hospital smiled, but his eyes were somber. "If you feel that's an odd blend of science and religion, you're welcome to the opinion. The results, in Seth's case, were astounding. You saw an example last night, in 3–1. I could give you a hundred others."

"Is he cured, then?"

"Seth was never mentally ill—only mentally troubled."

"If that's true, why don't you set him free?"

"Unfortunately, that's a question for which there's no reasonable answer. Seth has been with me almost ten years. He's part of Valley now. I won't say he's indispensable. I do know he's devoted to his work, no less deeply than I. Naturally, I can't guarantee that the complex causing his aberration won't recur. In any case, I've no way to release him."

"Seth told me you've asked the State Psychiatric Board to review his case. If *you* say he's cured, how can they refuse you?"

"You're forgetting two facts, Dick. Seth is here on a suspended sentence: the charge is still attempted murder. His own mother signed his commitment papers. So far, she's refused to ask for his release. My hands are tied, when the State House ignores my request for a review— and the next-of-kin does likewise. All I can do is prescribe domiciliary care for Seth, and continue using him as my assistant."

"What of his music, sir?"

"Did he speak of that?"

"Surely he deserves a chance to develop it?"

"I think he does. So do others who have heard him. Perhaps his music is more important than my clinical excuses for keeping him here. Have you heard him play?"

"Only the guitar, Doctor. As I understand it, the piano is his real instrument."

Dr. Moore's eyes were veiled now, but his weary smile was unchanged. "This is the time he practices in the auditorium. Since you're off duty, why don't you slip in and listen?"

The hospital auditorium stood in no-man's land between the private pavilion and the first of the six wards—a colonnaded building set off in three acres of beautifully mown lawns. Seth's presence was apparent, long before Rick could enter the lobby, via a half-open door. Prepared though he was for brilliance, he found the Chopin impromptu that poured from the concert grand onstage a revelation—and a refreshment of the spirit.

Intent on the keyboard, the slender performer seemed unaware of the visitor's entrance. Groping his way to a seat in the shadowed orchestra, Rick realized he was not the only listener. When his eyes had adjusted to the dimness he saw that many of the orchestra seats were occupied. Above him, in the twilit reaches of the gallery—reserved, by iron tradition, for the Negro inmates—nearly every place was filled. There was no applause when the Chopin ended—only a deep sigh, as though each of these lonely men had offered the same tribute.

Rick would learn later that Seth was used to an audience, even when he played informally: the listeners (forewarned that this was the musician's practice session) gave no obvious sign of their presence. Today, as his fingers glided into a Beethoven sonata, Seth did not even raise his eyes from the keyboard. Yet, even now, Rick sensed a communion between pianist and listeners. The audience, he realized, were patients from the open wards, who had stolen a precious hour of liberty to come and listen. Their rapt, almost devotional silence was a finer tribute than any ovation.

For over an hour, the musician ranged through the treasures of the pianoforte—refreshing his memory from open scores, but playing most of his selections entire, with an easy assurance that astounded his newest listener. His repertoire ranged from Bach to such moderns as Debussy and Ravel, from simple folk melodies to the bravura work of Lizst and Scarlatti. From time to time, he abandoned melody altogether, to thunder his way through octave études and chromatic scales that seemed the work of six hands rather than two. The playing ended with a brooding tone poem which Rick guessed was an original composition. It was a striking finale to a performance that was virtuoso in the best sense. The music flowed from those dark, sure fingers as naturally as Seth's own breathing.

Unschooled as he was in musical theory, Rick recognized its pattern. The composition was a melodic rendering of Seth's own story—and, by extension, the story of every patient at Valley who still clung, however dimly, to hope. The first movement, black with dissonance, sketched the despair of a mind groping in the night of madness. The second, an *andante cantabile* filled with tentative melodies that seemed to melt into thin air, was a celebration of that same mind's first hesitant steps toward recovery. The third, a ringing *allegro con brio,* was a bridge between madness and sanity, on which the freed spirit trod exulting. The finale, a masterpiece of towering chords, drew a glowing picture of triumph and self-assurance in the world outside.

Despite the examples about him, Rick found himself on his feet when the pianist left the keyboard, applauding until his palms stung. Seth Randall, recognizing him with a nod of greeting, came slowly down the orchestra aisle as the other listeners filed out with low, happy murmurs. The sound of a bell from the main building, warning of the approaching supper hour in the wards, did its part to hasten the exodus. In another moment, Seth and Rick were alone in the shadowed auditorium—moving, as by common consent, down the center aisle to the lobby, still lit by the declining sun.

Here, Rick settled on a bench and offered a cigarette, which the Negro pianist declined. Lighting his own, Rick prolonged the business a moment, to organize his thoughts. He was still enthralled by Seth's performance. Eager as he was to express his admiration for the Negro's artistry, he knew he must proceed with caution.

"I'm still bowled over," he told Seth at last. "Is this a daily occurrence?"

"Almost, Mr. Sloane. Sometimes I work privately: a musician's hands need constant strengthening, you know. That piano onstage is a vintage Knabe, and sweet as a nut. Today, I was playing for my own pleasure, nothing more. I can't tell you just when I sat down at the keyboard—but it was several hours ago."

"Don't you ever tire?"

The Negro smiled again, and settled on a facing bench. "Why should I? Music is my life. Or should I say it *was* my life until I came here? Thanks to Dr. Moore, I've had no reason to abandon it. We've found it helps the patients more than most therapies."

"I can see how it helped your audience today."

"We give weekly concerts. Every month, we put on a new operetta, with what talent we have. Of course, those are standard recreations, like our rival baseball clubs— and the contests for the best truck garden on the hospital farm. What we try for with my own music goes deeper. Of course we don't succeed too often, but it seems well worth the effort. Have you observed musical therapy, Mr. Sloane—as applied to mental disease?"

"I've seen a little of it in other hospitals," said Rick.

"What you did last night in the ward was something else again."

"The singing? That was only a short cut to cure insomnia. I've tried to do a good bit more at the piano."

"Like the tone poem you played this afternoon?"

Seth's face lighted up gratefully. "You do see, then? What it tried to say about a troubled mind?"

"Not just *about* a sick mind, Seth. It spoke to such minds direct."

"During my years at Valley, I've composed many such pieces. Dr. Moore says they're examples of what a medical man would call accessory circulation. A side circuit in my own emotional currents that allows me to bring my deepest unconscious feelings to the surface and express them in music. Until I came here, I'd no notion I possessed such a gift. Naturally, I've dedicated it to the service of our patients."

Seth rose from the bench and walked to the lobby door: there was a ring of pride in his voice as he went on. "Dr. Moore feels that all mental illness is only the abnormal functioning of those same currents. I was fortunate: as a composer, I could discharge the turbulence, explain it in music to myself—and to others. In most people, that same turbulence is short-circuited into emotional disturbances the layman calls insanity, for want of a better term. My task, as I saw it, was to speak to such people with my music. To convince them that the mind is stronger than the self—that it can find its own way from darkness to light."

"Let me see if I follow," said Rick. "You're telling me the successful artist learns to live with the dark side of his nature—and, in the end, to control it. A mental patient must make the same effort, before he can even begin to recover. Otherwise, all therapy is useless."

Seth faced back to the lobby. "You understand me perfectly, Mr. Sloane."

"Let me finish the picture. Such things can't be explained in words, even to a trained mind. The task is impossible in the case of the mentally ill—even when the intelligence of the patient isn't limited. Such patients need a far simpler road map to return to sanity. Your music provides it: I saw it happen just now. Or rather, heard it with my own ears."

"That is correct, Mr. Sloane. I could never have expressed the thought so clearly."

"Hasn't your music earned you the right to share your talent with the world?"

The Negro's face had been radiant while Rick blueprinted the function of his art. At this new attack, it clouded instantly.

"I'm sure Dr. Moore has explained I can never leave."

"If the charges against you were dropped—and your mother asked for your release—you could leave tomorrow."

"To my mother, I'm still insane." Seth's voice had hardened, and he refused to meet Rick's eyes. "She feels I'm safer here."

"Surely, if your case was reviewed———"

"I'm afraid that's impossible. Besides, I've found my lifework. Why should I go outside?"

"Are you satisfied with it?"

Seth's chin lifted, and he met Rick's gaze squarely. "Are any of us really satisfied? Ten years ago, I burned with ambition to be a concert pianist. I wanted to prove that one of my race could succeed in that field. How can I deny that I regret a lost opportunity? It's just too late to talk of might-have-beens."

"It isn't too late, Seth. You're barely thirty. Your talent's at your fingertips———"

"I've found peace of mind helping Dr. Moore. Don't ask me to go back to a dream that can't come true, Mr. Sloane."

"Why couldn't you do both? Tour the world as a pianist—and work here too, between engagements?"

"I know you mean well, but it's something I can't

discuss further." Seth moved toward the lobby door, as a second bell sounded in the main building. "If you'll excuse me, I'm needed on the ward to help with supper trays."

Rick made no move to detain him: he knew that he had pushed the Negro far enough. When he strolled back toward the main building a moment later, he was not surprised to observe Dr. Moore seated on a bench beside the path. After all, he had been sent to the auditorium with a purpose.

"Sit down, Dick. You look puzzled."

"I've just talked with Seth, Doctor."....

"In that case, I'm sure you grasp my problem."

"I've also heard him play. Will you agree his music belongs to the world?"

"We've no argument there," said Dr. Moore. "But you must see now why my hands are tied. I've no legal way to release Seth. Even if I could, I'm not sure he'd go——"

"Would you consent to a recording, if it could be arranged?"

The director gave Rick a startled glance. "Oddly enough, I was asked that same question a little while ago—by Miss King."

"Miss King?"

"Walter Case's niece. The lady who gave us our phonograph albums. Didn't I mention her yesterday?"

"I remember now." With a great effort, Rick kept his voice serene. "Does she know Seth too?"

"She knows both Seth and his work. A few weeks ago, she called here, to ask what his chances were. Now she plans to drive out again tomorrow, to discuss the possibilities of a recording."

Once the shock had registered, Rick found he could accept it. "Does Miss King have a specific plan in mind?"

"Not so far. First, we must learn if Seth is willing. If she gets his consent, she'll ask her uncle to foot the bill."

Again, Rick found he was swallowing hard before he spoke. "What would you say her chances are?"

"Mr. Case has always been generous to us. He built our theater as a memorial to his wife; he gave us our private pavilion. Surely he'd write one check more—to help a talented inmate."

"May I offer an even better suggestion?"

"Of course, Dick."

It was too late to retreat. Rick spoke a half-formed plan aloud, knowing he must improvise.

"Have you heard of Tony Gates?"

"I'm afraid not."

"He's head man at World-Wide Broadcasting. He controls the record company of the same name; it's a studio affiliate. We met in Italy during the war. We've been friends ever since——"

"Good enough friends to insure Seth a hearing?"

"Please don't think I'm boasting, sir—but I'm sure Tony would audition Seth if I asked him."

"Mr. Case could still help."

"I don't think so, Doctor; in the musical world, the amateur backer is always suspect. Besides, if we had Tony behind us, top professional attention would come automatically. Miss King is bound to agree it's sound procedure, if she knows the recording field——"

"How soon could you get in touch with Mr. Gates?"

"A phone call should do it, if he's in New York. May I work on that angle tonight, and report to you tomorrow?"

"Of course, Dick. Forgive me for gaping, but you sound remarkably like a worker of miracles."

"Perhaps I do, sir. From now on, I'll stop talking and perform."

"Use my office, if you wish to telephone now."

"I'll call from town. It's easier to talk with Tony when he's out of the studio. When do you expect Miss King?"

"Around noon tomorrow. Can you be up that early?"

"I'm off duty tonight, Doctor. If you'll excuse me, I've a date with Jed Bragg."

Tony Gates (whose name had come to Rick's lips unbidden) was a power in his field. Their friendship was based on the firmest of underpinnings—mutual self-respect, and the knowledge each man could help the other. Rick's telecasts were a prime source of revenue to Tony's network. Tony had been an expert liaison between commentator and sponsor.

More important still, this was not the first time Rick had led talent to the broadcaster's door. Three years ago, he had brought up a calypso singer from Jamaica who had since achieved a reputation second only to Belafonte's. Last summer, he had repeated the service with a girl from a Left Bank *chansonnier*—and Lili Morel's first album had sold over three million. . . . Remembering these happy circumstances, Rick carried ten dollars in change to the nearest phone booth, and put in his New York call in a glow of confidence. The idea of a Seth Randall recording had been a bolt from the blue. All that remained, at the moment, was to perfect his strategy with Carol King.

A half-hour later, the long-distance operator had pinned down Tony Gates in a wall booth at 21. Rick needed but a few minutes more to convince Tony that the discovery of a lifetime awaited him at Valley Hospital. The glow persisted after he had left the phone. Tony, who planned to be in Nashville on Tuesday to settle a local studio problem, had agreed to fly down to Eldon by chartered plane, with a brace of technicians in tow to appraise the theater acoustics.

Rick's endorsement of Seth, it seemed, was all the incentive Tony needed to make the journey. He had even promised to address his old friend as Richard Sloane, for reasons that were Rick's affair. (Tony Gates, whose daily bread was earned via subterfuges that would have shamed Machiavelli, could take a simple alias in stride.)

The date with Jed Bragg was for poker in the room above the Valley Stream firehouse. Tonight, Rick could welcome this apparently harmless interlude, though he had already divined its purpose.

Besides Jed, the members of the card club were a service-station operator, a butcher, a clerk at the town hall, and two loaders at a farmers' co-operative. It was another cross section, at strictly local level. Braced as he was for identical opinions, Rick was not surprised to learn that the entire club supported Governor Stead and all his works. It also believed (as though sparked by a single brain) that the school closings, however disruptive, were the inevitable response to pressures from the North.

The game was five-and-ten, with pot-limit raises and no wild cards. It was rustic poker at its worst and Rick soon perceived the players could ill afford even modest losses. A master of the game since his cub days, he was careful to plunge tonight, dropping several large pots with good grace and praising the skill of each winner. When stories and limericks went round the board, he was just as careful to contribute his share of feebly vicious anti-Semitic and anti-Negro jokes—and to agree (as stridently as any beer-brave voice in the room) that the white man was destined to remain king in the best of all possible worlds, now and forevermore.

When the game broke up just short of midnight, Rick felt he was one with the group. He did not need the cordial invitation to join the next session to prove his visit had served its purpose. Jed himself (leaning on his car door downstairs before departing for a weekend of dalliance in Eldon) added the final note, along with the revelation that Rick had awaited.

"Try to make it again your next night off, Dick. Maybe you'll draw better cards."

"I'll do my best."

The fox-faced attendant dropped his voice to a conspirator's whisper, though they were quite alone on the village street. "How'd you really like to be one of the boys?"

"I thought I was in now—while my money lasted."

"Take another look at us. This is Valley Stream's volunteer fire company—so that upstairs room is an all-purpose clubhouse. Would you guess we're a cell in the Knights of Freedom?"

"What's that, Jed—a retread of the KKK?"

"The Klan got a bad name years ago, but it stood up for things the South believed in—a long time before our integration shinola. Way I see it, the higher-ups figured we needed something even better. Now we got the Knights."

"Were tonight's card-players the only members in Valley Stream?"

"Hell, no. We got two more cells in town. Counting Smithville too, we can muster a whole troop. Fifty Marchers and ten Horsemen. The Horsemen are like squad leaders in the Army. All you do is supply your own mount. The Knights will stable it."

"What's your job—to burn out colored towns?"

Jed chuckled. "Our slogan's action through nonviolence. We don't give orders—we persuade. 'Course, we're just starting to roll politically. We're running our first slate in the next primaries."

"You're making your lodge sound mighty serious."

"We have fun on the side. Maybe you didn't realize, but tonight's liquor was free—and we get other expense money too. Our main job's to get things done the Southern way."

"What's that supposed to mean?"

Jed's starveling face, seen in the dim glow of the dashboard lights, seemed more vulpine than ever. "Good government, for example. Primary day in this state, every Knight sees to it that at least five people vote the right way."

"Who decides that?"

"We do, of course; we always back the best men.

Fellows who know how to keep the Yankee lawyers out and the niggers in the groove. The kind of politician who makes it hot for mackerel-snatchers and Jews——"

"Who gives the final word?"

"Our Grand Masters—at headquarters. 'Course, we don't know *their* names—but you can bet some pretty big men are under those robes. If you stay at Valley, you'll be smart to join up."

"What's it cost?"

"Not a red cent. Like I said, all you do is take the oath to back our candidates. We even supply the robes. If a fellow works extra hard and needs money, he can borrow through the local leader."

"Who puts up the cash?"

"Nobody knows for sure—but it sure proves there's important folks behind us. Some say the paymaster's in Central City—but that's probably scuttlebutt. The big thing is, there's hard money on hand, if a man can prove he needs help. All you do is get up on your hind legs and carry out special assignment."

"Such as——?"

"Well, just as an example, there's a gas station out on Route 6 that wouldn't give credit to our local cycle club. A couple of us dropped in on the owner quiet-like, and talked him into changin' his views. We got fifty apiece for that tour of duty. Not bad, for a half-hour's work."

"How much do they pay for bombing?"

Jed Bragg's lips curved in a sly grin. "Didn't you hear me say the Knights don't believe in violence?"

"Not for the record, you mean?"

"If you're thinkin' of that last job in Central City, the answer's no. My cousins there are all Knights: they say we had no part in it. Just the same, I think we ought to vote the fellows who did it a bonus."

"From what you've told me," said Rick, "I reckon they got their reward."

The fox-faced attendant chortled, and slapped Rick on

the back. "Why play hard to get, Dick? You know you belong with us."

"I may not stay at Valley long. I like to travel."

"So did I—once. But this Knights deal could turn into something big. Hell, if they give me a real promotion, I could quit hospital work entirely. So could you, if we moved up the ladder together——"

"I'll think it over, and let you know."

"When you say the word, I'll put up your name. The Knights need you. If you stay here, you'll need 'em even more."

"I'm beginning to see that, Jed."

"Come to our next meeting in Eldon. We're throwing a real outing next Saturday, with some red-hot speakers. Maybe it'll open your eyes."

There was no threat in the words, but Rick detected a note of disappointment in the attendant's voice as he withdrew his head from the car window and drove off in his own. Obviously, Jed Bragg was the sort of jackal who could not be put off indefinitely. Driving in a long detour to find a public phone booth, Rick told himself things might move too fast for comfort on this front as well.

When he called the *Times-News* in Central City, he was careful to ask for Theo. As he had hoped, Judd answered promptly.

"You can speak up, Sloane. I'm in a rewrite booth."

The photographer listened calmly, while Rick described his latest talk with Seth, and the plans he had made for a recording.

"It sounds like a good deal to me: I'm sure Bob would approve. At the very least, it should give friend Walter a jolt. Maybe we'll learn something from his reaction."

"The big problem's Carol. As of now, we've got to keep Case out of the picture."

"I can see that," said Theo. "If you ask me, she'll play along. She was in to see Bob today—to get the low-down on Seth. Just how he was locked up ten years ago, and why."

Rick whistled softly. This was an unlooked-for development. "Was she surprised when she learned Uncle Walter was behind it?"

"If she was, she played it close. After all, this recording plan makes sense, from her viewpoint—now she knows that Case had the colored boy committed. If she can prove Seth's really talented, she might get her uncle to turn off the heat."

Theo was right, thought Rick. Carol's actions had been consistent from the start—and Seth's welfare was behind them all.

"Does Case know she's coming here tomorrow?"

"I think not. He's been in Texas since Monday."

"That's a break for us."

"So it would seem," said the photographer. "What's your next gimmick?"

"To have Tony Gates do the recording, before anyone can interfere. Incidentally, he plans to put Randall on film as well as tape. If he looks well, he's giving him a spot on the network."

"Fair enough. Why shouldn't things turn out that way?"

"They will, Theo—if I can persuade Carol to say nothing, until we find just what he have. I'll lay odds Tony gives us a national telecast. *Then* we can see how Uncle Walter jumps."

"Do you think Carol will agree?"

"I don't see why not, if it's put to her fairly."

"Suppose she guesses who you are?"

"That's another thing I'll play by ear tomorrow."

9

THE STAFF RECREATION ROOM at Valley Hospital, on the second floor of the main building, had a set of wide windows that looked down on the visitors' parking lot beside the gate. Shortly before noon, Rick moved an armchair to this vantage point and settled behind a newspaper for his vigil.

He had sent a note to Dr. Moore, informing him of Tony Gates's enthusiastic reaction to his phone call; he had suggested that Tony be given carte blanche. Knowing he could not afford to seem anxious, he had not asked for an introduction to Carol King. . . . Instead, he had stated that he would be in the lounge if she wished to discuss the plan in detail. Weighing each word of the note, he concluded it had the virtue of candor: until he had measured Carol's reaction, he could do no more.

Shortly after twelve, when the maroon Triumph swept up the drive, he knew it was hers, long before he recognized the two figures behind the smartly raked windshield. Carol was wearing a polo coat and a gypsy bandanna. Rick was more startled than surprised to note that Hal Stacey was beside her, looking oddly naked without his Leica. Fearful that the camera reporter would attempt to follow her through the gate, he was relieved to note that Hal had settled in the car, after the briefest of exchanges.

The minutes ticked by after Carol had vanished into the rotunda, and Hal did not stir from his slightly bored repose beneath the wheel. Rick began to hope that the visitor, satisfied with the bulletin on Tony Gates, would be

153

content to leave him the field. The hope was dashed when Dr. Moore's secretary appeared in the recreation room to inform him he was wanted.

Following Miss Todd to the director's office, he kept his fingers crossed. As he had hoped, the blinds were down against the glare of sun on the lawn, and Carol was seated in a chair which faced the light. When Dr. Moore presented him, he managed to bow formally, with the desk between them: his spirits leaped when she looked up with no apparent sign of recognition. They had met just four times—in the gloom of a New York nightclub, aboard a dim-lit plane, in the bustle of a cocktail party, in a shadowed hospital room. Why should she connect this slightly flamboyant Californian with the man her uncle had ordered from the state?

Carol leaned forward in her armchair, and extended her hand. He had no choice but to take it.

"This is a pleasure, Mr. Sloane——"

"Well, my dear?" said Dr. Moore. "Do you think he's real now?"

Carol smiled, and settled again in her chair. Watching her anxiously, Rick felt the situation was still in control.

"You'll admit this is rather hard to take in, Mr. Sloane," she said quietly.

"How so, Miss King? I'm sure there are other hospital attendants who love music——"

"I'm referring to the miracle you wrought with a single phone call."

"Your friend Gates has just been on long-distance, Dick," Dr. Moore explained. "He's arriving on Tuesday. From his viewpoint, I gather the recording is already a *fait accompli.*"

"Only if you and Miss King approve."

"We do approve, Dick—most heartily. It still seems too good to be true."

"Tony's always been willing to gamble on talent."

"I must confess I'm bewildered by our electronic mirages," said the director. "Is it possible to have Seth perform in our auditorium—and transfer the performance to a television screen?"

"It's really quite simple," Rick said. "The Nashville studio will probably send a sound truck. There will be microphones in the proscenium, and a portable one for the announcer. The actual picture cameras will work from the wings—with another in the balcony for long shots."

"Must there be an announcer, Dick?"

"You can handle that part, if you wish," Rick ventured to address Carol directly. "Don't you agree, Miss King?"

"I've been persuading him to do just that," she said.

"What about Seth?"

"We talked the whole thing over this morning," said Dr. Moore. "What I suggested was a repeat performance of the concert he gives each Saturday—as a benefit for the hospital. He seemed willing enough."

Rick had hoped for this reaction from Seth, after their talk in the theater. The director, he saw, had chosen the ideal approach. Had he turned down this chance to send his music beyond the hospital walls, the Negro pianist would have been less than human.

"There should be no hitch, then," he said. "May I suggest the job's done soon—if Miss King agrees?"

"I agree completely," said Carol.

Dr. Moore got up from his desk. "I must leave you now. They're waiting for me at a staff conference—and you probably have details to discuss."

Rick walked with the director to the door. A glance into the outer office told him that Miss Todd had departed on her lunch hour. He was alone with Carol King—and the light was still behind him, until she rose to open the window blinds, bathing the office in bright sunlight.

"I had to be positive," she said. "It was an excellent disguise."

The game was up, he saw—though he continued to play it. "I don't know what you mean, Miss King——"

"You should wear longer sleeves," she said. "I wasn't sure, until I saw your arm."

He glanced at his right wrist, and the cresent scar that was a memento of a fishing accident. With all his care, it was ironic that this small blemish should betray him: only a woman would have noticed such a detail.

"You're Rick Jordan," she said. "Don't deny it."

"And if I am——?"

"Why did you come here?"

"You mean, after your uncle warned me off?"

"At the Central City Hospital, you said you were going North."

"I needed time, Carol—to put the puzzle together. Now I'm back to work out the ending."

"What puzzle?"

"The Seth Randall mystery. Why he's been a ten-year victim of persecution."

"On my uncle's part?"

"You'll admit that much, then?"

"Seth was sent here with good reason."

"Perhaps he was—ten years ago. He's cured today."

"I can see that now. I'm doing what I can to set him free."

Rick stood above her for a moment, taking what comfort he could from her unwavering eyes, and the slight smile that had never left her lips. It was impossible to doubt her sincerity—and just as impossible, even now, to tell her the whole truth about Walter Case.

"Now I've met Seth and know him—will you believe my motives are honest?"

"I believe you, Rick."

"Does that mean you'll permit me to retain the disguise?"

"Perhaps. If you'll give your real reason for being here. You didn't come to Valley just to help Seth's musical career."

"I want the Walter Case story too," he said. "And I think Seth is the key."

"Why can't you leave my uncle be? He's never sought publicity. Let him finish his life as he began."

"I'm not sure any of us have that right, Carol. Not the way the world is moving."

"I've apologized for his behavior at my party," said Carol—and he could see, by the sudden change in her tone, that she had sensed his drift. "I'll admit he's harsh at times—even tyrannical. Surely you can forgive him that?"

"I've been a newspaperman for twenty years. I don't mind Tory insults. This evil goes deeper."

"Evil?"

The die was cast now: he did not draw back. "I chose the word deliberately, Carol. In my opinion, your uncle is an evil man—the most dangerous this country has known. I'm asking you to let me prove it."

He had expected rage, frozen incredulity—even tears. But Carol King did not budge. Whatever the outcome of this strange encounter, he knew she would listen with an open mind.

"You've no right to ask that," she said at last.

"I've every right, if what I say is true. You half-believe me now, or you'd fight back."

Carol closed her eyes. When she spoke again, it was an almost soundless whisper. "I won't pretend I haven't wondered. These last weeks especially—after you left Central City. Things *have* happened I couldn't understand——"

"You're on my side, then?"

"Not yet, Rick. I can't promise quite so much. Not until I've made up my mind."

"Will you give me a free hand—until I've found my proof?"

"Tell me your plans. I'm not sure I can endorse them."

"At the moment, I'm improvising," said Rick. "Seth is my only real source, and he's unwilling to talk. The fact he's consented to the recording is more than I dared hope for."

"Suppose he makes the recording. What will it accomplish?"

"Tony Gates will introduce a musical genius to the world—and Walter Case will be reminded that the genius is still a prisoner. It'll be a real test of your uncle. If he's what you hope, he'll permit Seth to go free——"

"Why can't I ask that favor of him now?"

"We'll get the same result, through Tony. If I'm wrong about Case, I'll be the first to admit it——"

"What if you're right?" asked Carol.

"You're still in the clear, so far as Seth is concerned—and you're still the devil's daughter by adoption. We can work together to expose him."

"I could never spy on him, Rick."

"Events may change your mind," he said quietly. "I'll gamble on that."

Carol got to her feet. Her voice was as strained as her manner. "Apparently we've reached an understanding," she said. "At least for the time being." She moved toward the door like a sleepwalker, then shook herself alive, and faced him directly. "I won't thank you for what you've just told me. I'm praying that you're wrong. Meanwhile, you have my trust."

"I'll try to be worthy."

"How soon can you arrange the recording?"

"Within a fortnight, I'm sure."

"Uncle Walter will still be in Texas. Should I come to Valley for the actual concert?"

"I think it's better if you stay clear altogether. Besides, the big thing is the filmed telecast. Not what happens here."

"Good-by, Rick," she said. "I hope I haven't promised too much."

"You've been most kind," he said. "Few Southern ladies would be so patient with a visiting Yankee."

Again, she turned toward the door. "I can't stay a moment more. Hal must be back in Central City by three."

The mention of the camera reporter's name was a jarring note. Elated by Carol's surrender (partial though it was), Rick had forgotten Hal Stacey entirely.

"Does he know why you're here?"

"Of course not. I told him I was paying a duty call on Dr. Moore. He insisted on keeping me company."

"I needn't warn you to hold your tongue in his presence—even though he is your fiancé."

"I won't say a word, Rick—and he's my fiancé no longer."

Their eyes met and held. "Would you mind repeating that?" he asked.

"I haven't broken the engagement, formally. I don't intend to—until I've made up my mind."

"About Case?"

"About us all," she said. "I told you I'd had my doubts lately. They began with Hal."

He had taken her hand to say good-by—and, for a moment, he felt her sway toward him. He just missed taking her in his arms, to comfort her as she deserved— but he was glad he had resisted the impulse when she broke free and hurried from the office. The burden of proof was on his shoulders now. Until he had established his case, he had no right to trespass.

The arrival of Tony Gates at the hospital (muted at Rick's urgent plea) accomplished its purpose smoothly.

Rick had feared that the exuberant network president might overplay the situation—but Tony, for once, had sensed the dramatic advantages of the soft sell. He had come down from Nashville (he said simply) to observe an artist at work, to endorse a good friend's judgment, one more time. . . . Seth (who received the great man in the director's office) had taken his proposals in stride. At the audition that followed, his performance was all that Rick had hoped for. A date had been set for the concert, and Tony Gates had flown back to New York to call his crew together for the taping.

The recording was made as a typical Saturday concert
in the hospital theater, with Seth the solo player. Dr.
Moore had made the introduction for the benefit of the
picture cameras. A copy of his remarks was sent North, as
part of the printed matter to go with the two albums the
concert had yielded. Since the telecast addressed a nationwide audience, some of the sentences were slightly al-
tered:

Tonight [said Dr. Moore] it is my pleasure to speak
to you from Valley Hospital, on an unusual occasion.

Seth Randall, the solo pianist you are about to
hear, has been one of our patients for the past ten
years. He has asked me to explain the circumstances
surrounding his appearance, so you may judge not
only his performance, but what lies behind it.

Seth was committed to this hospital with a diagnosis of homicidal mania. At first, he was able to make
but little progress. If I, as attending physician, have
helped to show him the road back to mental health,
my contribution was incidental. It was Seth himself
who discovered that he, and he alone, must make
that sometimes painful journey.

In his case, he was helped by the fact that music
had been almost the whole of his life before his
commitment. Therefore, unlike so many others, he
had a goal from the start. Once he turned to the task
of continuing and developing his musical talent, the
way back was fully half-traversed.

In Seth's case, progress was also helped tremen-
dously by his desire (evinced almost from the first)
to share his great talent. Since his return to the
keyboard, he has given generously of his music, both
on and off the wards. Each week at this time, the
hospital auditorium has been filled with listeners. As
tonight's concert will illustrate, his original compositions—which are thematic studies of mental illness,

and living pointers for its cure—have done much to lead others from the slough of despond, to uncover talents and capabilities they did not know they possessed. This ability to give of oneself to others is the final test of a cure, as it is the final test in the maturing of the human personality.

Tonight's concert will prove, at all levels, that Seth Randall is a great musician. But we of Valley Hospital know he is far more than a piano genius: to us, he is the living epitome of One we refer to as The Master, Jesus of Nazareth. Despised and rejected of men, he has learned to triumph over adversity. In that triumph, he has gained the love and respect of us all.

I could not present you to Seth Randall the virtuoso pianist without paying tribute to Seth Randall the healer.

As the head of Valley Hospital ended his introduction, the camera picked up the slender Negro at the keyboard of the concert grand. Despite Tony Gates and his pleas, Seth had refused to dress for the occasion. The audience beheld him in his familiar hospital garb—a long-skirted doctor's coat, a white shirt open at the throat; he did not rise when he spoke, and his voice could not have been more casual had he been chatting with friends on the ward.

"Dr. Moore honors me above my deserts. He knows—and all of you know—that he is responsible for what I am today. I thank him from the bottom of my heart for this chance to play for all America, just as I have played so often for you———"

As he spoke, the cameras had panned to the audience, showing the rapt faces, the air of expectancy that was Seth's finest tribute. His voice continued on the microphones, vibrant with the same assurance, the same calm purpose. "Tonight's program will be in three sections. The first will include works by Bach, Mozart, Chopin, and

Beethoven, illustrating what is ordinarily called a classical program. The second will be an American section, featuring the music of my own people. The third will be compositions of my own—tone poems which I dedicate to all of you."

Seth had begun to play as he finished speaking: there had been none of the pretentious pauses that sometimes feature the appearance of the professional pianist. From the projection booth (where the sound equipment had been installed for the occasion), an announcer fed the titles of each composition into the recorder. Between numbers, Seth spoke briefly of the composer's message and his meaning.

From the start, Rick had seen that this very casualness (like the pianist's garb and his own deep sincerity) was far more effective than any deliberate attempt at showmanship. He had not needed Tony Gates's own glowing moment at the microphone when the concert ended to realize that this was a musical bombshell, packaged and ready for the television screens of America. . . .

When it was over (and Tony and his crew had left in a barrage of good wishes) Seth sat with Rick for a moment in the darkened orchestra. At Rick's insistence, there had been no mention of his name as a principal architect of the program. Watching from the wings, he had been glad to note that Seth had gone through the entire grueling recital with no evidence of strain. From first to last, the Negro had merely been playing for his friends, ignoring the bunched spotlights, the staring camera's eyes, and the jungle of microphone cables as though they had no real existence.

"How did it seem, Seth? Like visiting another planet?"

"Only until I began playing, Mr. Sloane. Then I forgot everything in the music. I always do."

"You didn't mind, then?"

"Not at all. Tonight, I played for Dr. Moore and the

hospital. I hope it will help to put them on the medical map of America."

"What of your own future?"

"My future is here."

"Suppose this telecast is a success? It could open the last door that keeps you inside."

Seth smiled in the half-dark. "You've been a real wonderworker," the Negro said quietly. "But there are miracles even you can't accomplish. My freedom's one of them."

Rick did not pursue the topic. Just before he departed, Tony Gates had said that tonight's program was already penciled into a choice sustaining spot a week from Sunday. Tonight's performance had clinched the date beyond question: until the actual telecast, Rick knew he could only wait and hope.

Meanwhile, there was a call to be made in Eldon. Not that he expected the visit to produce results: on the contrary, he was sure that Seth's mother would be even more reticent than Seth himself. He still felt he must approach her, if only to round out the pattern.

Seth's mother was listed in the files as Mary Randall. He drove to Eldon on his first free afternoon to seek her out.

He found the address easily—a neat, white-painted cottage on one of the side streets in colored town. Parking beneath a tulip tree at the crossing, he sat for an instant without moving. The siesta silence of three o'clock told him he had chosen the right moment for his call. At this hour, most of Eldon's Negro men were busy elsewhere. The women (following the Southern custom) worked within their gaunt frame houses, shuttered from the eyes of passers-by. The only sound to break the quiet was the low hum of voices from the windows of a school in the next block, where a class of dark-skinned first-graders chanted the final lesson of the day.

Rick had come in haste, forcing himself to make the

journey and disliking the errand in advance. So far, he
had no clear idea of what he would say to Seth's mother,
or how Mary Randall would respond. If his guess was
accurate (if she held the key to Walter Case's antago-
nism), he could hardly expect her to surrender it to a
stranger.

There was still a certain value in the direct approach,
even though the gulf between them was too wide for
leaping. Mustering a composure he was far from feeling,
he stepped out of the car and opened the gate in the white
picket fence that divided the Randall yard from the road-
way.

On closer view, the house (like the well-raked yard)
reflected the pride of the owner. Camellia bushes framed
the front portico: there was a neat chicken run beside the
kitchen stoop, shaded by the inevitable chinaberry tree.
Rick saw that the house next door was a Negro parsonage, an extension of the church that stood on the corner.
The two dwellings stood almost cheek by jowl, thanks to
the smallness of their lots: but there was a quiet dignity
about both houses no visitor could escape. Already, it
seemed natural that Rick should find Mary Randall living
in the shadow of the Afro-Baptist Church. Sight unseen,
he felt that she belonged there—no matter how clouded
her past had been.

When he stepped up to the portico, he noticed that the
front door was open. The house (a "shotgun" cottage, with
a hall that led from front to back stoops like a
breezeway) seemed empty at first. Then, hearing the hiss
of a hot iron from the kitchen, he saw that a woman was
hard at work there. When she turned in answer to his
knock, he could sense her recoil at the white face framed
in her doorway.

"My name's Richard Sloane, Mrs. Randall. May I
come in?"

The polite address, he saw, had done nothing to ease her
alarm: in the South, white men seldom addressed a Negro
woman in such respectful terms. Yet the fear (if fear was

the proper term) was gone in an instant. When Mary Randall set down her iron and moved to unlatch the screen door, she seemed entirely composed.

"Please come in, sir. I was working, and didn't hear your step."

Seth's own good looks had prepared Rick, in some measure, for what he saw. In the uncertain light of the shuttered living room, his mother could have passed for a white woman. Then, as she raised a blind, he saw that she was a light octoroon, still beautiful at fifty despite her snow-white hair and the deep lines of unhappiness in brow and cheeks. Even in a work dress and scuffed slippers, Mary Randall had the air of a lady. The gesture that made the visitor welcome was as unaffected as it was gracious. Before they had exchanged a dozen words, Rick sensed that this was a formidable antagonist, whose defenses were already in perfect order.

"What can I do for you, Mr. Sloane?"

"I'm from the hospital."

"I guessed that. Is it about Seth?"

"Yes, Mrs. Randall."

"Is he——?"

"Seth was never better. I'd like to talk with you about his future. Perhaps I should say his musical prospects."

The living room in which they stood, though sparsely furnished, was in excellent taste. The air of modest affluence was echoed in the spinet piano that stood against one wall, the console phonograph and television set between the two windows, and the tall glass bookshelf whose contents looked read. There were pictures of Seth on the piano. Above the books, an enlarged photograph showed him as a youth, in evening dress, at the keyboard of a piano. A special bookshelf contained a dozen fat volumes which obviously held his early press clippings. A folded *Times-News* lay on the table, open to the feature story Bob Partridge had run on the hospital concert. (After careful consideration, they had decided to run it without side comment, in the hope that it would induce Case to show his hand.) Picking up the newspaper, Rick prayed it would serve a like purpose here.

"I see you've read of the concert, Mrs. Randall."

"Yes, Mr. Sloane. It came as a great surprise to me."

"Next Sunday, the highlights will be telecast on film, coast to coast. I hope you'll be tuned in."

"Did Seth send you? Or was it Dr. Moore?"

"I'm here on my own," he said quickly. "I was present at that recording. There's no need to tell you of your son's talents—or how they've matured. When you tune in this Sunday——"

"Why are you here, Mr. Sloane? To ask for Seth's release? You must know it's impossible."

"When did you see him last?"

"Ten years ago, just after he was sentenced."

"You gave up all hope when he was sent to Valley?"

"I had no choice. He'd almost killed a man. It was either that or prison."

"Surely the case can be reviewed——"

"How much do you know of this?" she asked: her voice was almost harsh.

"I've read the hospital report."

"Then you know the man my son attacked was *white*. Such cases aren't reviewed in the South."

"Wouldn't this man reconsider—if he knew Seth was cured?"

Mary Randall's face remained a mask. "I've told you it's hopeless," she said at last. "You'd best believe me."

"Do *you* think your son is insane?"

"He must have been—to attack a man like Walter Case."

"It was the bodyguard he wounded."

"Does that matter? He was out of his mind—and they locked him up, for his own protection."

"Dr. Moore has told me he's entirely well. He'll release him tomorrow, if the State Psychiatric Board moves for a review. It would help greatly if you asked for such action."

"I've told you it's impossible."

"Even if it meant your son could be famous tomorrow? Perhaps the greatest pianist of his race?"

"Even then, sir." Her voice, like her manner, was unchanged. So far, Rick realized, he had failed utterly. Only the weary air of resignation was real, the steadfast resolve not to yield an inch.

"Would you consider visiting Seth at the hospital?"

"No, Mr. Sloane. I was told it would make him worse."

"By Dr. Moore?"

"No. By the doctors who advised his commitment."

"That opinion is ten years old. Don't you think Dr. Moore is right, when he insists Seth is well? Can't you believe he could change?"

"Here in the South, some things never change. Dr. Moore says my son is happy at Valley Hospital. He's doing useful work there. That's quite enough."

"Don't you *want* him to go back into the world?"

He saw that the question had shaken her. For a moment, her eyes met his directly—and her voice was almost soft when she answered. "Of course I've wanted him back, Mr. Sloane. At first, I thought the loss was more than I could bear. Then, when I heard of his work at the hospital, I knew he had faced the problem, and conquered it. He was always brave, you know—even as a child. Brave and proud and headstrong." She paused, and seemed lost in a memory she could never share. "He's put pride behind him; he's serving out his sentence. He has the strength for that—just as I have the strength to live alone."

"Mrs. Randall, Seth has paid for that one blind moment of rage, a hundred times over. He deserves this chance to resume his career. You're his mother. Won't you give him a helping hand?"

"I couldn't. It's something I wouldn't dare——" She broke off abruptly, and turned aside. Rick saw he had breached her defenses at last, and pressed his advantage.

"Whom could it possibly hurt?"

"It isn't a question of hurting," said Mary Randall. "No hurt lasts a lifetime——"

"Not even yours?"

"I've learned to bear it. Even if they'd let him go, Valley Hospital is better than prison."

Rick decided to take another tack, while he held the initiative. "One of the biggest men in music is sponsoring Sunday's telecast," he said. "His name is Tony Gates. He believes in Seth's talent. He's convinced that an artist of his caliber, even though he's a Negro, can occupy a high place in America. I'm sure he'd employ psychiatrists, famous men whose opinion must be respected everywhere, even in the courts of this state. If they testified Seth was well, couldn't he go free?"

"Free for what, Mr. Sloane? The chain gang at Turpentine Farm?"

"Mr. Gates would employ lawyers too. They'd fight for him—right up to the Supreme Court."

Mary Randall took a deep, sighing breath and he saw she was trembling. A tear formed in the corner of her eye and rolled slowly down her cheek. "You still don't understand, Mr. Sloane. You don't know the South."

"I was born in Virginia——"

"You've forgotten, then. How vengeful it can be—how it refuses to change its ways."

"Isn't this worth a trial—after ten years?"

He did not press her further as she sank into an armchair, knitting her fingers as if, through that action, she was gaining the strength to control herself. The vistas he had just opened, he felt sure, were persuasion enough. She could not banish them from her mind forever.

"What would you have me do?"

"Write to Walter Case. Or, better still, go to him direct—"

There was no mistaking her reaction to his plea: had he struck her across the face, she could not have flinched more violently.

"He wouldn't even see me——"

Rick steeled himself against any pity for her suffering. "Why? Because he's a millionaire contractor, and you're a Negro? Don't call him a monster until you've proved it."

"I'm calling no one names," she said stubbornly. "I'm only trying to make you see things as they are. They won't let Seth go."

"Who are 'they'? Case himself? The Psychiatric Board? The political machine?"

"It's bigger than any one man, Mr. Sloane. It's the whole South—keeping my people in their place. Are you asking me to go against that tradition?"

"I'm afraid I am, Mrs. Randall—for your boy's sake. Now I've had a chance to know you, I don't think you'll refuse."

He saw that he had pressed her enough, when she rose abruptly and left the room. He heard her draw a glass of water at the kitchen tap and drink it down. When she stood in the doorframe again, she was in complete command.

"Believe me, Mr. Sloane, I'd take this risk—if I thought it could do the slightest good."

"Promise me just one thing, and I'll go at once."

Mary Randall smiled, for the first time. Her whole face was transformed, giving him a glimpse, however brief, of the carefree charm she had known as a girl. At the moment, she was Seth's image when he sat at the keyboard.

"Don't think I mind this visit," she said. "You're a good man—I can see that. You came here for good reasons."

"Will you tune in on your son's program this Sunday—and let me have your opinion afterward?"

"Yes, if you wish."

"I won't trouble you again, Mrs. Randall—if you can honestly say that such talent doesn't belong to the world."

The smile faded—and Mary Randall's eyes dropped to her hands. The fingers were still tensely laced.

"Yes, Mr. Sloane. I think I can promise that."

"Until Sunday, then. Thank you for letting me say so much."

In his car again (needing a moment more to collect himself) Rick drove to the corner nad parked before the square white porch of the Afro-Baptist Church. There was a sound of organ music inside. Obeying a sudden impulse, he entered the building by a side door.

The dim-lit pews were empty. He hesitated in the vestry, until he could make sure that the man at the organ console was alone. Then, as the old revival hymn faded, he followed the side aisle, just as the organist was stepping down from his bench. Judging by the alpaca clericals, the stooped, aged Negro was also the minister. In these rural churches, it was not unusual for the pastor to double in brass, at the organ or in the choir.

"My name is Richard Sloane," said Rick. "I'm from Valley Hospital. Will you forgive the intrusion?"

"This is God's house, sir," said the pastor. "We welcome everyone. Can I be of service?"

The man's name, Rick found, was Dr. Stuart Howell (the fact that he was a doctor of divinity, with diplomas from both Tuskegee and a New York seminary, was stressed gently). For nearly forty years, he had been shepherd of the Eldon flock. When Mary Randall had come to town as a bride, he had sold the newlyweds their first abode, a house in an adjoining block, behind Sam Randall's general store.

Like the widow's present cottage, the store had been church property. Because of her good management, they had paid off the mortgage and owned it, free and clear, at the time of Sam Randall's death. The widow Randall still retained an interest in the store, though she had resigned its actual management to others. Ten years ago, she had bought her present house (it was also church property). She had lived there quietly ever since, seeing few neighbors, and rounding out her income with fancy laundering.

Dr. Howell had volunteered these facts freely. From the first, it was evident to Rick that he had been questioned more than once about the Randalls. At the time of Seth's commitment, he said, officials from the State House had descended on Eldon, to take depositions on Sam Randall's death—which, as Dr. Howell remarked, had been the apparent cause of Seth's mania. A coroner's jury had already called the death an accident. Seth's father, so the story ran, had been drunk, stalling his car on a railroad crossing and dying under the wheels of a passing freight. No one had questioned the verdict. In the months before his death, Sam Randall had often been drunk—and there had been other brushes with death before the accident. . . .

"Was Sam a bottle man?"

"I wouldn't say that, Mr. Sloane. Sam was one of those happy-go-lucky fellows who hadn't a care in the world, or an enemy. He'd inherited the store from his father. I'm afraid it was pretty badly managed, until Mrs. Randall took over——"

"I gather Seth and his father were close——"

"They were inseparable. Sam was aware of his shortcomings—he had enough common sense to leave the store management to his wife. He gave the boy all his affection, even though he couldn't set him a good example. And it was he who encouraged Seth in his music. He had his first lessons at this organ console, before his parents decided he should go North to study the piano."

"I'd like to ask a difficult question, Dr. Howell. Did Seth think his father met with foul play?"

The ancient Negro's eyes were clouded now. Obviously, this was a white man's question that could never be answered fully.

"No one knows what Seth had in mind, sir. From what I hear, he'd gone clean out of his senses from grief."

"May I ask your opinion on Sam Randall's death?"

"I think the coroner's jury was right. There's one thing about Mary Randall—and I can't say I blame her for it. She kept a tight hold on the purse strings. She fed Sam well, and clothed him from the store—but all she gave him was tobacco money, and precious little of that. How could she do more, when he'd only spend it on liquor?"

"You said he was drinking heavily before he died."

"So he was. No one knew where the drink money came from. Some say he'd been lucky with the dice. In any case, Mary had no way of stopping him. I think his death was his own doing. It's my guess he was asleep at the wheel, when the car stalled on the tracks——"

"Perhaps you're wondering why I've asked you these questions, Dr. Howell. We're hoping at Valley Hospital that Seth's case can be reviewed. Regardless of his motivation—or lack of it—we feel he's paid the penalty. Do you agree?"

"Mr. Sloane, are you asking me to answer as Seth Randall's friend, or as the pastor of this congregation?"

"I'm asking man to man. Your reply will go no further."

The minister led the way to the vestry. Following him into the small room, Rick noticed that his shoulders seemed bowed, as though the weight they bore was too heavy for a single mortal. Still without speaking, Dr. Howell picked up a copy of a Harlem weekly that lay on a table, and turned the pages to point at a photograph of Thornton Blanding, the famous Negro lawyer and a militant champion of civil rights.

"You recognize him, of course."

"Yes, Dr. Howell."

"If you'd asked Thorn Blanding what you just asked me, the answer would be a ringing *yes*. Of course Seth deserves to go free. In the North, this same lawyer would have mobilized the resources of the NAACP to win his freedom. It's another story in Eldon——"

"Do you call that justice, Dr. Howell?"

"I call it the Deep South. Here, my people must make

haste slowly. Don't say that's the voice of Uncle Tom speaking; and don't call me an old man who's learned the value of caution. I won't deny that both accusations are partly true. There's still no better way."

"Even in a case like Seth's?"

"His mother must answer that, not I," said the minister. "If she feels there's no hope, I'd take her opinion as final. This isn't the best time to open a closed case——"

"From what you've told me, Dr. Howell, no time's appropriate. Seth is already thirty——"

"Mr. Sloane, I've shown you lawyer Blanding's photo with a purpose. Will you read the story beneath it?"

Rick took up the Negro weekly a second time, and skimmed through the extended caption. The lawyer (a kingpin in the NAACP) was at present embarked on a tour of the South, with the avowed intention of attacking the problem of civil rights in key sectors. One such spot was the town of Eldon, where he was expected within two weeks, to argue before the local courts in behalf of a token integration in the town's only all-white school.

"It seems Mr. Blanding has the courage of his convictions."

"He's a fine man, and a fine lawyer—a crusader for the right, in the best sense. He is also as dogmatic, in his way, as the most dedicated states'-righter." Dr. Howell turned the photograph face down, with a gesture of frustration. "The cynic who called the NAACP an Association for the *Agitation* of Colored People wasn't too wide of the mark. When Thorn Blanding comes to Eldon, he'll rub fur the wrong way, on both sides of the fence. Especially at the State House——"

"Meaning, of course, that Mary Randall would be speaking to closed minds, if she asked for a review of Seth's commitment now?"

"I won't state that as a fact, Mr. Sloane. Perhaps she could make her appeal at the top. I've never questioned her on that score—I didn't feel it was my right——"

They walked to the church porch together. Across the

way, the all-Negro school was letting out: the recess yard
overflowed with chattering eight-year-olds, most of whom
paused to remove the shoes they had worn to class before
starting barefoot for home. In many cases, Rick noted, the
shoes were wrapped carefully in newspaper, then tucked
into the schoolbags. In Eldon's colored town, leather was
too precious to be wasted, once the white man's rules had
been obeyed in the classroom. . . . He turned to Dr.
Howell, hoping the minister had not misunderstood his
grimace. These children, after all, were happy enough:
they were still too young to feel the goad. Ragged as
jackdaws and chattering just as gaily, they had yet to
discover their world was content to pass them by.

"Say what you will, Mr. Sloane," the pastor murmured.
"For each Seth Randall, there are thousands like those
children there. We've a long road to travel before we can
walk together."

"But we must make a beginning somewhere—a better
beginning than we've yet made." Rick s glance took in the
rounded roof of the white high-school auditorium, visible
on a hill just outside the town. It was painfully new in
contrast with the sagging frame building from which the
Negro children had just poured.

Dr. Howell's eyes followed his glance. "The gap is not
quite so wide as it seems, Mr. Sloane," he said. "Industry
is growing fast in the South; we are no longer a strictly
agricultural region. Few Negroes work in factories yet—
but the number will increase. Give them time to better
themselves economically. The rest will follow."

"How much time?"

"A generation at least—perhaps more. Until they've
earned their self-respect, it can't be forced upon them.
Visitors like Thorn Blanding can only delay that kind of
social evolution."

"Don't forget there are powerful forces against you.
They're growing stronger."

"You mean the Knights, I suppose."

"Or the White Citizens' Councils. Do labels matter?"

Dr. Howell smiled. "You spoke of powerful forces, Mr. Sloane. There are powerful ones on our side too. The conscience of the Christian people of the South, to name just one. It can't remain silent forever."

"I wish I had your faith."

"I know the shadow is deep today. Sometimes, even I think this is a land God forgot. But the road leads up-ward: I'd give my life to that belief———"

"You've given most of it now."

"What does one life matter, if the human race moves forward? Someday, we'll learn to tread that road."

10

THE WAIT for the telecast was a bleak limbo for the newest ward attendant at Valley Hospital. Positive that he had exhausted his last lead, his prevailing mood had alternated between despair—and the illogical hope that this was the darkness before dawn. It was almost a relief to fulfill his half-promise to Jed Bragg and drive into Eldon to witness the conclave of the Knights of Freedom.

A note from Bob Partridge had informed him that the *Times-News* would cover the conclave *sub rosa:* the editor had given him a precise description of the car his reporter would use and its probable parking place. In a cryptic postscript, he had promised to bring Rick up to date on events in Central City. Until the rendezvous, he had suggested it might be wiser to risk no further phone calls.

The Knights' outing (as the conclaves were called locally) was held in the early evening. Aware that all such demonstrations followed a similar formula, Rick had purposely arrived late He was in time to witness the last, death-defying antics of the *Eldon Elites,* as the winners of the night's motorcycle contest slammed round the cinder track, to mount a wooden ramp and zoom into space like crazy comets. Attendants in asbestos suits lifted a flaming hoop at each leap. Hunched above their handlebars, the cyclists shot through the blazing circles as precisely as circus performers, hitting the cinder track again without a single spill. Then, re-forming in a double line, they vanished in the night.

A roar of cheers sped them on their way. Working through the crowd that covered the high ground on three sides of the meadow, Rick saw that the five acres within the cinder circle were packed with white-robed figures, massed by platoons as precisely as any well-drilled army. As numbers went, the army was not too large—but it made up for its lack of size in the iron grimness of its discipline. He needed only a glance to see that each platoon had its lieutenant—a man whose conical hood was a foot taller than the rank and file and emblazoned with a scarlet "F."

At the open end of the meadow stood a high-stilted platform, bristling with microphones. Floodlights were massed about it, on the roofs of the vans that held the sound equipment. Behind the platform, on a man-made knoll, stood a huge cross of pitch pine. It was unlighted as yet, though a flambeau blazed in the ground nearby. The tallest Knight of all, arms folded beneath his robe, stood waiting to ignite it.

The antics of the cyclists, Rick realized, had been only a clowns' prelude. So, in a way, was the jousting now taking place on the cinder track, where a dozen fully robed Knights (mounted on horses caparisoned in white) were brandishing lances and pretending to unseat one another as they circled the field. Each passage of arms was greeted by the same cheer, and a fanfare of bugles from the sound truck.

Viewed by day, the solemn mummery would have seemed grotesque. Played out against the night, with a thousand spectators gaping from the hillsides, it had an eerie magic of its own. Rick had witnessed similar preludes to mass hysteria in other corners of the globe; the memories did nothing to diminish his anger at each howl from the meadow.

A year ago, he had risked his life to cross by junk to the Chinese mainland. He had heard that identical mad baying in a field outside Canton, where professional agitators had whipped a Youth Group into a lather of hatred against Americans and all their works. He had seen exact parallels in Prague and in Warsaw, before the Communist take-over. In each case, the routine had been the same: only the language had differed. Tonight, when the first robed figure climbed the platform, he could have written the man's speech to the last artful pause, the last thundering climax.

The words were chanted rather than spoken in the formal sense, almost as though they were demented blank verse. This, too, was part of the technique of rabble-rousing—since the first crowd had formed at the first cave mouth:

> Over in Central City, there's a kike called Partridge—
> A Partridge is a Southern bird, but this bird ain't
>   Southern!
> I reckon you might call him a crow, or maybe a
>   buzzard—
> One that flew in from the North like a cuckoo—
> (A cuckoo, folks, is a bird that nests where he ain't
>   wanted!)
> We all know the Jews gave Partridge a newspaper—
> A paper he calls the Times-News—
> A paper that dares to tell you and me how to
>   think!
> Folks like us, born and bred in the South—
> Folks whose ancestors died in the War between the
>   States!
> Now Partridge is askin' these same folks to be nig-
>   ger-lovers!
> Jew-lovers! But don't worry, folks. Don't worry one
>   mite!
> Scum like Bob Partridge won't be with us much
>   longer.
> Folks in Central City have had a bellyful of his lies.
> Any day now, they're dipping him in tar—
> Givin' him more feathers than a buzzard ever had—

*And shippin' him back to Yankee-land—express col-
    lect!*
And when they do—
I'm sure you good people will cheer 'em on!

The speaker was mouthing his diatribe as clumsily as a
schoolboy, and sawing the air with gestures that should
have shamed a rustic orator. This, of course, was deliberate, a mountebank's caper on which better speakers
would build. But the man's bellows were broadcast clearly,
with none of the feedback squeal that so often distorted
outdoor broadcasts. The Knights' technicians in the sound
trucks, like the Knights' speech-writers, knew their job
thoroughly.

So did the white ranks that hemmed the platform. At
the first pause, their roar of agreement swept like a wind
across the meadow, so violently that the flambeau beside
the cross danced wildly. Rick had been braced for that
roar. What sickened him was the fact that most of the
watchers on the hillside cheered just as loudly. Somehow
he had refused to believe that ordinary Americans, even
in a piney-woods town like Eldon, would yield to the
compulsion of mass hysteria. . . . It was true that laughter
was mingled with the cheering, and a few catcalls were
heard at the fringes. But there was no blinking the fact
that this massed audience was responding with a single
voice.

The speaker had increased his tempo now. Blank verse
had shaded into a fast-chanted prose that seemed jumbled
only to an untrained ear. Buffoon though he was, the man
had learned his lesson well. In each sentence, the key
words were pounded like hammer blows.

"Now this Partridge—this *buzzard*—is tellin' us we
must let *niggers* in our *schools!*

"He don't tell you what's happened in *schools up
North!*

"He ain't explained the schools up yonder ain't *safe* for *white* kids!

"He don't mention the crop of *mongrels* they're raisin' in *Yankee-land!*

"He ain't said a word about the *nigger gangs* that run *New York* and *Chicago* and *Boston* nowadays!

"All he tells you is take your *black brethren* and plump 'em down at the same desk with *white children!*

"Well, folks! Maybe the *niggers* are *Bob Partridge's* brothers! But while there's a *God in heaven,* they ain't *yours* or *mine!"*

Again, the roar of approval, from both Knights and spectators, threatened the guttering flambeau. When the speaker resumed his harangue, his voice dropped into the lower decibels, until it seemed almost pleading:

"That's why your neighbors have formed the Knights of Freedom. It's to keep buzzards like Partridge from takin' over—like the carpetbaggers from the North in Reconstruction days. That why the motto of the Knights is just four words long: *Keep the South Pure.*

"Folks, what do those words mean to you? I know what they mean to me—and to every man in the Knights.

"Keep the South Pure means *Keep Down the kikes!*

"It means *Keep Down the Catholics!*

"It means *Keep Down nigger-lovers!*

"It means keep down *everybody* who ain't a *God-fearin' Protestant.* Because only the Protestant knows that *black's black* and *white's white,* and it's *God's holy ordinance* they must *live apart!*

"Over in Central City not too long ago, you heard what happens to people that mix *black* and *white.* Folks, that's only a sample of what's about to happen to *Partridge,* if he don't shut his trap an' head for the tall timber!

"I tell you, hangin's too good for the likes of *Partridge.* Back in the *old days,* when we knew how to handle *traitors* in our midst, they'd have cut that man to pieces! Yes, folks, they'd have cut off his lying *tongue,* and nailed it to his forehead, and stuck his *head* on the nearest *fence post* as a warnin' to others!

"But I've said enough about *Bob Partridge,* and that rag of a *newspaper* he edits. Pay 'em no more mind, folks. Like I told you at the start, they ain't going to rile us much longer. One of these days, that whole *Times-News* building's going to blow up, just like that *Catholic school* blew up a few weeks ago. And when it does—I hope *Buzzard Partridge* is sittin' spang in the middle of the *nest!"*

Again, catcalls mingled with the cheers as the orator retired from the platform—but the cheers won handily. He was succeeded by a second robed figure, who launched into another tirade. The new speaker, though his voice had a nasal twang, seemed far better educated than the first; Rick judged that he was a local merchant or lawyer. His subject was the Catholic Church, which he denounced in a fury-laden rhetoric, studded with every symbol in the bigot's dictionary. The bombing of the parish school, he told the crowd, was retribution laid upon the Sisters for mixing races. The Church of Rome would stop at nothing to gain converts. From this platform of eloquence, the speaker needed only a moment to bring the Pope by jet plane to Washington, to capture the government.

Rhetoric took over entirely, at the expense of logic, when the speaker insisted that American Jewry was hand in glove with this underground cabal. Unless they were beaten down and returned to their ghettos, he warned, Jews would soon control the country. They already controlled its moneybags, its mass-communications media, and its pink-tinged eggheads. To prove his points, he named names and quoted figures—usually in billions, which seemed astronomical sums indeed to an audience whose average income did not exceed two thousand a year. . . . The man spoke well, his ragings on leash, his timing as exact as a Broadway star's—and the crowd loved it.

Inured as he was to such diatribes, Rick felt his gorge rise. How could Americans hear this nonsense without a single open protest and keep their self-respect? Most of the listeners, he felt sure, were decent citizens, a world removed from the insensate rabble; they were the descendants of pioneers who had left Europe to escape this same brew of half-truths, intolerance, and naked venom. While his anger lasted, he felt the familiar need to break through that shield of disciplined masqueraders—to snatch the microphone from the liar's grasp and remind each listener of his heritage.

The impulse died—but he was still trembling with rage as he moved through the crowd to climb the nearest tree. It was a massive live oak, and its lower branches were already heavy with watchers. Finding a limb well above the ground, he was in time to hear the wail of a siren from the turnpike. For an instant, he could half-believe the police were arriving to disperse this witches' sabbath. The false hope died when the custom-built limousine came into view behind a wedge of motorcycles. It was obvious the Knights expected its arrival.

An overflow crowd had formed at the open end of the meadow. The nearest of the white-clad platoons, shouldering among the spectators, soon formed a corridor for the oncoming car, exactly as riot troops would have opened a passage through a mob. The limousine had already swung from the pavement, without slackening speed. As it bore down on the platform, a huge "F"—in white and red neon—blossomed above its hood. The welcome that greeted its arrival dwarfed the earlier salvos of cheers. Even the speaker, breaking his harangue in mid-sentence, had hastened to welcome the new arrivals.

First out of the limousine was Hal Stacey—and the fact he had dared to appear in civilian garb among those hooded figures was proof of his new status. So was the insolent way he pushed the Knights aside, to mount the nearest sound truck. Here, on a ready-made observation platform, he adjusted his Leica, and snapped the first of a series of flash bulbs. The murmur that had greeted his appearance tapered off. It was evident that the camera reporter had been expected at this stage of the conclave—and, though some of the Knights resented his presence, the squad leaders silenced them in advance.

There were two other figures in the limousine—both of them too tall to seem real in their scarlet and white disguises and towering scarlet hoods. They made a vivid contrast to the dead-white phantoms that hemmed them. Each received an ovation as he stepped from the car. The group of minor speakers all but groveled as they hurried forward to grip the newcomers' hands, and elbowed one another for the honor of escorting them to the platform. While the strange euphoria lasted, Rick could almost believe that the Knights' machine-tooled discipline had gone by the board. Then (with a wry grin at his own stupidity) he realized that even this welcome had been rehearsed.

A bellow from the loudspeakers broke off the cheering. Quiet clamped down on the meadow while the newcomers climbed to the platform, followed by the last speaker. Stalking to the microphone, he informed the Knights that tonight's outing was rarely privileged. Central City had sent the Grand Chaplain of the order to introduce the final speaker of the evening, who was the Grand Leader himself.

At this announcement, pandemonium seized the phantom ranks, and for another moment the Knights capered like schoolboys gone berserk, pounding each other's back and shaking the heavens with their shouted rapture. Then, at a second bark from the loudspeakers, the controlled ecstasy ended as predictably as it had begun. The white ranks were still (and the watchers on the hillsides continued to stare into the floodlights with jaws agape) as the Grand Chaplain stalked to the microphone. The leader, aloof and majestic in the shadows, waited impassively, his hands folded in the sleeves of his robe.

When the Grand Chaplain addressed the microphone, his voice was a grating anticlimax—the timbre of exhorting evangelists the world over, a sound that wavered between a whine and a high, womanish scream. Tonight, he said, was the first time the Grand Leader of all the Knights had honored Eldon with his presence. In the circumstances, it seemed only right to precede his address with a prayer.

As the wail continued, magnified beyond all reason by the skillful sound-mixer in the van, Rick had the nightmarish certainty that the Grand Chaplain was only a walking phonograph, whose needle, like his ideas, was jammed in a single groove.

"O God—we are gathered here tonight—in the humble desire to serve Thee—and to follow Thy teachings——"

Like the other speakers, the chaplain threw his words in bursts. With each phrase, his womanish voice seemed to rise in pitch. Then, pausing to draw breath, he began again, in a lower timbre, mouthing each phrase as greedily as a drunkard whose thirst was limitless.

"We read in the Holy Word that Thou hast made men white, red, and black, to occupy different stations on this earth. We know, O God, that if Thou hadst wished them to occupy the same place, Thou wouldst have made all men one color. We also know that just as Thou didst select one people to be God's Own, excluding lesser breeds, Thou hast selected the people of our great land, the white Protestant Americans, to rule the others. We know that Thy avenging sword will scourge all dissenters from our midst. *Selah!*"

"*Selah!*" The crowd rumble was precise as a cue in opera, permitting the solo performer to ride on without a break.

"O God, we know that in the past Thou hast granted the wishes of Thy servants—when they prayed for strength to confound Thine enemies. And we do so pray tonight—that Thou wilt sow confusion among those who seek to hinder Thy holy purpose. We read it was the Jews who crucified Thy Son. We know it is these same accursed people who now stir dissension in our land, setting men against men, religion against religion—though it is plainly stated there is but one true religion, that which is set down in the Holy Book——"

There was more—far more than Rick could force his ears to receive. The balderdash of the hate-mongers had been bad enough. This distortion of the Word of God was beyond the pale. He came back to what the evangelist was saying with a wrench of the will, as the man reached his peroration.

"Show us the way a militant, Protestant Christianity can serve Thee! In our trouble and discord, open our hearts to the message of our Grand Leader, whom Thou hast raised up amid our tribulations! Send us the spirit of Thy Son our Lord and Savior Jesus Christ—who triumphed over the plots of the Jews, yea even the shameful death to which they condemned Him, to rise again from the dead and lead us to Thee. In His name we pray—Amen."

"*Amen.*" The word rose like a single sigh from the massed ranks of the Knights as the Grand Chaplain surrendered the microphone. Rick saw that all he had heard so far (including the tumult of the Leader's arrival) had been a build-up for this moment. Looming against the starlit sky, the red-robed figure seemed almost as tall as the cross on the knoll behind him. He bowed twice—once to the group of speakers beneath the platform, and again to the massed ranks of listeners. Then, as he lifted his right arm in a commanding gesture, the guardian of the cross stepped forward to ignite it.

Rick had expected a fresh burst of applause as the flame ran up the wood. Instead, aping the gesture of the Leader, the Knights raised their right arms in unison. It was a silent salute to their emblem, to the sign of man's hope they had perverted to symbolize their own cause.

"Keep the South Pure!" the Leader shouted.

"*Keep the South Pure!*"

The roar shook the branch on which Rick had perched. He needed a moment to realize that the bellowed slogan had been picked up by most of the watchers around him. Every eye but his own seemed fastened on the blazing cross. Only a trained newspaperman (whose job it was to note detail) would have thought to watch the Leader, rather than the unthinking puppets who had just obeyed him. The man had fumbled at his robe before he spoke, to bring forth a wire which he attached to an outlet in the microphone cord. When his voice erupted from the loudspeakers, it was not quite his own, despite its bell-like resonance. . . . The Grand Leader of the Knights of Freedom, for all his godlike bearing, was not yet ready to reveal his identity, even by chance. He was using a throat microphone, whose tone distorted his voice, enough to make recognition impossible.

"Brother Knights of Freedom—I salute you!" he cried. "I salute every thinking man in our audience, for I know you would not be here tonight if we did not believe and feel as one———"

The Leader's manner, like his voice, exuded sweet reason: it scarcely mattered that the words themselves were commonplace. Sensing the mass hypnosis about him, Rick found that he was fighting hard to keep his own critical faculties alert. It would have been far easier to move with the herd, to take this welcome at face value.

"This is not only the largest gathering of the Knights in the Eldon district. Tonight is also a red-letter day in the history of our organization. Tonight, as it were, we come of age—our purpose formed, our credo established. Heretofore, we have been occupied in setting up our organization—in perfecting our discipline—in devising ways to recruit members. Tonight, it is my privilege to tell you what we stand for, what we intend to accomplish in this Southland of ours, which we all love so dearly———"

It was a calculated pause, and the Grand Leader made the most of it, roaming the platform like the restless, blood-drenched ghost he resembled. Repelled though he was, Rick could not help admiring the technique. Compared to the other speakers, this was the master mind, whose words seemed to issue from the heart.

"In New York and in Hollywood, the radicals who control all means of communication have tried to deny us an outlet. We have still made our voice heard all over America, and this is but the beginning. At long last, people everywhere are beginning to realize that we—and we alone—can be trusted to solve our own problems of race and color. In sober truth, those problems were well on their way to solution when the Supreme Court in Washington first dared to interfere, with its unenforceable ruling on civil rights. The Southern Negro had learned to dwell among us in peace. Year after year, his lot improved. He was better fed and housed, better able to succeed in the work of his choice, better able to educate his children in the separate but equal schools we provided. He was attaining an intelligence level thinking men of the past would not have believed possible. Given time—and the proper safeguards—he might even have been granted equality at the polls.

"I say it again, and it cannot be said too often. Our Negro problem was *solved*. We Southerners had faced up to it within our borders, on terms both races accepted. We had shown an inferior being his place in the scheme of things—and we had given him good cause to rejoice in his lot."

The Leader paused and raised a fist to heaven. When he spoke again, his voice was a shout.

"Then, ten years ago, the court in Washington—the same court that had endorsed the separate-but-equal doctrine that was the keystone of our success—reversed its ruling. Overnight, we were told we must share and share alike with our Negro wards. We answered then that such sharing is impossible. I repeat our answer now!

"You all know the sorry record of the years between— when that same court, and its minions, sought to change the unchangeable, to alter a fundamental law of nature by

man-made statutes. Yet these same lawmakers, and the
liberal crackpots who finance them, have refused to surrender. In their stubborn desire to control the South—
even today, after a decade of failure—they scheme to
pervert the rights guaranteed free men by our Constitution. They seek to poison the minds of our children with
the false claim that all men are equal, whatever their race
or color.

"To the shame of our border states, I must admit they
have achieved some measure of success with their impossible vision of Utopia. Here in the Deep South, the true
South, they have only a toehold—and I say to you that
we will drive even those few invaders from our midst!

"The future of the South lies with us. We must control
it ourselves, or be controlled by others——"

Breaking out of the spell of the man's voice, Rick
dropped from tree to ground, ignoring the growls of the
listeners who thronged the lower branches. Hypnotized by
falsehoods (at the same moment his reason rejected it),
he was finding it difficult to breathe. His first thought was
to leave the hillside, to seek out the *Times-News* car and
Bob Partridge's reporter. A few tentative thrusts of his
elbows convinced him that flight was impossible. Tight-
packed as the crowd was, he could not force a path
without distracting their magnetic attachment to the
speaker.

"They accuse us of condoning violence," the Leader
shouted. "Now our purpose is formed, we admit the
charge! When our right to exist is threatened, we must
tear down the enemy's strength before he tears down
ours. From this day forward, we will welcome recruits to
the Knights, not by the score but by the thousand. Each
joiner will pledge himself to save our traditions. It was no
accident that the South took up arms to defend our way
of life one hundred years ago. It was no accident that we
could emerge with our heritage intact after we had bowed
to the most brutal military occupation this country has
ever known. It was an act of God that preserved our

civilization—and God is with us now, as we speak again with a single voice.

"Let us make that voice heard, to the farthest corner of America. Let us drown out the mewlings of Bob Partridge and his ilk. We will always deplore violence—but if violence is needed to waken our people to their peril, so be it!"

The speech ended on that ringing affirmation: Rick knew the show was over when he saw Hal Stacey close the leather flap of his Leica and leap from the sound-truck roof. Bowing to all sides, the Grand Leader entered his car in a surf of cheering—and, like a clever performer who refuses to outstay his applause, drove off with siren wailing. The Knights, forming by platoons, marched out of the meadow in its wake, as precisely as they had come, to enter their own cars, parked in a vast double ring beyond the cinder track. The cross, still blazing fiercely, lighted their somber departure—and the crowd, its nerves keyed to concert pitch, began to disperse in turn. . . . Even this abrupt finale, Rick realized, was calculated. An audience sent away hungry would return for more.

Careful to show no sign of haste, he moved with the crowd, waiting under the wheel of his own car until most of the others had driven on. As the parking area cleared, he identified the *Times-News* car easily—a gray Buick sedan something the worse for wear, with the driver perched on a mudguard, smoking a corncob pipe and chatting affably with the last of the passers-by. Incredulously, he saw it was Bob Partridge himself, in a farmer's hat and blue jeans, with his shirttail out and a stubble of beard that would have disgraced the sorriest woolhat.

"Howdy, neighbor," said Bob. "That last fellow sure put the Yankees in their place—didn't he now?"

"What are *you* doing here?"

"Covering for the paper, of course," said the editor, in his natural tones. "Keep on driving, and don't look so startled. None of these hayshakers know me. I wanted a firsthand look."

"Is there some place we can talk?"

"Halfway House," said Bob, in the same dead-level whisper. "A tavern on Route 80, two miles west of town. I'll go ahead, so don't drive too fast."

He was under his wheel with the instructions, kicking the starter. A moment later, the gray sedan nosed its way into the file of farmers' cars, threading a corduroy road in the piney-woods that led to the turnpike. It was only when he had taken his place in the file that Rick had a clear view of Bob's rear window—and realized the woman in the polo coat and gypsy bandanna (who had made herself small in the back seat) must be Carol King.

The Halfway House was only a short drive from the meadow, but there was no sign of Bob's car when Rick nosed into the parking lot. The place was crowded: many of the spectators, and some of the now-disrobed Knights, were drinking in the taproom. The place, he gathered, had been ill-chosen—if the editor had intended it as such. Bob's strategy was apparent when a familiar station wagon turned in from the pavement, and Theo Judd leaned from the window to address him.

"Meeting's down the road," he said. "Don't lose my taillight: I'll take you there."

Rick followed the station wagon for a fast three miles, then swung after it into a road that traversed the lawns of a state park, to end at a picnic grounds beside a lake. The gray sedan stood on the shoulder, beside a row of tables. Theo slid to a stop on the opposite side, an example which Rick followed. The woman in the polo coat did not stir as he got out. Positive it was Carol, he made no move to join her when Bob Partridge's voice addressed him from the darkness. The editor was seated at a table in a tree-shadowed corner, still smoking his pipe and looking invincibly rustic.

"Sorry to be cloak-and-dagger," he said. "But Hal Stacey was at that pub. I ducked out in time." He beckoned to the photographer to join them. "Get any good angles, Theo?"

"A few. I'd have done better if I could have joined Hal."

"Why didn't you try?"

"And get my head blown off? Every Knight in that front rank was a Case bodyguard."

"Did you say *Case?*" Rick demanded.

Bob tamped his corncob. "The man with the doctored microphone. It was friend Walter all right. It's a fact I can't print, of course. Not until we catch him with his hood down."

"When did you find this out?"

"Only tonight. Hiring a stakeout has been damned expensive, but it finally paid off. That limousine was seen leaving the private entrance of the Case Building. We know just who was inside."

Rick glanced toward Bob's car, and the immobile figure in the rear seat. "Does *she* realize it was her uncle?"

"Miss King knows more than that," said the editor. "Don't disturb her yet awhile. Listen first to what I can tell you. It isn't much."

"Talk fast, Bob."

"This is one of the few outings Case has attended. The fact he delivered tonight's main jeremiad may be significant. I think they're heading for a showdown—now that they've taken off the wraps and endorsed violence. It could come at the next big clambake—a monster rally they've scheduled the night after tomorrow at the Stadium. If you ask me, Rick, this was only a rehearsal for the main event."

"What's your plan?"

"To be at the Stadium too—in force."

"You're sure to be spotted there."

"Not if I'm under a bedsheet too."

"Are you planning to join the Knights?"

"I can't go that far in person. But several hundred Central City businessmen have enlisted in the ranks to keep me informed. Now they're starting a drive for new members, we plan to enlist more. The purpose of this Stadium meeting is to induct recruits. It's a mass laying-on of hands, with the Grand Leader doing the anointing. We may unfrock him sooner than you think."

"Don't tell me you want a free-for-all at that rally, Bob. Not if those goons are armed, as Theo says. Why not fight them on their own ground? Prove there's no future in violence?"

"You can't kill a bad idea with a good one," said the editor. "Not when the bad idea's built into local mores. Besides, they don't preach hate and violence every time. The last Stadium outing was a pageant of Southern history; the one before was a Broadway musical—with a professional company, and free drinks for everyone."

"Bread and circuses?"

"It worked in Rome," said Bob. "Right now, it's working fine for Case."

"So you'd fight back with brass knuckles at the next rally. There must be a better answer."

"I've waited six weeks, Rick. What leads have you given me?"

"Didn't I pin down Case?"

"Naming the dragon isn't enough. You've got to supply a St. George and a few lances."

"Give me time, Bob."

"Time's running out. I may not even be here to print your story."

"Come down to earth. What can you accomplish with your vigilantes?"

"They'll be beachheads in enemy country." The editor raised a soothing hand before Rick could speak. "Don't think I'm short-changing your contribution. You zeroed in on Case—and you've brought his niece into our camp. She may be of real help later."

"Isn't it time I talked to Carol?"

"Rick has a point there," said Theo. "I'll be hitting the

road with our story, Bob. Unless you want to take it in yourself."

"You can be my copy boy tonight," said the editor. "There are three belts of tape in my car: take 'em to the desk—we're holding the space." He turned to Rick with a shrug. "It took doing, but I had a sound crew in a parked car, with a directional mike. Tomorrow we'll run the Grand Leader's speech, word for word. Not that I'm sure it's a good idea. He may even want *Times-News* publicity——"

"You can't be that discouraged, Bob."

"I am tonight," said the editor. "The way that crowd cheered, I wonder how many of us have the right to call ourselves Christians. It doesn't help to say the audience was mostly redneck—born and raised to think the world's flat." He waved Theo toward the gray sedan.

The two men at the picnic table sat unstirring while the photographer roared back to the highway in his station wagon. In another moment, Carol crossed the road to join them. Thanks to the upturned collar of her coat, and the gloom beneath the trees, her face was only a white blur when she sat down between them. Rick sensed that she was still on the defensive—like a witness at a trial, who hesitates to commit perjury, yet is determined to say no more than the law demands.

"I'm glad you aren't too surprised," she said quietly. "Mr. Partridge would have warned you I was coming— but there wasn't time."

"Do I understand you've found your uncle out?"

"I've found him out."

"From what source?"

"The best source of all—himself."

Rick listened without comment while Carol gave her story. Once it was told, he could grasp it well enough. Like all empire-builders, Walter Case had found the mountaintop a lonely eminence. Starved for a true confidante, he had turned to his niece at last, to open his mind and heart. . . . Since Carol was the substitute for the daughter he had never had, he could only wonder why Case had waited so long to speak out.

"When did he tell you?"

"Two nights ago. He asked me to dine with him alone——"

Rick could picture the setting perfectly: the frosty elegance of the widower's mansion, the perfect food and wine, the secrets poured forth in the baronial study. *Bob's right,* he thought. *Case is ready for his first real move. What's more, he's positive of victory. So positive, he can share his secret with a woman—the only woman he trusts.*

Word for word, the pattern the industrialist had sketched to Carol had matched the credo he had stated—with such savage bluntness—to Rick himself. When she had finished her recital, Rick could take comfort in the fact he had prepared her, in some measure, for this revelation. The shock was still appalling.

"I gather he asked you to approve?"

"More than that," said Carol. "He wants my help—all the way."

"Did he promise you the moon and the stars if you'd give it?"

"Yes, Rick. The moon, the stars—and part of outer space."

Rick glanced at Bob, but the editor's face was impassive as he touched a match to his pipe. "Tell Rick how you answered him, Miss King."

"I asked for time," said Carol. "I pretended I couldn't picture an America where one man is lawgiver and thought-provider."

"Did he believe you?"

"Of course. He was wise and kind, according to his lights. That's what frightened me most—the dreadful assurance he's *right*. That there's no other way to save the world."

"Self-doubt isn't a drawback of dictators," said Bob. "Finish the story, my dear."

Carol covered her face with her hands, but no tears came. "This wasn't an easy decision, Mr. Partridge—I've told you that. But I had no choice, after Uncle Walter spoke his mind. I knew I must come to you."

"Did Case swear you to secrecy?" Rick asked.

"Of course not. He trusts me entirely. It still hurts—to think I've betrayed that trust."

The rest was soon told. Using Theo Judd as an intermediary, Carol had arranged a meeting with Bob, to give him a repeat performance of her evening with Case. There the matter had rested until tonight. . . . Meanwhile, she had managed to continue her routine office assignments. Meeting her uncle often during the business day, she had not betrayed her desertion by a flicker.

"You're positive he doesn't suspect you?"

"He couldn't, Rick."

"What about Hal?"

"Hal is much too busy these days to ask me questions."

"You've still to break your engagement?"

"So far, I've said nothing on that subject. I was afraid I'd upset Uncle Walter needlessly."

"We're in the clear, then," said the editor. "What comes next?"

Rick spoke slowly, with his eyes on Carol. "You can't print this story, Bob—what purpose would it serve?"

"None, at the moment," Partridge agreed. "Some of my readers might believe it. Most people would call it a plant—and damn Miss King out of hand."

"What would you suggest? That she stay at Case Construction, and keep her ears open."

"She'd be invaluable there—if she'll take the risk."

Carol's hand was in Rick's now, though he had no memory of taking it. The sharp pressure of her fingers was the answer he needed.

"I'll do what has to be done," she said. "Right now, I never felt more helpless."

"If you'll keep your head," said Bob, "you can accomplish a great deal. For a start, you can go to Case and say you'll meet his terms."

"I *can't* do that——"

"You can pretend. From what you've told us, he's hungry for your approval."

It was too dark to see, but Rick was sure that Carol was weeping now. Then, as her fingers tightened again and her chin lifted, he felt his heart leap in answer. For the first time, he knew he could count on this woman to the last trump, that Carol King would find no task too heavy.

"Just what must I do, Rick?" she asked. "Must I be a spy for your sake?"

"For *all* our sakes," he said. "It's the only way."

As though by unspoken consent, they rose from the picnic table and moved toward the gray sedan. While Bob transferred the tape recorder to the trunk rack, Carol and Rick (alone for the first time) found themselves kissing—as naturally as though that brief, heart-bursting embrace had been ordained.

"When did you know?" he whispered.

"From the beginning. When did you?"

"From the beginning too. We started even, Carol."

"Does it help—saying it aloud?"

"You haven't—yet."

"I love you, Rick Jordan."

"I love you, too, Carol."

It was a litany of a sort, and they spoke it like two solemn acolytes. When Bob returned, they stood aside quite calmly, and said good-by in normal tones. The editor of the *Times-News* contented himself with a single gimlet glance before he handed Carol to her seat and put the car in gear.

"I hope you thanked the lady, Rick?"

"I tried, Bob. I'll never really find the words."

"We can both say that twice," said Partridge—and drove down the road that led to Central City.

Rick stood in the dark for a moment, until the taillight of the gray sedan was lost in the rush of traffic on the turnpike.

It was only when he had taken the lonely road to his lodgings in Valley Stream that he remembered Seth's telecast tomorrow. He had said nothing of Seth and Mary Randall—nor could he feel the omission greatly mattered. Now that his game at Valley Hospital was played out, it seemed of small importance, when measured against the sacrifice of Carol King.

SETH'S HOSPITAL CONCERT, telecast from film at Wide-World's New York studio the next evening, was witnessed by every inmate of Valley who could secure a ward pass. Reception on the recreation-hall set was ideal: the impact of the entire show, including the addresses by Dr. Moore and the pianist himself, was all that Rick had planned. When it was over, he prayed the end would justify the means. He had expected the applause of the patients. Only Tony Gates could report the outside reaction.

Seth had been on duty during the broadcast. It was in character that he refused to witness his own performance. From his viewpoint, it had been a contribution to the hospital's welfare fund and nothing more. He had shown no interest whatever in this electronic aftermath.

Dr. Moore shrugged off the Negro's *sang-froid* when he paused to congratulate Rick after the program had ended.

"People like Seth are above such things as material success," he said. "I know it's hard to take in, but his is a completely unselfish personality."

"He must realize the publicity will help his albums—and the hospital."

"Seth feels he did his best at the keyboard, the night of the recording. The telecast and future sales of his records are things beyond his control. Like all men who have made their peace with God, he is also a complete fatalist. Perhaps he's luckier than most of us."

With night duty awaiting him, Rick had no time to debate the problem of Seth Randall. The following morning, he slept late deliberately, leaving strict instructions with his landlady to refuse all calls. When he came downstairs in the early afternoon, New York was on the phone for the third time.

Tony Gates, speaking from his Madison Avenue stronghold in the husky whisper he used to cover real excitement, confirmed Rick's hopes instantly. Last night's telecast had been a smashing success at all levels. The public had inundated the studio switchboards; the New York critics had turned handsprings, to endorse one of the most refreshing talents in years. The verdict had been echoed in Hollywood. Tony's own record company, besieged by orders, had tripled its original cutting. . . . Once again, Rick promised to do what he could to effect the musician's release. Informed by his landlady that Dr. Moore had urgently requested his presence, he drove to the hospital in a glow of accomplishment.

The director was pacing his office when Rick knocked for admission. He pointed to an envelope on his desk.

"Mary Randall sent me this, by one of our workers who lives in Eldon," he said. "It contains an open enclosure you'll find interesting."

Remembering his interview with Seth's mother, Rick was prepared in some measure for the two notes Dr. Moore thrust upon him. The letter to the director was entirely formal. It requested a review of Seth's case before the State Psychiatric Board. It stated forthrightly that Seth, in his mother's opinion, now deserved to resume his musical career. Noting that only Walter Case could arrange for Seth's full pardon, Mary Randall planned to appeal to him directly—as the enclosed note to Mr. Richard Sloane would explain.

The note to Rick was even briefer:

Dear Mr. Sloane:

I have kept my promise and tuned in on Seth's program. You have won your argument. If he will consent to leave the hospital, I will no longer prevent him.

You are of course aware that other legal obstacles stand in the way. Just one man can remove them. His name is Walter Case.

Dr. Moore would release my boy tomorrow if these legal barriers were lowered.

Will you go to Central City and plead Seth's cause with Walter Case? Will you say that I beg him, as Seth's mother, to forgive and forget?

Mary Randall

Rick returned both notes to the director's desk. Fighting for time, he braced himself for the rebuke he felt was inevitable.

"What do you make of this, sir?"

"I'm waiting for *you* to explain, Dick. Apparently your skill in miracles covers several fields."

"You don't blame me, then—for going to Eldon?"

"I'd have suggested it myself, if I'd hoped you could get results."

"Don't credit me, Doctor. It was Seth's playing that changed Mary Randall's mind. She'd thought of him as dead, ever since he was committed. Knowing the South as she did, she felt his case was hopeless. Last night, her television screen brought Seth back to life. It also proved to her, as words never could, that her boy was a genius. What else could she do but write those two notes? No mother could do less."

"I've already talked with Mr. Gates in New York," said the director. "Naturally, he's burning to start promoting Seth—and clamoring for his release. In all fairness, we must try to satisfy that demand. Mary Randall's change of heart should make our task easier."

"Let's trust you're right, sir."

Dr. Moore studied the two notes carefully. "Since you're responsible for this plea, I gather you're prepared to follow through on it."

"Of course."

"You'll go to Central City as she asks—and talk to Walter Case?"

Rick forced himself to speak calmly. "How can I be sure he'll see me?"

"I've just arranged it, by telephone."

"Did you talk to Case himself, Doctor?"

"It wasn't at all difficult. As it happens, he's working at home today. His secretary put me through at once, on his private wire. He'll be glad to see you at six this evening. He'll listen to whatever arguments you advance."

"Did you tell him who I am?" Despite his agitation, Rick could not help a faint smile at the double meaning. When Dr. Moore took the query in stride, he felt his taut nerves unwind.

"I explained your connection with Tony Gates," said the director. "I stressed your interest in Seth—and your own musical background. If you leave promptly, you can reach Central City in good time. Mr. Case said he could give you a whole half-hour. We could hardly ask for more."

Rick framed the next question with care. "You told him I was only a hospital attendant—and he *still* agreed to talk with me?"

"Walter Case is one of our leading citizens, Dick. Granted, he's an extremely busy man; he finds time to listen to anyone with something real to say. I've convinced him you bore such a message."

"I'll do my best, sir. Have you any pointers?"

"Just two: both of them favorable. Mr. Case told me he saw Seth's telecast, and was charmed by it. And, so far, there's been not a ripple of protest from the State House."

"What does that suggest to you?"

"A thaw, perhaps—from the top down. It's one thing to send an unknown Negro to a state asylum and forget him. It's quite another to persecute a musical prodigy who's just won nationwide acclaim."

Rick nodded soberly. Guessing Case's strategy from

afar, he could not risk an opinion secondhand. "Perhaps you should go to Central City yourself, Doctor."

The director shook his head vigorously. "I love my work here, Dick; I must keep my position invulnerable. From here on, I'm remaining strictly neutral."

"Meaning that *I'm* expendable?"

"You began this campaign to free Seth Randall. I hope you will see it through."

Rick glanced at his watch. "Just one thing more. Does Seth know of his mother's request?"

"I showed him both letters when he came off duty," said Moore. "You'll find him at the theater piano now. You'll still have time to stop there a moment, and discuss his chances."

"Will he accept the outcome?"

"Of course, Dick. Didn't I explain that Seth is a fatalist who believes in God?"

The thunder of Tchaikovsky's most famous concerto shook the doors of the theater as Rick pushed them wide. Seth sat at the keyboard onstage, lost as always in his playing, and sublimely unaware of the visitor's approach. Because of the hour, the dusky reaches of the orchestra were empty. Rick could rejoice in this piece of luck: it was a longish drive to Central City and he needed every moment.

"May I break in for once, Seth?"

The Negro closed the lid of his keyboard and turned on the bench. Expecting a certain tension, Rick was a trifle hurt by his detachment. From Seth's viewpoint, the gates of Valley Hospital must seem at least partly open at this moment. It was beyond belief that he could wait so calmly for the next outside bulletin.

"Dr. Moore said you might be going to Central City, Mr. Sloane."

"I'm leaving in five minutes, to keep a date with Walter Case. I needn't tell you why."

The pianist, still seated at the keyboard, flexed his

fingers. When he spoke, he seemed to reflect aloud—as though he were but half-aware of Rick's presence.

"My mother saw the telecast," he said. "I thought she would."

"Are you sorry she asked me to go to Case?"

"No, Mr. Sloane. Not if it's what she wants."

"Don't you want freedom too, Seth?"

"My wish is to help Valley Hospital, and Dr. Moore. If I can help on the outside—if they feel I've served my time here, so be it. Apparently, both the director and my mother hope I'll be released. Do you?"

It was a fair question—and there was no way to answer it honestly. Obviously, there was more to Walter Case's affability than met the eye. At the moment, Rick had no choice but to accept his show of surrender at face value.

"Would I drive eighty miles on a wild-goose chase?" he asked.

"You might, Mr. Sloane. For my sake. Don't think I'm not grateful—but it's hard to believe a man like Walter Case can relent so easily."

Again, Rick forced himself to seek refuge in the first evasion that came to mind. "Put it this way, Seth. He may have forgotten you existed, until last night's telecast jogged his memory——"

"People like Walter Case never forget an injury."

"Be honest. Would you have preferred to leave matters as they were?"

"No, Mr. Sloane. Now this thing is started, I realize you must see it through. Just as I realize my mother couldn't help tuning in last night. Do as you think best in Central City. I won't reproach you."

It was a gentle dismissal, the resignation of a philosopher who has long since despaired of the white man's logic. Rick leaned on the piano a moment more. He had reached the end of the road with Seth Randall—but was not yet willing to take his leave.

"I'd shield your mother, if I could," he said. "Unfortunately, now she's made her plea, she can hardly stand aside."

The Negro pianist rose at last, and put a comforting hand on Rick's shoulder. "Don't reproach yourself, Mr. Sloane—no matter what comes of this. God sent you to Valley Hospital—not the devil."

"Thank you for saying that, Seth. I'll always remember it."

"Whatever happens today, I'll bear it. So will my mother. We're good at bearing things."

Driving toward Central City by way of Eldon, Rick knew that a hospital attendant named Richard Sloane was dead and buried. He was not yet prepared to close the grave. When he took the turnoff to colored town, and stopped again at Mary Randall's bungalow, he was still in character.

He was relieved to find the house locked and empty. A neighbor informed him that Mary was working at the far end of Eldon, and would not return until late afternoon; he left a note in her mailbox, explaining he was en route to Walter Case, and would telephone from Central City after the meeting. As an added precaution, he gave his forwarding address as Richard Sloane, care of Carol King's apartment. . . . The safeguard was routine. He would remember it later, and thank heaven for his journalist's caution.

Two hours later, still wearing the mask of Sloane, he entered Central City and registered under that name at the Hotel Cavalier. Carol's apartment phone did not answer. A cautious call to her office brought the information she was in Mobile, attending a convention of industrial designers as her uncle's deputy. Her secretary informed Mr. Sloane that Miss King was taking a night flight home, and would be at her desk tomorrow.

When he dialed Theo Judd, the photographer seemed more pleased than startled by his presence. The stakeout on Case, he said, was now perfected. The industrialist was still at his Crestwood mansion, working on the scale model of an opera house he was about to build in Texas. The detectives had covered all approaches to the house. The exact time of Rick's arrival would be noted—and proper action would be taken if he needed help. If he wished, Theo would be happy to drive him there.

"Would it be safer to use your car, Rick?"

"As of now, I'm without transportation. I sold my jalopy at a secondhand lot, and came to the hotel by taxi."

"I don't dig you. Aren't you still Dick Sloane?"

"Only on the hotel register. I'll explain when you get here."

Rick's next act was to dispatch a wire to Dr. Moore, formally resigning his post at Valley Hospital. The resignation was made without comment—much as he disliked the coldness of the words, there was no time for explanations. Two minutes later, he had removed his plastic scar and stripped to the buff to stand beneath a scalding shower. He needed that symbolic cleansing to rid himself of Richard Sloane (a nosy fellow, by any standards).

The hotel barber, a cheerful, middle-aged Negro, completed the metamorphosis that brought Rick Jordan alive again—shaving away the sideburns and mustache, clipping the duck-tailed hair into the crew cut he had worn since college days. The barber was making a final flourish of his shears when Theo Judd came in, stretched on the bed with a nod of greeting—and waited, with his familiar patience, for Rick to speak his mind.

"Pay for this, Theo. Add a dollar for a first-rate job." Rick went to his carryall to take out a suit. It was a pleasure to ignore Dick Sloane's nondescript garb, to don a broadcloth shirt, Peel shoes, and a tweed coat that had been cut to his measure on Bond Street. He was knotting a Charvet tie (in a color far gayer than his mood) when the photographer saw the barber out and locked the hall door.

"Don't let me speak out of turn," he said. "But I'll pant less obviously if you explain yourself."

"Sloane has outlived his usefulness, Theo. He's bitten the dust. Jordan rides again."

"In enemy country?"

"The fight's in the open now; the masquerade has served its purpose. I'd be a coward to hide behind it any longer."

"Case is expecting a call from *Sloane*. The stakeout picked that up, hours ago."

"I'm calling in Sloane's place. It's the fastest way to get inside the door. I don't think he'll risk mayhem in broad daylight."

The photographer listened gloomily while Rick described his mission, and his final talk with Seth. In the end, he shrugged and reached for his hat.

"Don't quote me on this," he said. "But I think you're trying to fill an inside straight."

"It's worth the try—if only to catch him off balance."

"I repeat, Rick: it's damned risky poker."

"So it is. Case has held every high card in the deck, from our first deal. Obviously, he can lie in his teeth about both Seth and Mary. Or he can send me about my business with a broken head. I still hope to learn something."

Knowing his man, Rick had expected the Case mansion to be far more splendid than it was; save for the immense apron of lawn that surrounded it, and the boxwoods that accented the height of its white-pillared portico, it was no more spectacular than the other showplaces of Crestwood, a steep bluff that dominated all of Central City. Theo let the station wagon coast past the gateposts, then stopped in the shadow of a privet hedge.

"It isn't too late to back out," he said.

"Do I look frightened?"

"Right now, you resemble a paratrooper about to hit

the silk on D day. Would it make sense if I followed you—as a kind of second wave?"

"Sorry, Theo. This is a one-man raid."

"Shall I wait here?"

"I'd appreciate that much support. Somehow, I don't imagine I'll be in there long. Are you sure your detective brigade is still alive?"

"They're watching, all right." The photographer consulted the dashboard clock. "Six on the nose. Show up by six-thirty, or we'll come in after you."

Rick grinned as he stepped out to the sidewalk. "If I'm not back in ten minutes," he said, "I'll deserve to come feet first."

At the Case gateposts, he remembered to wipe the smile from his face, to stride boldly up the drive with his shoulders squared. He had half-expected a guard on the portico, but the big house drowsed in the bath of late sunlight, with no visible sign of life. When he touched the bell, the answering chime spelled out emptiness. He was all the more startled when the door swung gently open, with no apparent touch of human hands. It was only when he stepped into a white-and-gold foyer that he realized the portal was operated by an electric eye.

"May I help you, sir?"

The butler who stood at the foot of the stairway was a model of his kind—tall, saturnine, and faintly forbidding, with a voice that managed to be both muted and resonant. Rick needed a second look to guess the man was Case's bodyguard as well. The nose had once been broken (though the repair job was excellent), and the gnarled hands could only have belonged to a former welterweight.

"Richard Sloane—to see Mr. Case by appointment."

"He's expecting you, Mr. Sloane. Will you follow me?"

So far, it appeared, his strategy was working with velvet smoothness. The gesture that ushered the visitor from foyer to library (and down a portrait-hung corridor that led to a glass-walled workroom) could not have been more deferential. Walter Case stood with his back to the open door, his head thrust deep into the scale model of an opera house. Blueprints lay on the trestle table beside him. Absorbed in his task, he seemed unaware of his major-domo until the man had given a second deferential cough.

"Your six o'clock caller is here, sir."

"Sit down, Sloane. I'll be with you in a moment."

"No hurry, Mr. Case." Rick used the voice of Dick Sloane for the last time. Settling on a sofa that stood across the room, he watched the industrialist with a certain wonder. It was clear that the man and his work made a perfect communion, that Case was deaf and blind to externals while the spell lasted. When he threw down his calipers and faced his visitor, he might have been a diver, emerging from the depths. In rumpled slacks, with his snow-white hair askew, he was far more human—and, while the illusion lasted, strangely vulnerable.

"I'm assuming I'm welcome," said Rick, using his natural voice. "I won't deny I've intruded deliberately."

It was the first time he had seen the industrialist startled—though there was no loss of poise, even in the first flush of astonishment. Only the snap of the pencil between his fingers, and the sudden jerk of his head betrayed the man's anger. Then, without a word, Case strode to the wall button. The butler's instant appearance underlined the discipline that was *de rigueur* here.

"What's this mean, Pollock?"

"Beg pardon, sir?"

"My appointment's with someone called Richard Sloane. This is Jordan, the columnist."

"I'm sorry, Mr. Case. The gentleman *said* his name was Sloane——"

The industrialist's fist smashed down on the roof of the opera house, so violently that the frail plywood structure collapsed beneath the blow. The gesture seemed to drain off his rage.

"Well, Jordan?"

"I came in Sloane's place—to deliver his message."

"What message?"

"It's from the Randalls, Mr. Case. Something you should have heard long ago."

It was a random try, and he had used it ad lib. His eyes did not leave Case, but he managed to watch the butler too. He saw that master and servant had exchanged a wordless glance; when Pollock's hand balled into a fist, he felt sure his visit had ended. Then, as Case put the wreckage of the model between them and flicked his fingers in a gesture of dismissal, he knew his shot had found its mark.

"You may go, Pollock. I'll talk to Jordan—since he's here."

The butler-bodyguard withdrew even faster than he had entered, his face a rich wine-red, the fist impotent at his side. Case had already gone to seat himself in a tall-backed armchair that dominated the somewhat Spartan workroom. With that move, he took back his dignity: the throne-chair added a foot to his stature, giving his voice the timbre of command.

"Very well, Jordan. How did you manage this?"

"I've told you. I'm acting as Richard Sloane's deputy. Or should I say his alter ego?"

"The man's an attendant at Valley Hospital. How'd you make contact?"

"By the simplest of methods. I *am* Richard Sloane. I've been working at Valley under that name."

"You couldn't. Someone would have known you."

"Not with my alter ego in place. I'm not just a newspaperman. When need be, I'm an actor too." Rick found he could speak easily now, that he was enjoying Case's stony stare. "While I was at the hospital, I made friends with Seth Randall. In Eldon, I heard the mother's life story. Now I've come to plead their cause. I trust I'm not wasting my breath."

"So you went to Valley after all. Even though I forbade it."

"I'm a reporter. I couldn't help going. Did you think a pair of high-school hoodlums would scare me off?"

"Who told you of Seth Randall?"

"Sorry. No reporter reveals his sources."

•"You've decided there's some connection between Randall and myself. Is that why you're here?"

"You can hardly deny you had him committed."

"Of course. In the judge's opinion, he got off lightly."

"Perhaps he did. He's paid his debt to society. Can you admit that too—or have you lost all sense of justice?"

"Jordan, would it startle you if I agreed this black boy should go free?"

The sudden change of front was not unexpected. It was already obvious to Rick that Case had permitted him to remain for just one reason—to assure himself that the message Rick bore from Mary Randall was, in sober truth, entirely harmless. Now, like a tiger with a kitten, he could afford to play awhile with his visitor.

"You'll admit, then, that your local courts permitted a miscarriage of justice?" Rick could feel the hollow echo behind his too-righteous demand. He knew that Case had sensed it too.

"I'm afraid that's a misleading phrase," said the industrialist. "Its meaning is a matter of opinion, so far as Randall is concerned."

"After ten years? When Dr. Moore himself says Seth is cured?"

"Let's go back to the beginning," said Case, with the same silky politeness. "You'll agree his attack on me was made wantonly—without apparent cause?"

"According to the records, yes."

"The colored boy was a maniac. A mental hospital seemed the only humane answer to his problem. Surely I was right to accept the judge's ruling?"

"Didn't you order that ruling?"

"Let's avoid conjecture, Jordan—and stick to fact. In

agreeing that Randall should be committed—I was acting from the best of motives. His own mother signed the papers."

"Why did you forbid me to visit the hospital, if you had nothing to hide there?"

"I wanted you out of the state. With your radical views, I felt we'd seen quite enough of you."

Rick breathed deep, and rallied for a fresh attack. For no good reason, he recalled a football afternoon at Chapel Hill, when he had carried the ball for the Tarheels against a far stronger Georgia line. That bitter Saturday, every ruse he had devised had smashed into an iron defense. In the end, he had been carried from the field—stunned and bleeding, and raging at the linesmen who had thrown all his plays for a loss. . . .

"You knew I'd come back, didn't you?" he asked.

"I feared as much," said Case.

"Must I add that I won't leave until I've cleared up this story?"

"Surely you'll agree you've failed so far?"

"At least I've reminded you that Seth Randall is alive."

"Don't expect me to thank you," said Case.

"You must admit he's a genius."

Case smiled thinly. "This time, I'll bow to experts in the field. Some of our American Negroes have been passable performers in the entertainment world. This seems to be one of them."

"Is that why you didn't stop the concert?"

"You may not accept this, Jordan, but it's years since I've thought of Valley Hospital and its problems. When I returned from Texas, I learned—quite by accident—that the hospital had filmed one of its concerts for a telecast. Naturally I tuned in last night, along with other citizens of my state. Today, I'm prepared to give credit to talent, since credit is due."

Case's strategy was now clear enough, his defense invulnerable. Rick had anticipated just such a defense. It was no less disconcerting to hit the wall full strength.

"Does this mean you approve of my contribution?" he demanded.

"No, Jordan. In fact, I find your meddling insufferable. Until you wormed your way into Valley, this colored boy was content. His mother was prepared to leave well enough alone. Now, thanks to a floodlight of notoriety, Randall is bound to have thoughts beyond his station——"

"Only if he's released from the hospital."

"He'll be released, in record time. The mother's changed her tune, and the telecast is national news. The Psychiatric Board will have no choice."

"Haven't I won, then?" The question was automatic: Rick knew his stymie was complete.

"To my mind," said Case, "your accomplishment seems of doubtful value. This Negro, by his own account, had found his niche at Valley. How can you be sure he'll succeed among white musicians? Or that his mania won't recur?"

"You'll admit he deserves the chance?"

"I admit it freely," said Case, with the same maddening calm.

"Won't you concede that his career is assured—now you've granted him his freedom?"

"I said he *deserved* a chance, Jordan. Because of his mental instability, I'm not at all sure he'll profit from this change of status. I've already told the mother as much."

"You've seen *Mary Randall?*"

"I talked with her by phone—an hour ago. She called me from Eldon to ask for her boy's release."

Case's eyes had dropped: listening intently for a change in his dead-level tone, Rick was sure it had softened, however slightly. He could understand Mary Randall's intervention perfectly. Tortured by her decision, realizing she had erred in sending her plea by another, she had taken her courage in both hands and called the industrialist direct. . . . Was it possible that Case was human after all? That a mother's cry for help, however belated, had struck a spark in that flintlike heart?

Rick risked a direct question, knowing in advance the answer would tell him nothing. "My errand was needless, then?"

"Quite needless, Jordan. She persuaded me, with no help from you."

"That's untrue—and you can't pretend otherwise. It took a national telecast to prove you'd gone too far in your persecution. And I'll tell you more. If I've the patience to wait, you'll overreach again."

"Those are strong words, Jordan. I'd call them boastful—if you'd a real achievement to boast about."

Rick rose from the sofa. Despite the ice-cold dismissal, he knew he had flicked Case on the raw.

"That telecast was just the shock you needed to prove your word isn't always law," he said. "It also proved you can be hoodwinked, as easily as one of Stead's wardheelers. Right now, for the first time in years, you're boiling mad. You're sorry you've behaved like a fool in the case of Seth Randall——"

"That's quite enough, Jordan."

"Correction, sir. That's only the beginning. From now on, our war's in the open. I'm staying in Central City until it's won."

"If you're wise, you'll leave my state at once."

"Save your threats," said Rick. "I'm aware that your bodyguard's outside that door, itching to take me apart. *You* know that Bob Partridge has his stakeout. Either I leave with a whole skin, or you'll be slapped with an assault warrant——"

"Why did you come here? I've told you nothing."

"You've told me a great deal. The last time we met, when you spelled out your plans, you were completely honest. Ruthless, more than a little mad—but you spoke your mind. Today, you're lying—and you're afraid. I'm learning why, if it's my last assignment on earth."

"Get out of my house!"

"I'm on my way. But I insist you're lying. And I'll go on saying it, until Seth Randall gives his first New York concert. Then I'll believe you've cut his chains."

"Get out, I said!"

The order was screamed, and Case half rose from the throne-chair as he uttered it. In a space of minutes, he had aged ten years; his body had shrunk, as though that bellow had taken all his breath, and his face was a mummy's mask of hate. Rick stood for a moment in the door. When no words came, he turned on his heel and left the house.

"Ten minutes exactly," said Theo. "I was ready to call the marines."

Rick got slowly into the station wagon. The image of Walter Case, all passion spent save rage, was still etched in fire on his brain. Try as he might, he could not put down a rising sense of dread—the inevitable aftermath of a head-on collision with madness.

"Feel like a playback now?" asked the photographer. "Or shall we save it for headquarters?"

"Take me to a phone first."

In the booth of a corner drugstore, he found that Mary Randall's phone did not answer—nor did the Afro-Baptist parsonage. He hung up with a certain relief. In a way, both calls were needless—and he had been unwilling to resurrect the voice of Richard Sloane.

"On to Bob?" asked Theo.

"Whenever you say. I've done my day's work."

Judd listened in soothing silence while Rick played back his encounter in the Crestwood mansion. Thanks to his training, he found he could repeat the Case monologue, almost word for word. The sense of dread persisted—the certainty that Case's reversal had a motive that eluded him.

The photographer summed up, neatly enough. "Maybe

I'm oversimplifying, Rick—but it sounds like a prime example of the devil quoting scripture."

"He spoke to Mary Randall. He had to."

"You're damned right he did. Case is no mossback. He knows what a national telecast can do to sway public opinion."

"Will Seth go free, then?"

"Like a shot—now you've forced the issue."

"Did Case give in to spike our guns?"

"Could be, Rick. One thing's for sure—he made the decision before he laid eyes on you."

Rick nodded a slow agreement, as the station wagon threaded the downtown traffic. Theo's sturdy common sense was a much-needed antidote for the nightmare of half-truths he had just endured. "In another moment, you'll convince me I should have stayed clear today."

"By no means. Hitting Case in the solar plexus was what the doctor ordered."

"You agree, then? He *is* afraid of something?"

"Of course. It's always a shock to Napoleon, finding he isn't quite infalliable."

"Did Mary Randall swing the balance, then?"

"If you ask me, Rick, she was a reminder he'd have to give ground. There's nothing Napoleon hates more than retreating—but not even Walter Case can sell motherhood short. Not when her son has just proved he's a genius on everyone's living-room screen." The photographer chuckled, and swung the station wagon into the back alley of the *Times-News*. "Your arrival capped that unpleasant admission. Let's trust that friend Walter passes a restless night. He deserves to."

It was a homecoming of sorts to whisk up to the city room in the freight elevator, to slip into the editor's office by the private door. Bob, they discovered, was not expected until midnight. Theo, prowling outside for news, returned to report that Partridge was presiding at a meeting of his impromptu vigilantes. It had been called in haste, at the home of a local builder (who happened to be Walter

Case's chief rival), to lay plans for tomorrow's conclave at the Stadium.

"We're infiltrating in earnest now," said Judd. "Bob has nearly five hundred recruits in the Central City Knights alone. Several hundred more will be inducted tomorrow. If we don't run out of bedsheets, we might break up that rally."

"A riot can't help matters now. I wish Bob would hold back a little longer."

"He won't give up on the hunch that Case is trying something big tomorrow. If he's right, we can use a few strong-arm squads."

Rick nodded gloomily, and settled in the editor's chair. He, too, was convinced that Bob Partridge's instinct could be trusted, that the enemy was about to strike. It was agony to sit tamely and await the blow.

"What's our next move, Theo?"

The photographer sat down across the desk, and took out a pack of dog-eared cards. "Can I challenge you to a little gin? I'd suggest poker, but our rewrite desk is busy."

"Can you play gin at a time like this?"

"With the greatest of ease," said Judd. "So, my friend, can you. We're both experts at waiting. It's a talent we share with soldiers and lighthouse keepers."

Dinner arrived on cafeteria trays, without spoiling the solemn tempo of the game. Twice in the next hour, the cards were put aside for phone calls. The first came from Bob's detectives, a routine reminder of a change of shifts in the stakeout. Case had received no further callers, and was presumably dining alone.

Rick made the second call on impulse, to inform his New York editor of his whereabouts, and to ask that a staff man be flown to Central City to cover the Knights' outing. The *Record*'s welcome did little to raise his spirits. He had risked his reputation on the Walter Case story —with no tangible result, beyond Seth's promised release. As the leaden evening dragged on, he could believe this card game might last forever, with no change in his luck.

When the wall clock hung on eleven, and the first edition of the *Times-News* had come upstairs, Rick threw down his hand at last.

"Pick up your ill-gotten gains, Theo. I'm lowering the blinds until morning."

"Bob will be along in the next hour."

"You can describe my day in a dozen words. Is it safe to walk to the hotel?"

"Reasonably, I think. There's an extra private eye in the lobby. We'll take you over, just to make sure."

At the Cavalier, Rick paused at the desk to ask for messages—remembered in time that he was registered as Dick Sloane, and moved toward the elevators. Theo fell into step beside him. At his nod, the detective had settled in one of the lobby armchairs.

"Did you notice the gray suit behind the second pillar?" he asked. "The face belongs to Frank Lamb—one of Sheriff Colt's boys. Believe me, he's anything but lamb-like."

"Does he have orders to dismember me later?"

"I'd say Colt sent him here to make a routine check. As of now, they can't risk turning you into a corpse."

"I hope you're right: it's a pleasant thought to sleep on."

"Our man will keep Lamb company until morning," said the photographer. "I'll share your room, if you like. We might even go on with our game."

"Thank you, no. Tonight, I'm making sure I sleep."

With the aid of two Seconal capsules, Rick fulfilled his resolve. It was a powerful sedative, but a much-needed one; at all cost, he had felt he must escape the treadmill of his frustration, the fear he had been outguessed from the start. . . . Struggling to waken in the dawn, convinced the phone was ringing, he realized the dosage had been excessive, that he should have calculated the side effect of a wearing day. At the moment, he could ignore imponder-

ables, as he dropped back into the deepest slumber he
had ever known.

When he wakened again, the day was far-advanced.
Long before he could focus on the bedside clock, he
realized a fist was hammering at the hall door, that Theo's
voice was added to the din.

"Are you all right, Rick? *Are you there?*"

"Coming, Theo!" He tried not to curse too audibly
while he fumbled with the burglar latch on the door. A
veteran newsman would hardly waken him without
cause.

"I rang your phone twice," said Theo. His face bore the
marks of a wide-awake night, and his voice echoed his
weariness. "If you've slept since midnight, you're
lucky."

"What's happened, Theo?"

"We haven't a complete story yet. Mary Randall died
last night. In Eldon—when her house burned down. One
of those colored-town fires that swept the whole block.
The story was on the eight o'clock newscast."

"D'you mean that Case——?"

"Bob will do the translating," said Theo. "That isn't the
whole bulletin. Seth must have heard that news report.
He's broken out of Valley Hospital."

12

"STOP BLAMING YOURSELF," said Bob Partridge. "It could have been an accident. We've yet to prove it wasn't."

"Walter Case set that fire. Why pretend it *happened?*"

"Don't be positive yet, Rick. Not until the story's in. The fire began in the parsonage woodshed: that much we're sure of. They were trying to roast Thornton Blanding—the NAACP lawyer."

"Why did the fire spread?"

"How could it help spreading, with tinderbox houses all around it? Seth's mother wasn't the only one hurt."

"She was the only one who died. This thing was planned, from the moment Seth appeared on the telecast. Mary Randall signed her own death warrant when she picked up her phone yesterday."

Though he was visibly shaken, the editor of the *Times-News* had maintained a judicial calm since Rick's arrival. Only the familiar clenching of his fist as he paced his office—and the uppercut he administered to a phantom enemy—suggested his inner rage.

"Flagellation will get us nowhere," he said. "After all, it was Miss King's idea to launch Seth as a pianist—not ours."

"I made the launching possible."

"I've talked to Moore, long-distance. Carol King wasn't the first music-lover who wanted to open the asylum door. Last year, one of Moore's doctor friends from New York tried to pull the same wires. He even went to Eldon to argue with Mary Randall."

"You're sure of that?"

"Peter Moore is the sort of medico who sticks to facts," said Bob patiently. "Seth's light was too bright to stay under that bushel forever. Sooner or later, someone was bound to take off the lid. It's pure chance you turned up to do the job."

"Don't let me down easy. Remember, I was working from mixed motives."

"To hell with your motives, Rick. Any human being, given your chance, would have gotten Seth a hearing. How could you guess things would end this way?"

"It was murder, Bob. Why not face it?"

"I'm drawing no conclusions, until our reporter sends in his story. Will you give the desk a jog, Theo?"

The photographer stirred wearily in his chair. "It's coming in now, Bob—by phone."

"Bring me the copy, then."

"Do you want it in takes?"

The editor shook his head, and strode to the office door, to stare grimly into the city room. Now that afternoon had begun to change to evening, it was stirring to life again. "Sorry, Theo," he said. "I didn't mean to bark. Rick should read the story in one piece, so he can get the picture. Let's stop fighting it now."

Ten minutes later, with a carbon of the news account before him, Rick found he could read almost calmly. It had been a rough quarter-hour in Bob's office, while he had picked up the facts of the Eldon fire in snatches: in the end, the editor had proved a solid stabilizer. Now, with the first stark horror behind him, he saw that the sequence of events had its own bitter logic.

On the testimony of neighbors, Mary Randall had returned to her cottage at seven, after a day's work in a white household. As dusk fell, she had been seen ironing by the wife of Dr. Stuart Howell, who had paused for a moment to chat through the kitchen door. Mrs. Howell had accepted a parcel for mailing. A little later, the couple had driven off, to pick up Thornton Blanding at the Central City airport. So far as the *Times-News* reporter could learn, the Howells were the last to see Seth's mother alive.

The blaze had begun in the parsonage shed around midnight, and there was no doubt that it was of incendiary origin. The Negro fire company, a volunteer group, had been hampered in its efforts since the tires of its one engine had been slashed. When they reached the scene, with such equipment as they could transport by hand, the blaze had swept over the whole block. Only a bucket brigade, rushing water from the river, had averted a far worse disaster.

Ironically enough, the NAACP lawyer (for whom the blaze had apparently been set) had never reached Eldon. His schedule had been changed at the last moment to permit a stopover in Mississippi: the news had come too late to help the Howells, who had driven eighty miles to the airport on a fruitless errand. They had returned in the early morning to find both their home and their church reduced to ashes—and nearly a hundred of their parishioners homeless. Later, they had gone to the morgue to identify Mary Randall: neighbors had risked their lives to drag her from the blazing cottage, just before the roof collapsed. . . .

"Is it true the parsonage had been threatened?"

"There had been the usual notes and phone calls," said Bob. "Thorn Blanding is one of the most hated names in the woolhat league." He was scanning the top copy of the story and editing it at high speed. "At least, that was the motive as of midnight. Read on, Rick. You'll see it won't wash."

The county coroner, Rick discovered, was a painstaking man. Since Seth's mother had been the only casualty, he had performed a meticulous post-mortem examination. The results were startling. Charred though the body was, he had found that Mary Randall had perished in her bed, stabbed through the heart by a bodkin tentatively identified as an ice pick. He had fixed the time of her death with fair accuracy, a good two hours before the first alarm. Long before morning, the police had booked the death as murder.

"So Case burned out a city block to cover himself," said Rick. "Has he gone completely mad?"

Bob Partridge threw down his pencil, and handed the first take of the story to a waiting office boy. "Call it a tandem job," he said. "He planned to roast Blanding in that same bonfire—*after* his goon squad made sure Mary Randall would never come out alive. The pattern's routine by now. Blow up the evidence—or burn it— before the law moves in. He'd have succeeded one more time, if Blanding hadn't missed his plane. Or if Mary's neighbors had hung back five minutes more."

"It says here the whole town's up in arms. Is that the truth, or editorial snow?"

"This time, it's gospel," said Bob. "The fire jumped Division Street, and burned down four *white* houses. Justice will be done, if they trap those firebugs."

The police, Rick read, had already picked up several clues, including the license number of a car that had been seen parked on the edge of colored town. Special deputies had been sworn in, road blocks set up, and a state-wide alarm sent out. A heavy rainstorm had delayed the searchers, but the pack was now in full cry.

The *Times-News* reporter had gone on to Valley Hospital to round out his dispatch, while he awaited the next bulletin from the Eldon police. The story awaiting him there had been on the meager side. Seth had come off ward duty at seven o'clock: there had been a radio in the staff dining room where he had breakfasted. Other ward attendants had been present when the news of his mother's death came over the newscast. . . . Seth had hurried from the room before they could offer their sympathy. A moment later, he had been seen running across the lawn behind the main building, in the direction of the hospital laundry:

The Negro attendant (who had just received nationwide acclaim for his brilliant piano recital on a coast-to-coast telecast) evidently made good his escape via that building. He had worked for years as a "trusty" and carried a complete set of keys.

The fact that one of the laundry trucks was missing from the garage lends credence to this theory. At noon, the truck was found parked on the shoulder of the Central City Turnpike, some fifty miles from Valley Stream.

The Eldon police, already occupied with its intensive search for the arsonists, lost no time in broadcasting another statewide alarm for Randall. So far, there has been no further trace of his whereabouts.

Bob watched the last take of copy go to the composing room. "Too bad we can't interview Case on that last point," he said. "The truth would make a nice shirttail to our story—such as it is."

"You'll agree *now* that he was behind the fire?"

"Naturally—now the evidence is in. All we need is a motive. Unfortunately, only Seth can enlighten us."

"Do you think he's in Central City now?"

"Either that—or he's damned close."

"He means to kill Case. Is that what you're saying?"

"If he gets the chance," said Bob.

"Finish it. Will the state police shoot on sight?"

"My colleagues on the *Sun* have Seth's picture on their front page now. The caption reads *Homicidal maniac breaks out of Valley Hospital*. It's only a question of time before he walks into someone's sights." Bob broke off, to take the phone. For a moment, he talked briskly with his reporter in Eldon: the lines between his eyes had relaxed when he faced Rick again.

"Break number one for our side," he said. "They jumped the firebugs, and brought 'em in. They aren't talking yet—but they will."

"That doesn't mean Case will be implicated. He's too shrewd for that."

"Maybe—and maybe not." Bob swung viciously on another invisible foe. "They're giving us an exclusive on the capture: I won't break the story until our late final. It'll do friend Walter no harm to think his bully boys have done another perfect job. Meanwhile, we'll attend the Stadium rally—infiltrate, and pray."

"What can you accomplish there?"

"I'm still not sure. But I do know that Case is using that speaker's platform tonight for something really big. Everything he said to you yesterday confirms it. So, for that matter, does the murder of Mary Randall—and the state-wide manhunt for Seth."

"What's the connection?" Rick demanded.

"Yesterday, when you appeared from the blue and taunted him, his self-esteem was shaken, for the first time in years. In my opinion, last night's events have restored the balance. So completely, he may really blow his stack at the rally——"

"Prove he's God, you mean?"

"Exactly, Rick. The sort of Old Testament avenger who can strike at will. As of now, he doesn't realize he's goofed in Eldon. Why shouldn't he goof again at the Stadium?" The editor turned to snarl at the phone that had just rung at his elbow. His tone changed abruptly as he recognized the voice on the wire.

"Miss King, boy. She wants to talk with you."

Rick took the phone with a lifting of the heart. He had checked on Carol's flight at the airport, only to learn that her plane had been grounded in Montgomery by fog. It was good news that she had reached Central City at last.

"When did you arrive, Carol?"

"Only a moment ago. I'm calling from my apartment."

"Who told you I was in town?"

"Uncle Walter. I phoned his office from the airport. He

wants me at the Case Building in an hour. Thank Heaven I found you so soon——"

"Is something wrong?"

"There's a package here for you, Rick. It's addressed to Richard Sloane: Western Union delivered it last night. The return address is Mary Randall's house in Eldon."

"Stay put, Carol. And don't open your door to anyone but me. I'll be there in ten minutes."

Bob, who had listened shamelessly on the extension, faced Rick with excited eyes. "Could this be break number two?"

"We'll soon learn, Bob. Come with me, if you like."

"I can't leave this desk, until it's time to head for the Stadium. When I go, Theo will be my stand-in."

"I'll ring you the moment I have news."

"You have news right now. What's more, you've given me the first line for the editorial I'll be printing when we nail friend Walter down. Care to hear it?"

Rick paused, with one hand on the door. Eager though he was to join Carol, there was no resisting the blaze in Bob Partridge's eyes.

"You think he's really goofed this time, don't you?"

"Here's my line," said the editor. *"Playing God can be a risky business, if you're using mortal equipment.* Carry on, boy. It's your story now."

Case's watchdog was planted in the *Times-News* lobby when Rick and Theo emerged from the elevator. Expecting this obstruction, they were prepared to avoid it. While the photographer buttonholed the man (and opened a newspaper to point out an item), Rick stepped into a freight elevator which had just come up from the press-room to await him. A moment later, he had slipped into the alley and flagged a taxi.

Carol was waiting in her apartment foyer. The package lay on the table—a squarish bundle wrapped in heavy paper. When he had shucked off the outer wrapping, Rick found it was a bulky book, enclosed in a cellophane envelope with the edges tightly sealed. A letter was pinned to the flap.

"You say this came from Western Union, Carol?"

"The superintendent signed for it last evening."

Rick opened the letter: one mystery, at least, was solved. The *Times-News* story had mentioned an exchange of civilities between Mary Randall and the wife of Dr. Stuart Howell, just before the couple had departed for Central City. There had also been mention of a package that Mary had given the pastor's wife for mailing. Rick gathered that the Howells, finding the post office closed and noting the Central City address, had stopped en route to send this bundle by messenger. Before he could read half of Mary Randall's note, he knew they had performed a priceless service.

Dear Mr. Sloane:

I am sending this to you by a neighbor. It will reach you safely.

By the time you read it, you will have called on Walter Case. He will have told you that I have spoken with him on the long-distance phone.

Perhaps I should apologize for that phone call—after I had asked *you* to plead with this man for Seth's release. When I realized how badly I had behaved, it was too late to call you back. Asking Walter Case for mercy was not your task but mine. It was the act of a coward to send you.

As you now know, he has promised to do all in his power to speed Seth's release from Valley Hospital. He will also make sure the suspended sentence is dropped—*or so he says*.

In the circumstances, I must take him at his word. But I had my doubts, even as I write this note.

I cannot (in all fairness) explain why I have good reason to question this man's word. Or why I fear he has made me this promise, only to do some greater mischief later.

Should my fears prove groundless, I am asking your solemn promise to return the enclosed scrapbook unopened. Keep it close to you, until Seth is really free, until the cloud is lifted from his name. If the cloud remains—if the hope this man has lighted in my heart is snuffed out—use it as you think best to bring him to justice.

You are a good man, Richard Sloane. I know I can trust you to follow my wishes.

Thank you again, for everything.

Mary Randall

Rick heard Carol's soft-drawn breath as he looked up from the letter—and realized she had read it over his shoulder. He shook his head incredulously, like a man fumbling his way in darkness, toward a doorway he can sense rather than see.

"Did she know she was risking her life?" Carol asked.

"I'm sure of it," he said slowly. "She was a brave woman."

"Most women are, when a son's happiness is at stake."

"Why did she doubt Case's word?"

"The answer is under your hand, Rick. Break those seals."

Once he had stripped off the wrapper, he found the bulky volume was identical with the scrapbooks he had seen in the Randall living room. The note had given no instructions for its perusal, so he forced himself to turn the pages in order. The first contained a wedding photo of Mary and Sam Randall, taken over thirty years ago. The groom seemed ill at ease in formal garb, though he was a strikingly handsome man in his dark-skinned fashion. Compared to his slender, cream-and-ivory bride, he seemed almost another species. In her twenties, Mary

Randall's demure beauty was enough to take one's breath away.

"Exhibit A," said Rick.

"It's surely the beginning of something," said Carol. "I don't mean just a marriage."

"I feel like an eavesdropper—even with her permission."

Each page in the scrapbook, protected by a cellophane overlay, had an odd air of freshness, despite the remote dates. The next items in the chronology were Seth's birth certificate (registered at the city hall in Eldon), his baby photos, a family group in an A-model Ford. They were followed by other pictures—Sam and Mary on the porch of their general store, Sam in the sailor suit he had worn in the Second World War, Mary and Seth on the Tuskegee campus, with the statue of Booker T. Washington as background. Succeeding snapshots pictured Seth at his graduation. There was a clipping describing the award of his Julliard scholarship, and stories from New York musical publications, describing his student triumphs at the keyboard.

The next page contained three news items. The first was a story from the Eldon *Gazette,* telling of Sam Randall's death. The others were clipped from the Central City *Times-News,* recounting the details of Seth's assault on Walter Case, his sentencing, and his commitment to Valley Hospital. Red-ink underscores stressed Case's part in the commitment. At the foot of the page, a separate entry announced "the end of the Randall record," with a date now ten years old.

The remaining pages of the scrapbook were sealed in a special binding. Across it, a warning was written in the same neat hand.

To Whom It May Concern
This seal is to be broken only in the event of my death.

                                  Mary Bradley (Randall)

"Bob would call this the clincher," said Rick. "Will you hand me those shears again?"

The first three photos now revealed were usual enough: Mary Bradley as a young girl in a garden, a somewhat older Mary in a *bouffante* evening gown, singing against a nightclub background, Mary waving from a ship's rail in a snarl of confetti streamers. All of the three pictures were dated—the first two in the *Vieux Carre, New Orleans,* the last *En route to Havana.*

On the next two pages, Mary was shown dancing, on a floodlit outdoor floor, with the trunks of royal palms behind her. These photos were dated a year later, and labeled simply *Havana.* Her dancing partner, a shortish white man in a tropical mess jacket, had his back to the camera, and was not identified.

The next picture showed the same couple at a table, in the same grove of royal palms. Both were facing the flashlight now: the man had made a laughing, half-serious effort to hide his face, but there was no mistaking his identity. Walter Case in his twenties had been a *jeune elegant* in the manner born—and he was enjoying his evening quite as much as Mary. This time, the caption (*Havana "honeymoon"*) was needless.

The last two pages of the scrapbook underlined what was already apparent. On the first, a pair of facing photographs showed Seth at twenty, and Case at the same age. Both were precisely dated: there had been no other effort to stress the resemblance.

The final page contained a short note, the perfect coda for this bizarre photo montage:

My Dear Mary:

My father has ordered me to end all communication—and, as we both know too well, his word is law. I am sending you this note without his knowledge. It is a poor good-by, but better than none.

The few short years we spent together were the happiest of my life. Perhaps they were happier than

I deserve. You must be the judge of that. One thing is certain. There was a rapture about those years that was not quite of this earth, a joy of living I will never find in this world.

I need not explain why I must blot those years from my mind as though they had never been—and why I can never see you again, or the child you expect to bear. We are both Southern: we know that answer.

Your marriage to Randall, which our lawyers have already arranged, will protect your good name. Adequate financial provisions have been made for you both—and for the child as well.

My father has ruled that any further demands, either by you or Randall, will be made at your peril. It is a ruling I must respect.

> Walter Case

The letter, written on the stationery of Tulane University in New Orleans, bore a date thirty-one years old. Rick handed the scrapbook to Carol, who reread it slowly, with veiled eyes—as though she was reluctant to make the first comment.

"Did your uncle attend Tulane?"

"For three years," said Carol. "As a boy, he had a long illness, and was tutored at home. When he came of college age, he was far behind his classmates——"

"Did he go to Cuba to convalesce?"

"So I'm told." Carol's eyes were on the open scrapbook. "It seems he didn't go alone."

"First Havana, then college in New Orleans," said Rick. "With an octoroon mistress at both. A nightclub beauty from the Quarter, who bore him a son. We've proof of that much right here. How do we handle it?"

"If you used this book as a threat, could you save Seth's life?"

"I'm not sure," said Rick. "Your uncle may brazen it out. The scrapbook establishes Seth's paternity, beyond all question. It would hardly stand up as evidence if we brought a murder charge." He took the book from Carol's hands and closed it. The exultation he had felt (when the pattern of the Walter Case story had come clear at last) was subsiding rapidly. The years between, and the blind lust for power they had spawned, had fogged this early portrait beyond recognition. There was no point of contact between the lover who had penned that note of farewell and the monster of today.

"Why not go to him together?" asked Carol. "We can't help Mary. We might still help Seth. Or are we too late for that as well?"

"I'm afraid so. Your uncle has stopped listening to any voice but his own."

"Surely we can do *something,* Rick."

The phone had been ringing steadily. He lifted the receiver and handed it to her wordlessly. Carol's eyes were brimming, but her voice was firm enough when she took the message.

"That was his secretary, Rick. Just a reminder I'm due at the office. How can I face him now?"

"You must make the effort, my dear. We can't show our hand."

"You'll do nothing, then?"

"Not until I can get more evidence—the kind we can really use. This scrapbook explains a great deal. It doesn't establish his guilt." He looked hard at Carol—and took fresh pride in her, when he saw she had regained her composure. "If the firebugs are talking in Eldon, we may have our proof already. No matter what we turn up, this scrapbook will backstop us. It's of no value alone."

Carol moved to the foyer mirror to put on her hat: a few deft touches restored the damage the tears had done. "It's all right, Rick," she said quietly. "I won't disgrace you. What shall I say, if Uncle Walter asks me to attend the Knights' rally?"

"You must go, I'm afraid."

"He has a box at the stadium. He's planning to turn it

over to the Daughters of the Constitution. I'm sure he'll want me to sit with them."

"Has he admitted he holds office in the Knights?"

"He's allowed me to infer it. Will you be at the rally too?"

"I'm driving out with Theo. We'll be in the south parking lot, beside the *Times-News* radio truck. Come there at once, if you learn anything. Or call Bob, if you need to reach us sooner."

"I'll try to call before I leave the office," she said. "It won't be easy. My workroom is next to his, you know."

"Can you risk listening on the intercom?"

"I've kept it open for the last two days," said Carol. "The only private visitor he's had so far was Sheriff Colt. I could only pick up their talk in snatches."

"Do what you can, my dear. Just don't take chances."

"I'll be careful, Rick. Shall we leave together—or wouldn't that be wise?"

"You'd best go alone. I'll slip out later, by the side door."

Carol's good-by kiss sustained him for a moment. But he was pacing her living room in an agony of indecision when the phone rang. Lifting the receiver cautiously, he spoke only when Bob Partridge's booming voice had placed the call.

"I've a two-part bulletin for you," said the editor. "First, our friends in Eldon are dictating a confession: the police have promised my man a look when it's down on paper. Second, Case wants you to come to his office for an interview."

"Will you repeat the last item?"

"You heard me right. Walter Case is giving you an exclusive—for the Central City *Times-News* and the New York *Record*. Don't ask me why. He'll tell you."

"Did he call you himself?"

"He did—for the first time in over ten years."

"D'you think it's a sign of weakness?"

"What else can you call it?"

Rick stared hard at the phone before he spoke. "At the moment, I've stopped calling the shots in this game."

"What's up, Rick? Are you losing your grip?"

"It's *your* turn to listen, Partridge. I've opened one prize package today. I may not enjoy opening another."

Bob did not interrupt while Rick read the letters aloud, and described the scrapbook, page by page. Only an occasional chortle betrayed his reaction. When Rick had finished, he let his smothered laughter erupt.

"Stop at Western Union and shoot that book to my office," he said. "Friend Walter's over a barrel at last."

"I'm not too sure of that."

"Give me that evidence. I'll show you how to print it."

"What'll it get you but a libel suit—unless you can pin Mary's murder where it belongs?"

"We'll do that, the minute those firebugs finish confessing——"

"The confession may not even mention Case."

"Why are you backing up, Rick? It isn't like you."

"I'm not. But I'm asking you to keep that scrapbook on ice, until I've seen Case."

"Suit yourself." Partridge's dour tone echoed his disappointment. "Just the same, I'm starting to block out a story to fit round your interview. Any idea what you'll be asking him?"

"No, Bob. I've given up asking this fellow questions."

"That's no attitude for a first-rate reporter."

"He's burned me once too often. I don't think he'd have called you, if he wasn't sure he'd won."

"Look, Rick! D'you want *me* to write that interview? Are you afraid to ace the dragon again?"

"I'm not afraid. I'll bring you back a story. But I'm not sure you'll care to print it."

"Damn you, boy—make sense!"

"Do I have to tell you why Case has sent for me? He's proving he's God Almighty, complete with thunderbolts. Can you sell that story to your readers?"

13

THE RECEPTION ROOM at Case Construction was completely worthy of the earth-molder who had straddled all the continents. Photographic proof of his genius loomed on every side; models under glass illustrated work in progress; maps of the two hemispheres, on facing walls, were pricked with scores of American flags, to show where Case bulldozers were breaking ground, from Greenland to Cape Town. Rick's ear (tuned to office rhythms) could detect no false note in the hum of activity from the open workrooms beyond—where stenographers drove a score of typewriters and men in shirt sleeves bent in myopic concentration above their drawing boards. If these were trembling wage slaves, he saw no visible sign. The slogan of Walter Case was service: these busy men and women were his docile lieutenants.

It was a strange feeling to give his name at the reception desk. Already, his suspicions were beginning to seem unreal as the tumult in his brain subsided. He had just proved that Case was pure evil, that megalomania had swept him beyond the bounds of reason. Here was other, no less convincing proof that Case was a servant of mankind, in the best sense. The paradox cried out for resolution—but it was impossible to believe he was on the verge of enlightenment.

The blonde receptionist favored him with a smile that was both brilliant and restrained. It was clear from her manner that presidents and maharajahs had waited here for admission. She could take his own modest arrival in stride.

"You're expected, Mr. Jordan. Miss Bonbright will be with you in just a moment."

The welcome (friendly yet casual) was a needed corrective. So was Miss Bonbright, a slender, dark-haired girl who was obviously a secretary's secretary, from the second defense line that stood between the head of Case Construction and unwanted visitors. Following her perfect figure through a suite of offices (beginning to empty fast at the day's end), Rick was aware of two sobering facts. First, his appearance in the heart of the Case domain was only an entry in an appointment book, an extra item on a great man's schedule. Second (and the conviction pressed on his mind like lead), Case had summoned him for just one purpose—to stress the perfection of his victory, to show that the wall dividing them was impregnable.

"If you'll follow that corridor, Mr. Jordan, you'll find Mr. Case in the last office. His personal secretary is with him now—but he wants you to go straight in."

The hall leading to Case's sanctum was on the austere side. So were the offices that opened into it: the furnishings were comfortable but sparse, and their most striking feature was the sweeping view of Central City. At first glance, this corner of the building seemed empty. Case's voice, booming in dictation, was the only sound to break the after-hours stillness. It was a shock to pause in the next to last door frame and catch a glimpse of Carol, immersed in a stack of sketches that littered a drawing board. He was glad her back was turned as he hurried on; until this ordeal was behind him, he dared not advertise his presence.

The grotesque travesty of normalcy continued when he entered Case's own office. The industrialist, lolling in a high-back swivel chair behind a glass half-moon of desk, waved him to a seat as easily as though his were a daily visit.

"Sit down, Jordan. This is my last letter of the day, and it's almost finished."

The respite, such as it was, gave Rick a chance to

catalogue the office. It was a tall, grave room, bare to the point of ostentation. Save for an intercom, the desk was swept clean as an admiral's bridge; the visitor needed a second look to make sure the swivel chair was mounted on a platform, giving the occupant an illusion of height he did not possess. There were two side doors. One, which evidently gave to Carol's office, was closed. The other, opening to a dressing room, stood wide to admit a shaft of late sunlight. . . .

"That will do, Morison. Close the door as you go out."

The secretary, a waxen-pale man who scarcely seemed to breathe, took up his notebook and departed on noiseless tiptoe. Case smiled at Rick with perfect composure as the door sighed shut.

"If you're surprised," he said, "you're concealing it admirably."

Rick forced himself to match the easy tone—even as he yielded to the insane conviction he had played this game before, with different weapons. "Perhaps I've lost my capacity for surprise."

"I hope to disprove that before you leave," said Case. When he smiled, Rick found it impossible to believe that this dapper pygmy was the same man who had ordered him from the house in Crestwood. "That's why I offered to submit to an interview. It seemed the quickest way to get you here."

"If this is really an interview," said Rick, "you'll have to start it rolling. I've run out of questions too."

"May I begin with an apology? When you called on me yesterday, I'm afraid I was insufferably rude. Will you admit I had good reason—if I confess it was bad manners to show my annoyance?"

"I'll admit it gladly. Is that the only reason I'm here?"

"Jordan, I'm about to tell you the story of my life. The complete story. It's a favor I've granted to no other living soul. All I ask is an impartial judgment. When I've finished, I think you'll agree I deserve that much."

"Say what you will. I m making no promises."

"I expect none," said Case. "However, I'll warn you in advance that *this* life story is not what you'd call good copy. As a man of the world, you'll find it's not without interest. Perhaps you've been shrewd enough to guess part of it already. If so, I'll merely fill in the gaps."

Case rose from his chair and entered the dressing room, leaving the door ajar. "If you'll forgive a bit of melodrama, I'll begin with the ending. Or, to be exact, the first of *several* endings. Be patient, please: I've learned to make this change in thirty seconds——"

Rick heard the swish of robes behind the door, a muffled whirring he could not define. A second later, the Grand Leader of the Knights of Freedom stalked into the office, ducking his head a trifle to ease his cone-shaped hood beneath the portal. The whirring continued as Case made the final adjustment to the microphone hidden beneath the robe, then spread both scarlet-draped arms.

"Keep the South Pure!" The deep-throated intonation shook the windowpanes. Then, with a sharp click, Case disconnected the microphone and spoke in normal tones, behind the thick red hood.

"Did I startle you, Jordan? That was my intention. Need I explain the costume?"

"Don't bother. I saw you perform at Eldon."

"It has amused me to wear it now and then—to sway the mob with mumbo-jumbo. The fools adore it—and mine is an empire of fools. All empires a₁e."

Case was gone with the words. There was another swish of robes behind the door, the snap of a buckle as though the masquerader had just shed a harness. Then the industrialist emerged to resume his seat behind the great glass desk. His manner was urbane as ever, his smile as benign.

"Don't think me rash," he said. "It's already an open

secret that I'm Grand Leader of the Knights. Tonight, I'm speaking in that capacity, at University Stadium. I'm using the occasion to consolidate my power beyond question. Or shall I be precise and say my unchallenged control of this state?"

"Is this part of the interview?"

"Of course. Didn't I say I'd hold back nothing?"

"May I have an advance copy of your address?"

Case tossed up his hands, in a gesture of comic despair. "Must you be the inquiring reporter forever? Can't we talk just this once as man to man?"

Rick took an iron grip on his whirling thoughts: already, his last remark to Bob Partridge had returned to haunt him. With an effort, he forced himself to match Case's porcelain grin.

"Don't say you were misquoted, then."

"All my speeches are extemporaneous. When one is swaying fools, one must be guided by circumstances. Tonight, as I say, the outcome is already ordained: the words are incidental."

"You're sure of that?"

"Quite, Jordan. My triumph—and I use the term advisedly—is based on a lifetime of preparation. Failure, at this point, is unthinkable."

"So we're back to the story of your life. The past this time, not the future."

"Exactly. The fact I can sway morons as I see fit is no accident. Once you've heard my history, you'll see this seizure of power was inevitable. You might almost call it my destiny."

"Shall we begin at the beginning?"

"By all means. Since I've already tried your patience, I'll be brief."

Rick held up a restraining hand. "Would it surprise you to discover I know the story now?"

Case did not stir in the swivel chair. "Not at all. I've called you a shrewd observer. I don't waste compliments."

"Put me to the test. You'll find we can cut corners."

The industrialist smiled again, and lifted one foot to the desk top. He still wore the six-inch elevators he had donned to give himself greater height in his robes.

"Go on, please. I'll correct you if you stumble."

"You were the ailing son of a tyrant father," said Rick. "The kind of father who coddled with one hand and flogged with the other. You were stunted in body, living in a cotton-wool universe. Because of sickness, you were years behind your classmates—if you'd been allowed to have classmates. Instead, you stayed at home, and grew up in your father's image. Until you were ready for college, you were fenced in by tutors. By that time, you were healthy enough, but you were sent to Cuba for a year of convalescence. You were then in your midtwenties, and it was your first real taste of freedom. Now, thanks to an unlimited allowance, you could do as you liked. Before you took passage to Havana, you stopped in New Orleans to pick up an octoroon mistress you'd established in the Quarter. If your father knew of the liaison, he didn't interfere. After all, it was the custom of your time and your class——"

Rick glanced sharply at Case, but the man gave no sign. "Mary Bradley was the only person you ever loved—and the first to show you real affection. Your relationship continued during your years at Tulane. When it was time to finish your education in the North, your father forced a break. Provision was made for Mary's marriage to Seth Randall, a storekeeper in another state, to give your son a name. That, too, was part of gentleman's code, when a gentleman's affections were involved. A subsidy was paid by your lawyers. There, presumably, the affair ended. Have I erred, so far?"

"The score is perfect," said Case.

"Later, when you proved yourself as a construction engineer, you were assured of your inheritance. You married well—for position, not for love. When your father died, you took over a prosperous business, and made it your personal empire. Like most sons of despots, you proved an even greater tyrant than your sire. Over the years, of course, your tyranny paid off in millions, until it became a way of life." Rick spread his hands. "The details are in the biography you had written to order last year—a success story that happens to be true. There's no need to repeat it now."

Case stared at the elevator, kicked it in mid-air, then tossed it through the dressing-room door. He spoke with his eyes on the ceiling, and his voice was still benign.

"You've done an impressive job of research, Jordan. I suppose I should be flattered."

"Have I left anything out?"

"I think not. It's beyond me how you learned the truth about Mary. I won't ask your source; it s no longer important."

"Did you love her once?"

"You might call it that," said Case. "I prefer to think of her as the symbol of my escape from prison. Until we met, I'd lived under twin shadows—my illness, and the need to obey my father's orders. They were the only orders I ever heeded. I'll always hate him for giving them."

"How long did the affair with Mary last?"

"Just four years. My tutors followed me, even in Havana. In New Orleans, my father insisted I crowd four college years into three: he'd have disowned me, if I'd failed to head all my classes. It was bearable, with Mary waiting on Bourbon Street."

"Do you feel you treated her fairly afterward?"

"The settlement was more than generous. She was glad to accept it."

"Glad?"

"She had her code; I had mine. We were both trained to follow them."

"You had no regrets, even then?"

"None. She was a pretty wench, who served her purpose. Ten years ago, when the boy attacked me, I'd forgotten her completely. When that business was settled, I forgot her again—until yesterday."

"And now you've killed her."

Case's smile did not change. "Jordan, I've called this our hour of truth: I'm prepared to prove it. I could pretend that Mary Randall died by accident, in the Eldon fire. That, of course, will be the official story. Actually, she was stabbed in her sleep, at my order. Just as her son will be shot down—now he's run amok again."

"He's your son too. Have you no pity left?"

"None. The boy and his mother belong to the past. I can have no such encumbrances when I move into tomorrow." The voice was ice-cold now. "We're confusing a simple story with an overlay of sentiment. Like a thousand Southern gentlemen before me, I financed a family in colored town, for reasons of my own. Sam Randall was a happy-go-lucky fellow—he'd been selected carefully. My lawyers assured me he'd make no trouble, so long as he was kept in drink money. Now and again, as Nigras will, he asked for more——"

"Blackmail?"

"That's too strong a word, Jordan. Our law firm was prepared to handle such demands. Later, I'm told, he boasted to the boy of his source of income——"

"Did Seth know Sam Randall wasn't his real father?"

"I suppose he picked up the truth somehow. Not that it troubled him; he was extremely fond of Randall."

"You just said you'd put the Randalls out of mind."

"So I had—but my lawyers sent me periodic statements."

"Did you order Sam Randall's death to stop his tongue?"

"Why should I concern myself with the ranting of a drunken darky? Sam Randall died by accident, under the wheel of his car."

"Seth thought otherwise."

"So he did. That's when I reached the end of my patience, and ordered him committed. There the matter ended—until a newsman named Jordan crossed our state line."

"You forgot them that easily—for ten whole years?"

"If you're a man of destiny, ten years is no longer than a busy afternoon. I'd seen how dangerous this mother and her son could be: it was my duty to put them out of mind. To rid myself of them completely, if they proved troublesome again."

"Then life and death mean nothing—when they're measured against your ambition?"

"Not my ambition, Jordan. My country's future."

Rick kept a tight rein on his tongue—and a weather eye on the door. He could hope he and Case were alone, now that the office had shut down. Yet it was quite possible a bodyguard still lingered (the whey-faced secretary—or Pollock, the ex-thug who served as butler). Even if Carol had used some pretext to remain next door, he could hardly ask her help—faced, as he was, by a mind that had crossed the border. Again, he recalled his last remark to Bob Partridge. If Walter Case had summoned him to prove his godlike status, he must listen to the end. He spoke carefully, fearful that a single word might push the man beyond the brink.

"Was it too great a shock to hear of Seth again?"

"That colored boy was dead and buried," said Case. "So was the woman. When they rose from the grave, I exorcised the ghosts."

"Why? Because an apostle of white purity could never admit his mulatto son was a genius?"

"Again we've blundered into sentiment, Jordan. Mulatto offspring are an inevitable by-product of our culture."

"But not for a man of destiny."

"I'll admit the difference. Now I'm about to take over my state, I can afford no stain on my record."

"I'm beginning to see why you were so anxious to keep me out of Valley."

"So long as the Randalls accepted the *status quo,* I was

prepared to ignore them. Unfortunately, that state of affairs couldn't last forever. The boy *was* talented. It was only a question of time before someone uncovered that talent and made him famous." Case leaned across the desk, with real concern. "Please don't reproach yourself, as the unwitting cause of his destruction——"

"You were always ready to strike, then?"

"They'd been found wanting ten years ago, Jordan. I couldn't risk a repeat performance. Nor could I permit the boy to rise above his station. Once he'd become a national figure, his whole past would have come to light. Such things are inevitable."

"So you ordered the parsonage fire——"

"Just as I've ordered a statewide manhunt, now that a maniac has escaped from Valley Hospital. All day long, I've waited for word of his death. He's bound to be hunted down by morning."

"How long have you had this power to decree executions?"

"Isn't it the privilege of every leader in history?"

"Don't you fear exposure?"

"Not within my own boundaries—where I control both the courts and the police. I'm making myself Governor in the next primary. From then on, I'll use my power openly."

"Why have you given me this blueprint—when you know I'm dedicated to exposing you?"

"For the best of reasons," said Case. "Even though we're enemies, I respect your intelligence. In your book, I'm a tyrant: so be it. I've shown you how tyranny can succeed, how it will become the language of tomorrow——"

"Will being Governor content you?"

"That's only a beginning. Already, I've agents in each of our Deep South states, working to spread my influence. When that bloc comes under my leadership, I'll move in on the North——"

There was no further need for prompting. Immersed in his vision, hypnotized by the purr of his own voice, Walter

Case forgot his visitor as he rehearsed his strategy. Group would be pitted against group, he said, race against race. When he had proved that one-man rule could succeed in the South, its success was assured elsewhere. Eventually, since government from strength could not fail to enrich its backers, its appeal would prove irresistible.

"How old are you, Case?"

The flow of verbiage ceased. For the first time, the man's eyes narrowed venomously, as the unwelcome thought sank home.

"I'm still in my fifties. I've time enough."

"What of the Soviet Union? Will you make peace there, or do you plan to rule the world?"

Case weighed the question with perfect composure. "I'll make peace, pro tem, with their current leader. *Real* peace, not an uneasy truce. America, for the first time in its history, will speak with a single voice—my own. Even Moscow must respect my power."

"Is such a take-over possible here? In a country as diverse as ours, can you persuade one hundred and eighty million citizens to do your bidding?"

"As I've told you, I'll persuade some, and coerce others. Most men can be bought. Give me five more years— ten at most. I'll destroy every man who dares to fight back—as easily as I've destroyed the Randalls."

"In a democracy?"

"America is a democracy only in name. Such experiments are doomed in the future. Most men are low-grade apes, who are happiest when they're taking orders. The Communist machine has proved that in our time. The Case machine will prove it here."

"I've asked you once why you've told me everything. Isn't it time you answered?"

Case leaned forward within the glass half-moon of his desk, and his smile was almost kind. "I've already complimented your intelligence, Jordan. Try using it. At the start, I warned you that this interview could never see print."

"Suppose I ask Bob to use it regardless?"

"I'll deny every word, of course. Just as I'll deny the preposterous canard that I fathered a son on a mulatto wench thirty years ago———"

"We've proof of that, at least."

"Print and be damned then. No one will believe such a lie about Walter Case. Ask your television sponsors to give me air time to call me the first all-American dictator. You'll lose your contract overnight."

"Don't be too sure of that. My contract permits me to say what I like."

"You can't say *that*, on a national hookup controlled by advertisers. Your New York paper will kill the story, for the same reasons———"

"Suppose you're mistaken?"

"My lawyers will bring the usual libel suits, which you'll be sure to lose. *I'll* shrug the whole thing off—and proceed as before. Who in this great, prosperous country of ours would accept such a bogey-man as real? You'd be laughed off the air waves———"

"I'm still asking why you've told me."

"For your own good, Jordan. I admire your spirit, even when it's wasted on a lost cause. Break your lances elsewhere in future, and leave me to my destiny. I'll see to it that you're spared—when the day of reckoning comes."

"D'you think I'd go on living in *your* America?"

"Believe me, you'll find no other place to hide."

The two men sat face to face a moment more, like spent antagonists who could summon no further blows. Rick got to his feet at last. Case did not speak as the visitor left his office—but the madman's chuckle that pursued him was more damning than a curse.

At street level Rick sat for a while before an untasted Scotch and soda in the bar across the way from the Case Building, watching the last workers depart for the night.

He did not stir when Carol King emerged, to enter a waiting bus that was decked with Confederate battle flags and jammed with a twittery aviary of females. The van-

guard of a dozen such vehicles, it paused to take on a
load of passengers, then roared off in the direction of the
University and the Stadium. Each bus carried a side banner, announcing that it was a transport for the Daughters
of the Constitution, a militant female counterpart of the
White Citizens' Council, already primed to cheer as loudly
as its menfolk, when the first recruit marched up the steps
of the inevitable flag-draped platform to join the Knights
of Freedom.

Carol, he could see, was anything but happy at joining
such company. She entered the first bus with a frozen
smile, and Rick's own spirits dropped a notch lower when
he recalled the sorry part he was forcing her to play. A
part which, like his own, had been barren of results so far
and promised even less. Since Walter Case had made her
promise to attend the outing, she'd had no choice except
to go through the motions of loyalty, in the hope that her
own role might play a small part in unmasking her uncle's
insane plan to turn a quiet corner of the South into a
political and racial battleground. And even though the
conviction of defeat was growing on the man she loved, as
he sipped the now-tasteless drink, he had no right to call
her back.

Ten minutes later, a familiar dead-black limousine
glided to a stop at the side entrance of the Case Building,
visible through a fly-specked window just around the corner from the bar, where Rick was sitting. The industrialist
emerged promptly; neatly precise in every motion, he
plunged for the back seat without glancing to the left or
right. In fact, Walter Case could have been any one of ten
thousand similar executives, hurrying to his own fireside
after a day of honest toil, his bank balance healthy with
black-ink entries and his conscience at rest.

Reluctant to return to the *Times-News* Building and
confess to Bob Partridge that he was as powerless to stop
Walter Case with words—spoken or written—as he was
with the television camera, Rick ordered another Scotch.
But before he could taste it, another man emerged from

the side door of the Case Building. As he headed for a black Volkswagen parked down the street, Rick leaned forward to study him, his drink forgotten.

Though Rick had seen Walter Case's butler-bodyguard, Pollock, only once or twice before, and then very briefly, there was hardly any mistaking the battered, ex-boxer's mug. Pollock, who was quite alone, carried a small zippered bag, as if he were off for the afternoon. Puzzled that the great man's personal bodyguard had not accompanied him to the station, Rick was even more perplexed when he saw Pollock shoehorn himself into the black Volkswagen and drive off—in the opposite direction from the one Case and his entourage had taken leading to the Stadium.

Suddenly, the most likely explanation of Pollock's behavior hit Rick like a blow between the eyes, lifting him from his seat and sending him hurrying to one of the two telephone booths at the back of the bar.

"Mr. Partridge is not in, Mr. Jordan," the secretary who answered his call said. "He's at the Stadium directing the news coverage."

"Who's in charge there?"

"Mr. Judd is in Mr. Partridge's office."

"Ring him, please."

"Where are you, Rick?" Theo Judd came on the line. "I've been——"

"I'm at a bar across from the Case Building. Case just left—"

"I know. A prowl car is following him and reporting by radio."

"Pollock just left the building too—alone and carrying a zippered bag."

"So what? He's small fry."

"Did it ever occur to you that Walter Case wants you to think just that?"

"You mean—— Good God! Pollock's gone to plant another bomb!"

"And you can bet it will be timed to go off at the height

of the festivities at the University Stadium. Can you get the police to put out an all-points alarm and pick Pollock up before he blows up another school—a black one this time? It would make a fine climax to that bed-sheet orgy out there at the stadium."

"We'll get him," said Theo firmly. "Chief Brandon's on our side—even if the state police aren't. I'll take care of it."

"Get going then," said Rick. "I'll be down there as soon as I can get a taxi."

There was a taxi stand across the street in front of the Case Building, with a single cab waiting; the driver was leaning against the door smoking a cigarette. Rick was halfway across the street, when four men hurried out of the building and into the waiting taxi, their white robes bundled, not too skillfully, into a canvas carryall.

The cab roared off, leaving Rick standing at the curb, fuming with impatience; but spotting a call box for the cab-company phone on the wall of the building outside the door, he hurried over and lifted the receiver.

"Can I help you?" a female voice with a strong Southern accent asked.

"I'm at the Case Building cab stand. And I need a cab in a hurry."

"Sorry, sir. I can't promise——"

"Where the hell are all your taxis?"

"On the way to the Stadium, most of 'em. Wait a minute, one is just reporting in." There was a pause during which he could hear her talking on the radio, then she came back on the line. "A cab will be there in about ten minutes," she replied.

"But I'm in a hurry."

"Sorry, sir. Everybody seems to be going to the Stadium tonight."

"I'll wait."

When Rick hung up the phone, he could well believe the dispatcher was right. Even though it was barely dusk, the crisscross of floodlights above the not-too-distant Stadium had begun to resemble a man-made aurora borealis. Once again, he was oppressed with the conviction of futility that had assailed him ever since he'd seen Walter Case emerge from the closet, looking ten feet tall in his lifts and conical hood, and somehow as frightening as any bogeyman from his own childhood. Somewhere, too, unless the Central City police force was unusually vigilant, Pollock would soon be intent over the death machine he had carried out of the building in the zippered bag, preparing it with loving care for the moment when it would sow destruction all around it at the prearranged signal from his master.

The ten minutes until a battered cab came to a stop before the door of the tall building seemed more like an hour.

"Ten blocks!" the driver muttered when Rick gave him the address of the *Times-News* Building. "I had two chances to pick up a load for the Stadium on the way here."

"Five bucks says you can make it in five minutes," Rick told him, and the cab scratched away from the curb when the driver gunned the motor. They made it in four-and-a-half, and Rick gave the driver an extra dollar.

"I hope it ain't you all them cops are lookin' for, mister," said the driver. "Jeez! The whole city police force must be here."

Rick hadn't noticed that the *Times-News* Building was flanked with green-and-white sedans, or that a brace of patrolmen guarded the door, peremptorily shooing passersby on their way. But as he crossed the sidewalk tc the entrance, there was no escaping the air of tension that dominated the scene.

The sergeant stationed in the lobby thrust out a detaining arm as Rick moved toward the elevators.

"Sorry, sir! No visitors upstairs tonight."

"I'm Rick Jordan—on assignment."

The man gave him a closer look, then dropped his arm.

"You can go up, Mr. Jordan, but if I was you, I'd get the hell out of here as fast as I could."

"What's happened?" Rick asked but knew the answer before he heard it. Walter Case's butler-bodyguard could have had only one destination when he placed the zippered bag he was carrying in the black Volkswagen only minutes after his master had departed in state for the greatest moment in his life. Just one act could give tonight's performance the climax Walter Case had been building up to for weeks, the final proof that he was stronger than all of his opponents put together—the destruction of the edifice symbolizing the newspaper that was his strongest opponent.

"When did they catch Pollock?" Rick asked and saw the sergeant jerk up his head, his eyes suddenly alert with suspicion.

"How did you——"

"I saw Pollock leave the Case Building and phoned Mr. Judd. I should have known then where he was headed for but, like a damned fool, it didn't occur to me."

"We don't know yet how he got in, Mr. Jordan, but we will," said the policeman grimly. "As soon as Mr. Judd called for an all-points, everybody in uniform and out was looking for Pollock. We didn't have any trouble findin' him, either; he came walkin' out of here like he owned the place, with a grin on that ugly mug——"

"Did you say walking out?"

"Empty-handed. We've got the building swarming with officers, lookin' for something we don't even know how to recognize. And if you don't think that's a hell of an assign——"

Rick didn't hear the rest; he was racing for the nearest elevator. The car whisked him to the city-room floor without a stop; but even in the relative isolation of the elevator shaft, he already knew that activities at the newspaper itself had come to a virtual halt, the pulse of the presses in the basement stilled in midflight. When the elevator door opened and he plunged out, he wasn't at all surprised to see that the city room itself, normally a madhouse of chattering typewriters at this hour, was as empty as a tomb.

Theo Judd was talking on Bob Partridge's private wire, the camera bag that was almost a part of him lying on the corner of the desk. The fact that the door to the editor's office stood wide open was evidence enough that the *Times-News,* for the moment at least, had ceased to function—at all levels. Moving toward Bob's office, Rick paused to glance through the door to the wire room. The corner was usually a controlled beehive, shuttling copy to each desk in the city room; tonight, with each light glaring down from the low ceiling, it was a sweatbox in a nightmare.

Incredulously, Rick saw that Pollock was planted firmly in the witness chair while a detective stood over him, slapping him methodically. Just outside the cone of light silhouetting Pollock and the detective was a burly man in civilian clothing whom Rick identified as Chief Brandon, the head of the city police—the one outfit in the state that had, so far as was apparent, escaped Walter Case's magic wand of corruption.

"Speak up, you son-of-a-bitch!" said the detective. "You've been interrogated before, so you know what's coming. Spill your guts now and save yourself one hell of a headache."

Pollock shrugged and the detective hit him again. Behind Chief Brandon stood several other men in plainclothes, waiting their turn at the "interrogation".

"We know you brought a bomb in here, Pollock. And it makes sense that your boss plans to explode it as part of that war dance he's doing out at the Stadium." Chief Brandon spoke heavily from the shadows. "We're all going to stay here until you tell us where it is so, if you don't, you're going to be blown to hell with the rest of us. Why not save yourself while there's still time?"

Again Pollock shrugged and, when the Chief nodded, the detective gave him a slap that rocked the chair in which he was sitting. Although Rick knew he was witnessing police brutality, he felt no impulse to protest; for no brutality, police or otherwise, could be worse than what Walter Case had ordered for the woman he had loved, the woman who had borne him a genius in music for a son.

Theo Judd came to the door of Bob Partridge's office. "You took long enough getting here," he said to Rick. "What delayed you?"

"All the damned taxicabs were headed for the Stadium."

"It will be packed. And Walter Case is obviously planning to blast this building off its foundation as a climax."

"It would have helped if your police had caught Pollock before he planted the bomb."

"Nobody's perfect," said Theo. "One of the loading-platform men had been bribed to let Pollock in the back way. The police have him, but he doesn't know anything that would help locate the bomb."

"Pollock does, but you're not going to get it out of him."

"Chief Brandon figures he'll start to crack as the deadline approaches. But if you ask me, that's cutting it too close."

"Why are you staying then?"

Theo shrugged. "It's my job, but there's no reason for you to stay. By the way, New York has been calling you for the last past half-hour—somebody named Ormsbee."

"George Ormsbee, my producer."

The telephone rang, as if on cue, and Theo picked it up. "For you," he said, handing the receiver to Rick. "New York."

"Rick?" It was George. "What's going on down there?"

"All hell's about to break loose and a lot of us are liable to be going there in the middle of it. Who told you?"

"Somebody's putting pressure on the network to interrupt. Says what's happening down there will be the TV newsbreak of the century."

"It could be at that. Who called?"

"Nobody knows, but he got through to the network president. Net's been on my tail for the last half-hour, and all I could tell them was that you were there on the scene but hadn't said a damn thing."

"I've been busy——"

"The Net's fit to be tied and everybody's on my tail because you didn't let us know what's happening."

"Cool down, George. Maybe we can make something out of all this." An idea was beginning to form in Rick's mind, a vague pattern that he recognized as part of his reporter's instinct. The trouble was that it was still far from clear.

"Here's what we have so far." Tersely, Rick summed up the events of the past few days for the director in New York.

"You think this high panjandrum of the Knights of Freedom really means to blow up the *Times-News* Building?" George Ormsbee asked.

"I'd bet on it. It's like Case to find a way to pressure the network into covering the explosion, and he's got the power to do it."

"For God's sake, Rick! He's not the President."

"He just might be, if I don't stop him. And right now I don't have the faintest idea how to do it."

"The first thing you'd better do is get the hell out of that building. You've got less than an hour-and-a-half."

"What?"

"Whoever's been pressuring us up here even named the time he wants Net to interrupt—a few minutes before nine o'clock tonight. If I were down there like you are, I'd be sweating out every minute."

The developing instinct suddenly exploded into a full-fledged idea, and Rick felt his pulse spurt with the realization that the way to wreck Walter Case and his whole empire might well have been dropped right into his lap by George's last phrase, "sweating out."

"You still there, Rick?" Ormsbee's anxious voice sounded in the receiver.

"I'm here," said Rick. "Hang on a minute while I talk to Theo Judd."

Theo had crossed to the wire room but came running at Rick's call.

"Anything gained on that front?" Rick asked.

"Not a thing. Pollock would rather take his chances on living through the explosion than what Walter Case will do to him, if he tells where the bomb is."

"That's what I figured," said Rick. "Where are your TV-broadcasting facilities located? In this building?"

Theo shook his head. "They're out beside the Interstate Bypass, where the tower is. What's up?"

"No time to explain. Get Chief Brandon in here while I finish talking to George Ormsbee." He turned back to the phone. "Listen carefully, George. Do exactly as I tell you and don't waste time squawking. The *Times-News* TV cameras are at the Stadium getting ready to broadcast the big Knights of Freedom rally there on a local hookup of maybe a half-dozen stations. I'm going to have the station put their picture on the cable to you in New York about a quarter to nine. Keep it on a monitor where you can see everything that's happening, especially at nine o'clock."

"I need to tell the Net what it will be."

"If we're lucky, nothing—except a lot of damned fools running around in bed sheets. But no matter what happens, keep that cable open and your eyes on that monitor, ready to cut into the whole network without warning. Tell Net I'll be responsible. Got it?"

"Yes," said George. "Now, for God's sake, get out of that building!"

"I've got a few things to do first. If they work out like I think they will, I'll be as safe here as I would be in a church—maybe safer, with five hundred Knights of Freedom after me, boiling-mad."

Rick turned from the telephone to see Chief Brandon standing by the desk, a frown on his rugged features. "You're not running the Central City police force, Jordan, and you're not the mayor," he said. "I'm not used to being ordered around."

"Sorry, Chief. I just found out when that bomb's set to explode."

"What?"

"Walter Case has been pressuring the network to preempt with a special news broadcast at nine o'clock."

"How could he——"

"Money, and power, can do almost anything, Chief. Tell me: do you have a portable polygraph and somebody to operate it?"

"The machine is at police headquarters," said the stocky police chief. "Our technician is off-duty, but he can be here with it in thirty minutes."

"Better make it twenty—or less," said Rick. "We've got maybe an hour before that thing is set to go off."

"All right—but if this is some reporter's stunt, you'll answer to me. And don't go away before I get back."

Chief Brandon was gone only a few minutes, and Rick used them to brief Theo Judd on what he wanted done at the TV station.

"There won't be any trouble," Theo assured him. "Mike Galvin runs that station like he owned it. He'd cover his own funeral, if he thought it was news."

"All right, Jordan," said Chief Brandon when he came back. "What's this all about?"

"You know how a polygraph—a lie detector—works, don't you?"

"Sure. Every high-school student knows it measures the physiological responses to emotion by making a graphic chart of the suspect's blood pressure, heart rate and respiratory movements."

"Does your technician measure the galvanic skin response, too? With electrodes attached to the palms of the hands to detect unusual sweating?"

"He can. It isn't always necessary."

"We can't take any chances; this has to be a complete test."

"On Pollock?" Theo Judd asked.

"Who else?"

"But we already know he's lying, or at least he isn't telling the truth by not telling anything."

"That's right, Jordan." Chief Brandon's tone was still suspicious. "What's the gimmick?"

"My director in New York just gave it to me over the phone by saying, if he were in my place, he'd be sweating it out," Rick explained. "Pollock can control his tongue and keep from telling us anything, but he can't control the autonomic—automatic—responses of his body. Your technician will get him connected up to the polygraph and ask him a lot of questions about where the bomb is. When he hits the right spot, Pollock will have a mental picture of that thing exploding——"

"And it's bound to cause a response on the polygraph." The police chief's tone had changed to one of conviction. "That's clever thinking."

"If it was me, the damned pens would jump off the graph paper recording the responses." Theo Judd mopped his face with his handkerchief.

"What we need to do while we wait is think of places the bomb might be," said Chief Brandon.

"My guess would be somewhere in the central core of the building," said Rick. "And low down."

"Pollock wasn't free inside the structure more than five minutes, and we caught him at the street level," said Brandon. "That's why my men are working upward from below looking for the contraption."

The telephone on the desk jangled sharply and Theo picked it up, listened briefly and started reaching for his camera with his other hand.

"We're on our way," he said into the phone as he hung up and turned to Rick. "That was Carol; she found out that Bob's got Seth Randall hidden in cur radio-TV truck at the stadium. Seth will talk to you there, Rick, but nobody else."

"I'll send you both in a police car," said Chief Brandon. "And don't worry about the bomb. Once we get Pollock hooked up to the lie detector, he'll tell us the truth about where it is—without saying a word."

14

"You KNEW Seth was at the stadium all the time, didn't you?" Rick accused Theo Judd angrily, as the police car, siren screaming and warning lights blinking, screeched around the corner and headed for the stadium.

"Bob's been handling that; he only let me in on it a couple of hours ago."

"Why didn't you call me then?"

"Bob's been letting you play your own hand, Rick. You agreed to let him play his."

"That's true."

"He's got to destroy Case now or lose the opportunity, maybe forever. You had your chance—with the interview this afternoon."

"And muffed it," Rick admitted bitterly.

"Maybe not. The intercom on Case's desk was open while he was boasting to you about what he planned to do. Carol said to tell you she took shorthand notes on it."

"Good girl."

"I could have told you that a long time ago. Seth told Bob he had no trouble escaping from the hospital, as the reporter in Eldon surmised. He kept the radio on in the laundry truck he was driving and when he heard, maybe forty miles later, that they were after him, he abandoned it and started walking. He was picked up by a Negro man and his wife from Michigan who dropped him off at Linden Grove. It's a Negro recreation ground at the edge of Central City, so it was simple for him to mix in with the picnickers until he got a chance to call Bob. The TV truck picked him up, and he's safe and sound in our trailer at the stadium."

"Seth was mad to come this close to Walter Case. His luck can't hold forever."

"Bob took no chances there, either. He's equipped Seth with a Knights of Freedom robe and a phony identification card; we've got a lot of our own people at the rally, too—under cover. If Sheriff Colt's men get suspicious and close in on our truck, Seth can always duck under the hood."

"He'd be still safer at police headquarters in town with Chief Brandon to protect him."

"Maybe you can smuggle him back later. Right now Bob has to know what's on Seth's mind so we can get the story written for the presses."

"They've been stopped. Remember?"

"Only until Pollock's sweating palms betray him. Fifteen minutes after that little cache of nitroglycerin is defused by Brandon's bomb experts, we'll have our rewrite men back at the typewriters. Carol's stenographic notes and whatever Seth tells you will be part of the early-morning edition. And by that time, Walter Case will be the one who's sweating."

"One more thing," said Rick as the police car rocketed toward the brightly lit stadium. "Was Seth armed?"

"No. Bob made sure of that."

"But he's there to kill Case—he *must* be. What other reason could he have for risking his life, when he could be over the state line now and home free?"

'Don't ask me," said Theo as the car entered the stadium area. "Jesus, what a crowd!"

The vignettes flashing past the window of the police car, as it slowed to negotiate its way through the crowd to the *Times-News* radio-TV truck, were as vivid as a surrealist nightmare: the massed, heraldic banners that ringed the velvet-soft football field; the white-and-scarlet robes that seemed to go on forever; the blur of spectators, tiered by thousands in the high-decked Stadium; the bunting-draped speakers' platform with the inevitable twenty-foot cross waiting to be ignited at the climax of the ceremony; and the tall figure in white-and-scarlet before it, casting a shadow of evil across the field, belying the usual meaning of the cross—all of it formed a blatant threat Rick Jordan knew he would never forget.

The south parking lot, placed to facilitate crowd management on football weekends, commanded an excellent view of the teeming, phantom-haunted field. The foursquare vehicle of the radio-TV truck, with its trailer, web of cables and elevated platform upon which stood the cameras with the dish antenna of the microwave transmitter, was at the very edge of the lot. The truck faced a gate that opened onto the field, and through it, the Knights of Freedom, regimented by platoons, still poured beneath the goalposts toward their positions around the speakers' platform.

The formal grouping was not quite complete, even though the speaker's voice, magnified by thousands of decibels, rolled from the loudspeakers and echoed eerily from nearby university buildings. A bit to one side, just outside the eight-foot wire fence that divided lot from field, stood a group of men in yellow-white robes. Several hundred strong, they pressed against the fence to watch the proceedings within. Some were hooded, but a few stood with heads still uncovered. These, Rick gathered, were the recruits to the Knights, whose formal induction would climax tonight's outing.

At that distance, the rantings of the speaker on the platform, though clear enough, seemed only an obbligato to the marching pageant. Rick noted it but dimly as he followed Theo Judd to the steps of the truck. The fact that Seth Randall was behind the locked trailer door was still hard to grasp, despite Carol's assurance to Theo on the telephone that he was waiting there.

"I'm going to see if I can find Bob," said Theo as he pressed a key into Rick's hand. "Incidentally, Seth knows that Dick Sloane was only Rick Jordan with a suntan. Bob figured it would save a lot of explanations."

At the trailer door, Rick turned the key in the lock and whisked quickly inside. He had expected a dimly lit interior, a fugitive crouched at bay. Instead, the lights were on above the emergency control panel, and the small monitors at one side showed two pictures of the events outside as seen by the TV cameras. One was centered on the speakers' platform where a tall figure in white-and-scarlet was shouting into a microphone before the outline of the cross. The spotlights centered on the speaker were placed so as not to shine directly on the cross but from behind it, casting a massive shadow of evil across the grass of the football field. The second camera was roving, panning the crowd for newsworthy close-ups.

Seth lay at his ease on a cot, seemingly as emotionless as a trained fighter, catching a catnap before his turn in the ring. A yellow-white recruit's robe, with a matching hood, was folded neatly at the cot's foot. More than any detail, it gave the scene its air of muted fantasy.

"Thanks for coming, Mr. Jordan," said Seth, as Rick checked the spring lock to make sure it could not be opened from outside without a key. "I'm glad to meet you a second time. When I learned the truth, I think I had half-guessed it already. Only Rick Jordan——or Aladdin—— could have done so much for me so soon."

"Believe me, Seth, if I'd had any notion how things would end——"

"Don't say you'd have left well enough alone. You were quite right to persuade me to make that recording. And even to ask my mother to plead for my release." Seth's tone was still oddly remote, his patient smile unchanged. "Above all, you mustn't blame yourself for the result. The choice was ours. Both of us knew the risks we'd run."

"Why didn't you tell me?"

"We couldn't betray my father. That was our bargain.

Of course you know by now that Walter Case is really my father."

"I've known for several hours—although I suspected it before."

"It was a bad bargain, Mr. Jordan—one we should never have made. We settled for second-best. Once a person has done that, he's lost his dignity—and dignity's a precious thing. But at least the problem's in the open now. The question now is, how do we solve it?"

Rick took the chair before the small emergency control panel, outside the cone of light from the ceiling fixture. Rushing against time to save Seth Randall, he had expected rage or blank despair—anything but this serene philosopher's air.

"Why did you come here, Seth? To kill Case?"

"Yes, Mr. Jordan. I felt he deserved death. But halfway to Central City, I realized that his death would really solve nothing. What he needs is forgiving."

"Forgiving?"

"Why not? Next to kindness, forgiveness is always in short supply in our imperfect world. Couldn't my father use a little?"

"He killed your mother. Not with his own hand—but he ordered it."

"I know that, Mr. Jordan."

"You *can't* forgive him. He's beyond redemption."

"No man is beyond redemption: I've learned that much at Valley Hospital from Dr. Moore. Not even a sick soul like Walter Case."

"The state troopers have orders to shoot you on sight, as an escaped maniac. Did you know that, too?"

"Of course. I was careful to cover my tracks. It wasn't too hard."

Rick felt as if he were battering a stone wall; yet, at all costs, he knew he must break up this mood of abnegation, if there was to be any chance of saving Seth from the certain death his own father had decreed for him.

"You said you came here to kill a man, Seth. That I

can understand. What are your present plans—now that you've changed your mind?"

"I haven't quite perfected them. I hope you'll help me there."

"Perhaps I can. We're ready to trap Walter Case at last. When this mass orgy is ended, there'll be warrants out for his arrest, on several counts. Murder in Eldon is one; Bob Partridge is ready to start printing the confession of the men who killed your mother and set the fires on Case's orders, as soon as we can be sure a bomb in the *Times-News* Building doesn't explode."

"So that's to be the big climax. They've got a pro-Knight radio commentator broadcasting directly from the stadium. I was listening when you arrived; he's been boasting about a big event."

Rick glanced at his watch. "It's set to happen in a little over fifteen minutes—unless Chief Brandon's men find the bomb."

"Pray God they do, or my father will have many more deaths on his conscience."

"Conscience?" Rick snapped, his own control breaking momentarily. "How can you say he has a conscience?"

"My mother loved him once, Mr. Jordan," Seth's tone was mildly reproaching. "That's proof enough for me that there's something in my father worth saving."

"I'm afraid the people he tried to kill tonight can hardly be asked to forgive and forget, even if the bomb doesn't go off. There's too much at stake to let him escape the punishment he deserves."

"I agree, Mr. Jordan. Walter Case must come before the law and answer for his crimes, but I will take no personal vengeance. Somehow, I must make him see why. Him—and all the other merchants of hate."

"He's past understanding, Seth. He wouldn't even hear you."

"Isn't it worth proving that a black man can still forgive a white?"

Rick had begun to sense the Negro's purpose, and the

magnitude of the risk he had run so deliberately. Knowing Seth's life might depend on his next words, he shifted his attack.

"Stop being a saint for a moment, and face the facts," he said bluntly. "Case means to kill you before morning, if he can track you down. We must get you out of here. There's protection waiting in Central City——"

"I don't pretend to be a saint, Mr. Jordan. Danger doesn't matter, if I can deliver my message."

"What message? To err is human, to forgive divine?"

"Walter Case killed my mother rather than acknowledge me. Now you say he'll kill me, too, because he fears me. Won't it help a little, if I prove his fears are groundless? That his only enemy is himself?"

Seth had risen from the couch like a man possessed. Striding the length of the trailer with shining eyes, he lifted both arms in a gesture of absolution—as though he were rehearsing an entrance on a far larger stage.

He's out of his mind, thought Rick. *While this trance is on him, there's nothing he won't do to prove his point.*

Searching for some way to reach Randall's rational mind, Rick suddenly saw what might be a possible answer—a portable tape recorder with battery power and a long-cord microphone lying on the floor of the trailer beside the cot on which Seth had been lying. Aloud, Rick spoke carefully.

"There's a recorder right here," he said. "Would you make a statement? Something I might use in my next column?"

Lifting the recorder to his knee, he held out the microphone.

It's only a subterfuge, he thought. *Still, it may break his trance. At the worst, it might delay matters a little longer.*

"I've already recorded my thoughts, Mr. Jordan; the message is quite brief. I hope you will edit it as little as possible when you use it." Seth stood above Rick now, smiling at the reporter's bewilderment. "I made the recording while I waited for you. Play it back and see if you approve; then use it as you wish."

Seth's hand touched the switch and, as the reels began to turn, his voice filled the trailer. Listening, Rick didn't notice that he had moved back into the shadows.

A new commandment I give unto you, that you love one another; as I have loved you, that you also love one another. By this shall all men know that you are my disciples, if you have love one to another.

Those are Jesus' words. What can I add to them? Two thousand years ago, they gave new hope to the world. Their meaning was never truer than today.

What can I say to *you*, Walter Case—now that the whole South knows your religion is not love but hate?

Tomorrow you must stand at the bar of justice to answer for the murder of my mother. You have planned to kill me too, because you cannot bear to call me your son. Perhaps we can never really meet, in this South you would remake in your image. Perhaps this is the only message you will ever have from me. Try to believe me when I say *Father, I forgive you.*

You can never ask as much from your fellowman. Tomorrow he will doom and damn you. But the son you would grind into dust forgives you with all his heart.

When there is so much hate in the world, one man's forgiveness may seem little enough, but it is a beginning. If more of us learn to forgive one another, is it too much to hope that we may someday love one another, too?

The voice died and the tape spun on in silence. Bemused as he was by the strange message, Rick didn't look up until he had switched off the machine. Only then did he realize that the shadowed corner where Seth had stood was empty, and the trailer door stood open. As he rushed to the threshold, he saw too, that the yellow-white recruit's robe was gone.

In his haste to reach the parking lot, Rick tripped on the bottom step of the trailer. An outthrust arm saved him from falling, and he found himself staring blankly into the face of Theo Judd.

"I was coming to get you," said the photographer. "Walter Case just started his spiel and Bob——"

"Have you seen Seth?"

"Wasn't he in the trailer with you?"

"He left a few minutes ago, while I was listening to a tape recording he had made. I'm sure he's under a robe——"

"So are three hundred other recruits. You'll never find him."

A shout had risen from the field. Climbing to the mudguard of the communications truck, Rick saw that the gate had been opened. Uniformed police were checking the recruits' cards, one by one, as the long file of candidates continued to move in for their induction. Understanding Seth's strategy now, and knowing he could do nothing to stop him, Rick dropped to the ground again— staggering a little, like a man shaking off a nightmare.

"Did you say Seth has a joiner's card?" he asked Theo.

"A doctored one. But he'll be safe enough, as long as he stays under that hood."

"Not if he reaches the platform."

"It's too late to stop him now." Theo looked at his watch. "Five minutes from now we'll know whether they got anything out of Pollock. I don't know whether I can stand it."

The last of the yellow-white file had just gone through the gate. Marshaled by white-robed Knights, the neophytes began to move through the serried ranks. On the bunting-draped platform, Walter Case, magnificent in his scarlet masquerade, was rising to the climax of his harangue. A few moments more, and the first of those recruits would mount the platform for the ceremonial laying-on of hands. If Seth were among them, Rick knew he was helpless. Even if he were somehow able to recognize the Negro among the neophytes and had stopped him, it would have meant certain death, with Sheriff Colt's deputies standing guard at the gate.

"Where's the best place to watch, Theo?" he asked.

"The press box. But you'll have to go alone. Bob wants all the pictures we can get."

Racing up the ramp leading to the press box, Rick found time to glance at the sweep-second hand of his watch and see that several minutes still remained before nine o'clock. Whatever happened now, the most important thing was that Theo's lens together with those of the TV cameras on their elevated platforms were about to frame a man's martyrdom. No power on earth could turn Seth Randall from his purpose now—or the inevitable last scene of the tragedy.

One thing only Rick Jordan could, and must, do. Having set in motion the dramatic forces that were meeting here head-on—by choosing to investigate Dr. Peter Moore and Valley Hospital weeks before—he must sear the final scenes of the horrendous denouement into his brain so indelibly that the picture would still be vivid when he sat down to describe it for his own column. He must, in effect, record the last act of the tragedy for the world to see in words and pictures that could not be denied.

Walter Case was well into his diatribe by the time Rick found a place at the back of the press box. Though it was jammed with reporters, all eyes were on the central figure of the bizarre drama, and Rick was thankful not to be recognized. Bob Partridge was once again the target for the speaker's scorn. But Rick was sure Walter Case's eyes were watching the clock on the podium before which he stood, even as his voice spewed hatred and venom and he windmilled the scarlet pennons of his robe, pounding every word home with clenched fists in a gesture of mailed power.

"Fellow-citizens, the Knights of Freedom were organized to protect you from the enemy. His fortress stands in our very midst—in Central City. You can see the building from every seat in this stadium. Once again I name the villain—Bob Partridge, and his nigger-loving *Times-News!*"

Involuntarily, Rick's eyes swung to the newspaper building, its tower a brightly lit beacon dominating the skyline. It was hard to believe that in a little more than a minute, the great building might start disintegrating from the explosion of a charge of nitroglycerin in its vitals. Even harder to believe was that the absurdly posturing figure in scarlet far below on the platform, dominating the field with its massed ranks of hooded figures, would literally have pulled the trigger.

"There, like a king on his throne,. sits the obscene vulture who calls himself Pártridge—croaking his song of evil. His very breath pollutes all that is precious in our Southern heritage. But I say to you that his days are numbered, that God's fist will strike down both Partridge and his lies!"

The volume on the loudspeakers was suddenly increased, and the voice of the orator, its pitch rising steadily, swept the stands like a hurricane.

"I say to you that we—the Knights of Freedom and agents of a God who meant this country to be ruled by white Americans—will level this fortress of falsehood! Yea, even as a vengeful Jehovah destroyed Jericho—till the walls came tumbling down."

The hurricane of rhetoric ceased abruptly and silence clamped down on the stadium. The speaker's timing had been accurate to the second; the sweep hand of Rick's watch was just touching the hour of nine. As the red-draped arm was lifted to point to the open end of the stadium and the brightly lit tower of the skyscraper that was silhouetted there like a beacon, Rick found himself holding his breath. In response to the hypnotic gesture, spectators and Knights alike were facing south to look toward Central City and the *Times-News* Building with the tall electric sign spelling out its name.

Only when a full minute had passed and the great building still remained in its place, intact, did Rick Jordan dare to breathe again. His desperate gamble for the life of a skyscraper had paid off, when Pollock had failed to control the physiological responses of his own emotions recorded on the polygraph. Walter Case, however, whipping his audience to a calculated frenzy, had possessed no way of knowing it. Confident that the timing in Central City would match his own, he had expected his prophecy to be punctuated by a blast powerful enough to rock the Stadium to its foundations—even at this distance—as the skyscraper was disintegrated into rubble. But in Case's twisted mind, the blast would have done far more than wipe out the last threat to his rule: by its sheer terror, it would have forged the final bond between leader and led.

The silence grew. Rick waited for the first sign of doubt—a single snicker, he knew, could break Case's spell beyond all mending. Instead, the speaker rolled smoothly with the missed cue. A flailing motion of his arm brought a snarl of trumpets from the loudspeakers as he strutted, rather than walked, to the far edge of the platform, and held out both hands, shoulder-high, in a royal gesture of welcome.

"Enough of Bob Partridge!" he shouted into the microphone—and only Rick, watching from the press box, could guess that Case was improvising wildly. "Enough of a man whose days are numbered! Tonight, as a fitting climax to this rally, I welcome our new recruits to our ranks. Let the candidates approach the platform so I may induct them one by one."

Rick leaned forward sharply: this was the moment he had feared. Hal Stacey, he saw, had just leaped the barrier to train his Leica on the platform. Theo Judd was close behind, jostling his rival for space. Somewhere in the background, a band blared out the inevitable "Dixie"; but the music was lost in the cheers as the head of the yellow-white line came into view.

The recruits marched in single file and the massed ranks of the Knights formed a wide lane to let them pass. Around the stand, the scarlet ring of guards fell back a dozen paces. When the first marcher reached the steps of the platform, a tall, robed figure (whom Rick recognized as the Grand Chaplain) blessed him with an uplifted hand, even as his free arm propelled him on his way.

Once he had gained the platform, the neophyte dropped to one knee before the Leader, who administered a silent laying-on of hands, then graciously waved him toward a standing microphone. Here, each ex-recruit—as the first act of a full-fledged member—shouted a slogan of his own choosing, then left the platform via a second stair, to join the ranks in the cleared space below.

The words—all of them brief—made up in vigor for their basic sameness. Most of the new-made Knights contented themselves with a shouted *Keep the South Pure!* Others mouthed a snatch of the Leader's own oration. Still others drew applause from the stands with their version of the rebel yell made famous in the Civil War.

For a few wild moments, as the line dwindled, Rick dared to hope that Seth had used this easy escape route. Then, as the last figure took the Chaplain's ersatz blessing and mounted the steps with a slow, almost fateful tread, he sensed that father and son were about to meet at last.

The suspicion deepened to a certainty when Case raised both arms (a trifle wearily, after almost three hundred such gestures) in a salute of welcome—and Seth, unlike the others, accepted the accolade without bending his knee. Even before he turned to the microphone, something in his ramrod-still aloofness brought a hush to the watchers. The Leader recoiled a step—but he made no attempt to interfere, as the last of his recruits adjusted the microphone to his own height and bent above it. Once Seth was positive that he had the ear of the whole assembly, he did not prolong the suspense.

"Father, I forgive you!" he cried—and the shout rang into the farthest reaches of the stadium.

Rick's ear, familiar with Seth's voice and tuned to nuances, caught the intentional slur in the accent. This, unmistakably, was a Negro voice. Even before Seth dropped his hood, every spectator had recognized that fact. The tone, like the gesture, had been deliberate—but the four words of the pardon were a challenge, a ringing invitation to Walter Case to drop his own disguise.

I forgive you, Father! May God forgive you, too!"

The spell broke abruptly, with the explosion of Hal Stacey's flash bulb. At that same instant, a babble of voices rose from the field and joined with others in the stands. In the press box, necks craned forward as a score of men fumbled for their notebooks.

"Who smuggled in the Negro?"

"It's Randall! I saw his picture in the *Sun.*"

"Who gave *him* a sheet?"

"Who's he claiming for his father?"

The roar from the stands drowned out the excited babble of the reporters. Forgetting his wish to remain anonymous, Rick pressed forward to the press-box rail. He was in time to see a beefy, white-clad figure (who could only have been Sheriff Colt) charge toward the platform steps—to fall headlong, when another robed Knight thrust a foot between his legs. Fistfights were starting to break out on the field, as spontaneously as brushwood fires in a drought. A roar of *Keep the South Pure!* was topped instantly in a surf of booing; Bob Partridge's vigilantes, it seemed, had proved useful after all.

It was only when the Grand Leader himself held up both hands for silence—and the gesture was backed by a blast of sound from the loudspeakers—that the babble stilled.

"Fellow-Knights! This man is an escaped maniac!" he

shouted into the podium microphone. "Deal with him, before he harms me! Kill him!"

By some miracle, the silence still held after that wildly bellowed order. Seth, at the microphone, did not stir, and something in his refusal to panic gave the lie to Case's shrill accusation. Significantly, not one man in the hired bodyguard had responded to their master's command. Even the sheriff, his hood knocked askew by the fall, did not rise from hands and knees as Seth spoke again into the microphone.

"I forgive you, Father. Can't you be done with hate?"

"Kill him, I said!" Walter Case screamed.

Anchored at the press-box rail, Rick Jordan breathed a short prayer: the next echo from the field would tell the story, that much was certain. For no reason the watchers could fathom, a defenseless Negro had just been threatened with death. The fact that Seth remained quietly at the standing microphone, while Case continued to harangue the audience, was only an added bewilderment.

"Kill, you fools! What do I pay you for?"

The bodyguard still made no move. Maddened by their refusal to obey his order, Case rushed headlong at Seth and wrested the microphone from his hands, forcing him to step back to the foot of the towering—and still unlit—cross. His voice magnified a thousandfold by the idiot loudspeakers, Case repeated the command to kill; it shocked each eardrum in the stands, and even sent waves of revulsion through the massed white platoons below.

Seth, making no move to cling to the one support the platform afforded, stood eye to eye with his father for that final moment. There was no mistaking the mutual recognition now. It was also glaringly evident that Case was hysterical with fear and hate.

The stadium was deathly still when the Grand Leader of the Knights whipped the automatic from his robe and fired, at point-blank range. The press box was a hundred yards from ground level, but Rick heard the thud clearly, as the bullet struck home in Seth's body. And, like every spectator in the stands and on the field, he knew that Case (facing an unarmed man who made no threats toward him) had killed in cold blood, for the sheer need of killing.

Seth's features were contorted with agony and his body started to sag but, even in death, he sought some contact with the living. As he reached out in a plea for help, his clutching fingers closed on the Leader's robe and, ignoring that final call for help from his own son, Walter Case jammed the automatic against Seth's dying body and pulled the trigger twice in rapid succession.

The bullets, thudding home at a higher level because Seth's body had been sagging forward, literally picked it up and slammed it back against the cross, at whose foot he'd been standing. Since they had entered the body at the higher level, the second and third bullets struck home in the plexus of nerves controlling Seth's arms. And as his body hung momentarily against the upright, they were suddenly extended in an involuntary gesture of absolution—oddly like, Rick thought suddenly, the gesture Seth had made in the trailer before he'd tried to hand him the microphone. At the same moment, the hand that had clutched at his father's robe was clenched by the powerful involuntary contraction of dying muscles, and the fabric of the robe was torn away. Stripping the Grand Leader of his disguise, as he instinctively backed away, Seth's final convulsion revealed Walter Case for what he was—a stumpy Napoleon on elevators.

Curiously enough, the cross that towered behind the platform became the next actor in this macabre dance of death. Set to be ignited as the last recruit left the stage, it hissed into flame at the very moment of Case's unmasking, sparking the sudden fury that erupted in field and stands.

Still at the rail, hearing the tide of curses in the press-box, Rick could not avert his eyes from the scene below.

The involuntary contraction of Seth Randall's arm and shoulder muscles had lasted but an instant, though long enough, he hoped, to be recorded by Theo Judd's camera and those providing the television coverage. He heard shouting all around him, and realized that his own voice was part of the din, baying for Walter Case's blood.

As Seth's body began to pitch forward again, his robe caught on a splinter projecting from the upright of the cross, making it teeter eerily above the drama of death being played out below. Rick noticed that Bob's vigilantes were no longer needed to stir a riot at ground level. The fistfights that had preceded Walter Case's act of murder were as nothing to the maelstrom of renunciation that swept the gridiron. Recruits and veterans alike swarmed toward the exits, many stripping off their robes as they ran. The rout changed to panic, as the mob clogged the ramps.

Case, still on the platform, howling his meaningless stream of rhetoric, seemed unaware that he had lost his audience. One of Rick's few coherent mental pictures, after the shock of the bullets thudding home into Seth Randall's body, was of Sheriff Colt, shouting to his employer to save himself. Seconds later the mob had swept Colt aside, along with the rest of the bodyguard, in its frantic efforts to quit the field. A jerry-built underpinning supporting the speaker's platform splintered under the press of bodies, just before the platform itself collapsed. While behind it, the flaming cross had started to totter even more wildly on its moorings.

It has Hal Stacey who first told Rick the game was up. Scrambling wildly to get in the clear, Hal emerged from the wreckage of the platform, losing his Leica in his attempts to escape and making no attempt to retrieve it. Theo Judd's footwork had been better, however; lingering a moment more, he lifted his camera to snap Walter Case one last time.

On the steps, as he sought to reach Case and drag him

to safety, Sheriff Colt roared a final warning. Then he, too, was scuttling for his life—as thirty feet of blazing pitch pine crashed upon the collapsing platform, pinning Walter Case across the dead body of his son.

15

CAROL HAD BEEN fighting hysteria when Rick drove her to *Times-News* in Theo's station wagon. She had won the battle by a narrow margin before he left her in Bob Partridge's office suite and rushed to his own manifold tasks.

Now, with a promise of dawn at the windows, she sat quietly beneath the droplight beside her chair, scanning the front page of the special postscript edition. Watching her from the doorway, Rick was sure that she had risen above the terror of the night. He moved forward to put an arm around her. Neither of them spoke, while they surveyed the product of Bob's labors—and his own.

The stories beneath the banner headline were now complete. From Eldon, the arsonists had confessed to Mary Randall's murder, naming Walter Case as the instigator. The story from the wire room, where Pollock had been interrogated—the pens of the polygraph recording every variation in his physical response to the emotions generated by the relentless questioning—revealed just how close the great building, now humming with the presses in the basement, had come to being destroyed. Dictated by Chief Brandon to a rewrite man shortly after nine, while the climactic ending of the conclave of the Knights of Freedom had been reaching its final climax at the Stadium, the account was hair-raising in itself.

The turning point came with a routine question about elevators that had brought a startling galvanic response from Pollock's sweating palms on the lie detector. Chief Brandon had followed the clue relentlessly, homing in on the location of the lethal machine, even as the clock ticked toward the moment of its detonation. And, when the polygraph pen, writing madly its up-and-down squiggles, had revealed the presence of the explosive in a service elevator, whose door had been jammed partly open with a metal slug to keep it from moving out of the basement, the bomb squad had removed the detonator with no more than five minutes to spare.

Bob Partridge himself had written the running story of Walter Case's jeremiad at the stadium, climaxed by Seth's cold-blooded murder, and the Grand Leader's own demise beneath the cross. . . . Rick's interview (backed by Carol's shorthand notes) was in the place of honor, since it established Case's motives in the man's own words. His biography was detailed from the beginning, with proper emphasis on the liaison with Mary Randall. It was illustrated on the break page, with a full photographic layout, taken from the scrapbook.

It was Theo's next-to-last photograph, however, that summed up the Walter Case story most graphically. Snapped at close range, it showed Seth, the glaze of death already dimming his eyes, standing before the fiery cross, arms outthrust in that dramatic, if involuntary, gesture of absolution; while Walter Case crouched before him, the automatic still in his hand, and his features distorted by the manic rage that had driven him to the public act of murder. So detailed was the photograph that it even showed the broken joist beneath the platform and the mob milling around it, as both platform and cross were beginning to collapse, sealing Case's doom. There, written, as it were, in letters of fire any reader could grasp, was a pattern of crime and punishment as simple as it was tragic.

Rick leaned across Carol's shoulder and opened the *Times-News* to an inside page. It showed the fire-blackened field an hour later, and the smoking ruins of platform and cross—which, in the end, had served as funeral pyre for both father and son.

"They tried to save the bodies," he told her. "Perhaps it's just as well they failed."

Carol looked up with tear-wet eyes, and made a brave effort to force a smile. "Are you as tired as you look?"

"Strangely enough, I don't feel tired at all," said Rick. "The aftermath will hit later, of course. Since we left the Stadium, I've been too busy to think."

"Did you talk to New York?"

"Twice. The *Record* gave us six full columns, and the same page of pictures. And I'm doing a special *Profile* this Sunday; the network is setting up the air time tomorrow. Fortunately there'll be plenty of videotape covering the events at the Stadium. George Ormsbee told me he kept a monitor going and even interrupted the network the last few moments—which means the whole country will be watching Sunday to see what happened before that."

"Can I go to New York too, Rick? I never want to see this town again. Not after tonight."

"Of course you're going with me. After the telecast, we'll take a two-week honeymoon-trip abroad." He took her hand in his, and looked down at her sternly, although his lips were smiling. "Two weeks, Carol; we can't afford more. Then we're coming back to Central City to help Bob finish this job. Tonight is only a beginning."

"Can't we stay in New York after we're married? I want to leave the South forever."

"You belong here too, darling. We have to do this job together. Read Bob's editorial and it will tell you why."

He turned the page. The editorial was printed under the *Times-News* masthead:

Playing God can be a dangerous business. Especially if the actor has only human equipment.

Last night, a madman named Walter Case, who

fancied himself as God, died at University Stadium. The fact that he took his own son to death in his final act of madness was a tragic loss for both the North and the South. Seth Randall was both a great musician and a great human being; yet his end did serve a purpose. It was he, at the very moment of his death, who stripped away the madman's mask, and showed us the true face beneath.

Walter Case was one of the country's great builders. He was also a true son of Satan, who could build skyscrapers—and tear souls apart. It was both ironic and appropriate that this great builder should die spewing his last litany of hate, on a jerry-built platform that collapsed beneath him.

The platform was fated to collapse, since it was built on a lie: the greatest lie of our time—that might is better than liberty, that the individual man is of less consequence than the faceless mob.

At University Stadium, last night, another preacher of this lie was consumed by his own fire. The threat of Walter Case has been scourged from our midst—but the battle for our survival remains to be fought.

Justice was done last night. But, as is so often the case in a democracy, justice was belated.

Here in Central City, we must never forget the martyrdom of Seth Randall. The would-be dictator will continue to flourish in our midst, so long as man's inhumanity to man remains a living thing.

Let us learn to recognize this atavism by his deeds, whatever his name, before his mask is torn aside to reveal his true identity.

In New York, the telecast was nearing its end. Seated at his desk microphone, Rick Jordan watched the monitor scene with brooding intentness. It had been a heartbreaking hour, but he knew it had served its purpose.

In film clips and photographs, in the framework of the newsreel and newsprint, he had told the Seth Randall story from its beginning, and the story of Walter Case was its evil counterpart. He had described Seth's work at Valley Hospital; he had shown portions of Seth's filmed recording. The scene had then shifted to the newsreel coverage of the last conclave of the Knights. Shot from every angle, the pageant at University Stadium had emerged in its true colors, with the Leader as its focal point.

Now, as the telecast moved into its final moment, both Seth and Case were on camera. The lens moved forward for a close-up, as the Negro took the microphone.

"I forgive you, Father! May God forgive you, too!"

The photomontage that followed was topped by the report of Case's automatic; the death scene on the platform dissolved into shots of the milling mob, while the sound track picked up the Leader's last screams. Then, as the blazing cross tottered and fell, the studio camera showed Rick Jordan at his desk.

"Last week in Central City," he said, "a man died. His only crime was that he had black skin—and a white father."

The studio camera pulled back, to take in the wall behind the desk—and a huge enlargement of a photo. One of the series Theo had taken, it showed Seth Randall in that final moment of agony before his death—his arms outspread in a gesture of peace, absolving a man who was beyond absolution.

"Seth Randall's death was not in vain," said Rick. "As proof of this, I am closing this program with his recorded words. Even then, he spoke in death's shadow. It was an end he had chosen deliberately, that other men might live better lives tomorrow."

The camera lifted, to show Seth's face. Rick rose from the desk and stood with bowed head as the sound track picked up the recording Seth had made in the trailer. The face in the photograph was still. Yet, as Rick heard Seth's voice, he was sure the lips were moving.

"*A new commandment I give unto you, that you love one another*——"